ESTATE OF MIND

A Den of Antiquity Mystery

TAMAR MYERS

AVON BOOKS
An Imprint of HarperCollins*Publishers*

This is a work of fiction. Names, characters, places, and incidents are products of the author's imagination or are used fictitiously and are not to be construed as real. Any resemblance to actual events, locales, organizations, or persons, living or dead, is entirely coincidental.

AVON BOOKS
An Imprint of HarperCollins*Publishers*
10 East 53rd Street
New York, New York 10022-5299

Inside cover author photo by Richard Johnson
Library of Congress Catalog Card Number: 99-94464
ISBN: 0-380-80227-9
www.avonbooks.com

First Avon Twilight printing: December 1999

Printed in the U.S.A.

10 9 8 7 6 5 4

Estate of Mind

Greg winked at me. "Hey Abby, how much will you sell this thing for?"

"One hundred and fifty dollars and ninety-nine cents."

"I thought you said it was a worthless piece of junk?"

"It is. But that's how much I paid for the frame."

"Tell you what, I'll give you ten bucks for the painting, and you can keep the frame. It's too fancy for me anyway."

"Sold!"

I went inside and got a screwdriver and Greg and I popped the painting loose from the frame.

"Well I'll be," said Greg. "This is a two-for-one."

I stared. The horrible copy of *The Starry Night* was just a loose piece of canvas. Still firmly attached to the wooden stretcher was another painting altogether.

With trembling hands I turned the new painting around one hundred and eighty degrees. "This one is mine," I said in a small, strangled voice.

Den of Antiquity Mysteries by
Tamar Myers
from Avon Books

BAROQUE AND DESPERATE
ESTATE OF MIND
SO FAUX, SO GOOD
THE MING AND I
GILT BY ASSOCIATION
LARCENY AND OLD LACE
A PENNY URNED
NIGHTMARE IN SHINING ARMOR
SPLENDOR IN THE GLASS

For Gwen Hunter

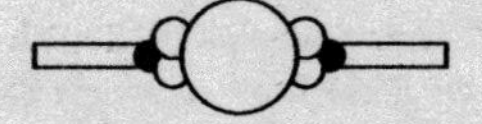

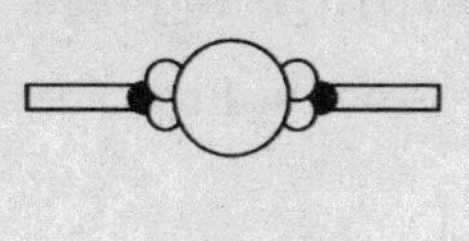

1

I've been in sorrow's kitchen and licked out every pot. But I haven't suffered half as much as Mama, to hear her tell it. So out of guilt I went along with her to the Episcopal Church of Our Savior in Rock Hill, South Carolina. I go to church regularly, mind you, but this was to the annual white elephant sale and potluck supper, and it was a Wednesday night.

"Junk," I whispered. "It's just junk."

"Shh, Abby. Someone will hear you."

"So what, Mama? Feel this sweater. It's 100 percent acrylic. You could grate carrots with it."

"It's a very pretty pink."

"Speaking of pink, can you believe this pink flamingo night-light?"

"Lower your voice, dear. You Know Who donated that."

"You Know Who?"

"The Queen."

I glanced around the parish hall, looking for a dowdy little woman with a hat and an obviously empty handbag. There were no hats to be seen.

"I don't think she can hear all the way from England."

"Priscilla Hunt is not in England, dear. She's right over there."

"Oh, *that* queen."

Priscilla Hunt is the uncrowned queen of Rock Hill. At least in her eyes. Not only is she the wealthiest woman in town, but she descends from one of the city's earliest settlers. Frankly, I have always been baffled by the amount of power Priscilla is able to wield, especially considering the fact that nobody likes her. She was standing alone, as usual, glaring at her archrival, Hortense Simms.

Hortense doesn't have a lineage worthy of a horse thief, but she is the Episcopal Church of Our Savior's resident celebrity and the second-wealthiest woman in the parish. She is also a confirmed spinster with a reputation for holding her nose so high, it's a wonder she doesn't require an oxygen mask. Confidentially, Hortense doesn't deserve to be famous just because she published a book on antique undergarments, even if the ones she wrote about were worn by famous people. *Of Corsets and Crowns* never would have made the *New York Times* best-seller list if Oprah hadn't mentioned it in passing. A woman who describes underwear for a living has no cause to put on airs, if you ask me.

"I wouldn't be surprised if the high and mighty Hortense chipped in with these cracked wooden salad bowls."

"I gave those," Mama said.

"Mama, you didn't!"

"I asked you if you wanted them, remember?"

I shook my head.

"Well, I did. Last Thanksgiving. And you said, 'no.' So don't blame me if somebody else snaps them up for a song. Abby, I would have let you have them for fifty cents apiece."

"I don't want the salad bowls." I waved my arms at the clutter spread across eight folding tables that flanked the room. "Mama, we're Episcopalians. Can't we do better than this?"

"What did you donate, dear? This auction is to benefit the youth group, you know. They're badly in need of a new van."

I hung my head in shame. As the owner of the Den of Antiquity, one of the Charlotte area's finest stores, I had plenty to donate to a church fund-raiser.

Mama gasped and clutched her single strand of pearls. "You didn't donate anything, did you?"

"I was going to, Mama, but I've been busy. It sort of slipped my mind."

"Bet that new boyfriend of yours hasn't slipped your mind, has he?"

I must have looked guilty.

"I knew it. Well, Abigail Louise Timberlake, I'm ashamed of you."

"Oh, Mama, you just don't like him because he's short."

"You said it, dear, not me."

"But, Mama, he's three inches taller than I!"

"You're four-foot-nine, dear. And besides, we don't know who his people are."

"Mama, you've met them, for crying out loud. You had lunch at his aunt's down in Georgetown."

Mama sniffed. "Appearances can be deceiving,

dear. You aren't really serious about this man, are you?"

Mama has her heart set on my marrying Greg Washburn, a handsome Charlotte police investigator. Greg is tall by anyone's standards, and drop-dead gorgeous. Buster, on the other hand, has a face only a mama can love—his mama, not mine—and is a coroner. But Buster is someone I can count on, while Greg is as faithful as a buck rabbit—just like my ex-husband. I had a trump card that I knew would sway Mama over to Buster's side, but I wasn't ready to play it.

"Maybe we should head over to the food tables," I said, by way of diversion. "Father Foss is about to say grace."

"All right, dear, but I'm not letting you off the hook for a prayer. We'll talk later. Can you make it for supper Saturday night? Or do you and that little man have plans?"

"Saturday will be fine," I said and, grabbing her arm, steered her toward the food tables.

We barely made it in time. As soon as the word "Amen" passed the good father's lips, the crowd reenacted the Oklahoma land rush. Not that I can blame them. Episcopalians rank among the world's finest cooks, after all. Potluck at the Church of Our Savior can be a treat.

But I was feeling a little off my feed that night. Lunch, earlier that day at Bubba's China Gourmet up in Charlotte, was more than just a memory. Bubba's moo goo gai grits and Beijing barbecue were still in my stomach, which in turn felt like it was somewhere down around my knees. But just to be sociable I put a watercress sandwich on my plate. Normally one would not find finger food at an evening potluck, but I blessed the kind soul who had provided it.

"Is that all you're going to eat?" Mama demanded, once we were seated.

"Shhh, Mama, the bidding's started."

"Do I hear a dollar fifty for these salad bowls?" Father Foss was saying.

"Two dollars," Mama said.

"Mama, you can't bid on your own donation!"

"Why not?"

Father Foss glanced our way. "Do I hear two-fifty?"

"Two-fifty!" I called. What the heck. Dmitri, my cat, could use a chow bowl.

Mama raised her hand. "Three dollars!"

"Four dollars!" I yelled.

Father Foss grinned. "Do I hear five?"

I stood up. "Ten dollars!"

"Do I hear fifteen?"

The room was dead silent, except for the snicker that escaped Priscilla Hunt's blue-blooded lips. We were Episcopalians, not fools. As it was, Dmitri was going to have to give me a lot of lap time to make that ten dollars well spent.

"Ten dollars once, ten dollars twice—sold to Mozella Wiggins's daughter."

Mama beamed.

I sat down and took a bite of my sandwich. In the meantime, Father Foss tried to unload a toaster oven that had seen better days—perhaps when Herbert Hoover was president.

Try as I might, I could not swallow that bite. I came dangerously close to gagging.

"What's wrong?" Mama hissed.

I chugged back half a glass of sweet tea and mercifully set the morsel on its way. "This is the worst sandwich I've ever eaten," I gasped. "The bread is so dry it should be patented by a sponge company. And that's parsley, not watercress!"

Mama kicked me with the pointed toe of her patent leather pumps. "I made that sandwich, Abby. I was too busy learning Tshiluba to cook a real dish. Parsley and bread were all I had."

"What?"

"Well, I had butter, of course. That's real butter, Abby. Not margarine or one of those disappointing spreads."

"Mama! What were you learning?"

"Tshiluba, dear. It's an African language from the Congo, formerly Zaire. *Muoyo*—that's how you say 'hello.' Literally, it means 'life.' "

I stared at her in wonderment. Forty-eight years, and the woman never ceases to amaze me.

"Why are you learning an African language?"

Mama said something that might even have been intelligible, but something even more curious had happened. There was some real bidding going on, and it was over a hideous copy of one of my favorite paintings, Vincent van Gogh's *The Starry Night.* I had seen the monstrosity earlier and would have laughed myself silly had it not been for the restraining influence of Bubba's lunch. My guess was that a neophyte oil painter had foisted his masterpiece on some undeserving relative at Christmas, and said relative had been waiting all year to dump the piece of garbage. Still, the frame on the faux Gogh was nice, and I had initially allowed myself the possibility of acquiring the painting for just that reason.

"Thirty-five," a female person called from the nether reaches of the hall.

I am comfortable with my height—believe me, I am. But even if I had been standing, I wouldn't have been able to see who had bid such an exorbitant amount.

"Mama, who is that?"

"I don't recognize the voice, dear. It's probably a Presbyterian. They're the ones with the money, you know."

"Forty-five," a male voice boomed. It sounded like that sleazeball Vincent Dougherty. He doesn't belong to any church that I know of, but he's a big deal in the Rock Hill business community. When the Catawba Indians opened their high-stakes bingo parlor on Cherry Road, Vincent opened the Adult Entertainment Center just across the street. Don't ask what goes on in there, but the city zoning committee rues the day they let that one slip by them.

I considered standing on my chair. "Mama, is that Vincent?"

"Yes, and don't you think it's ironic? Him bidding on a painting by another Vincent!"

"It's ironic all right. One disgusting thing bidding on another."

"Fifty," the female voice said.

"Sixty-five," Sleazeball countered.

"Seventy."

"Eighty."

"Ninety." I could tell by the tone of the woman's voice that this was her last bid.

I stood on my chair. It was quick hop up and then off. I'm sure that no one but Mama noticed. It was just long enough to see a beautiful black woman with cornrows. She was sitting near the door, next to a bearded white man in a black leather, grommet-studded vest. They were not Episcopalians, that much I could tell. And I didn't remember seeing them in the food lineup.

"One hundred!" I said and waved my arm like an F student who finally has the right answer.

Mama pinched me. "Abby!"

"One hundred and twenty." Sleazeball was determined.

So was I. Although Vincent Dougherty made a career out of peddling trash, he was not the type to throw his money away on junk. No doubt he too had recognized that the gold frame was valuable.

But how much was it worth? It had been a while since I'd been in a decent frame shop. And anyway, that was comparing apples with oranges. This was an old frame—hand-applied gilt on molded gesso. Had it been teamed with a real painting, its value would have been easier to judge. Still, it was worth more than one-twenty.

"One hundred and fifty dollars," I shouted, "and ninety-nine cents!"

There followed an equal mixture of guffaws and gasps.

Mama was one of those who gasped. "Abby, I thought you said it was disgusting!"

"The painting, Mama. Not the frame."

"Going once, going twice—" Father Foss paused and looked in Vincent's direction, but got no response. The sleazeball had met his match. "Sold to Mozella Wiggins's daughter."

"He doesn't know my name, does he?" I wailed.

"He's only been here a year, dear. And you've been gone—uh, how long?"

"Twenty-five years. But I come back for weddings and funerals."

"Those don't count, Abby. And neither does Christmas and Easter. A person should have God in their life on a more regular basis."

"Mama, since when did you start being so religious?"

"Since—"

She didn't finish her sentence because Father Foss was standing directly behind me, the painting under his arm.

"Congratulations," he said with a warm smile. "I wouldn't be surprised if this was the biggest moneymaker of the evening. On behalf of the youth group, thank you."

"Just glad to do my part," I said breezily. "And by the way, my name is Abigail Timberlake. The reason you don't see me in church on Sunday is because I live up in Charlotte. Which isn't to say that I don't go to church there. Well, actually I don't, but I could if I wanted to—"

Mama nudged me. "Abby, dear," she whispered, "you're digging your hole deeper and deeper."

"In that case," I wailed, "maybe I'll just hide in it."

Thank God Father Foss is a kind and gentle man. "Enjoy the painting, Miss Timberlake. It's certainly one of a kind."

"Let's hope so."

Father Foss smiled and returned to his auctioneer's post. I, quite foolishly, hoisted the painting on my shoulder and headed out the parish hall doors. After all, I was through buying for the night. But had I known then what I know now, I would have chased after Mama's priest and begged him to pray for me. I was soon going to need all the prayers I could get.

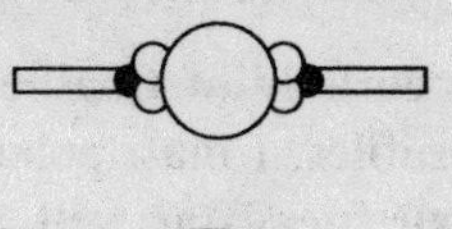

2

You already know that my name is Abigail Timberlake, but you might not know that I was married to a beast of a man for just over twenty years. Buford Timberlake—or Timbersnake, as I call him—is one of Charlotte, North Carolina's most prominent divorce lawyers. Therefore, he knew exactly what he was doing when he traded me in for his secretary. Of course, Tweetie Bird is half my age—although parts of her are even much younger than that. The woman is 20 percent silicone, for crying out loud, although admittedly it balances rather nicely with the 20 percent that was sucked away from her hips.

In retrospect, however, there are worse things than having your husband dump you for a man-made woman. It hurt like the dickens at the time, but it would have hurt even more had he traded me in for a brainier model. I can buy most of what Tweetie has (her height excepted), but she will forever be afraid to flush the toilet lest she drown the Ty-D-Bol man.

And as for Buford, he got what he deserved. Our daughter, Susan, was nineteen at the time and in college, but our son, Charlie, was seventeen, and a high school junior. In the penultimate miscarriage of justice, Buford got custody of Charlie, our house, and even the dog Scruffles. I must point out that Buford got custody of our friends as well. Sure, they didn't legally belong to him, but where would you rather stake your loyalty? To a good old boy with more connections than the White House switchboard, or to a housewife whose biggest accomplishment, besides giving birth, was a pie crust that didn't shatter when you touched it with your fork? But like I said, Buford got what he deserved and today—it actually pains me to say this—neither of our children will speak to their father.

Now I own a four-bedroom, three-bath home not far from my shop. *I* paid for this house, mind you—not one farthing came from Buford. At any rate, I share this peaceful, if somewhat lonely, abode with a very hairy male who is young enough to be my son.

When I got home from the auction, I was in need of a little comfort, so I fixed myself a cup of tea with milk and sugar—never mind that it was summer—and curled up on the white cotton couch in the den. My other hand held a copy of Anne Grant's *Smoke Screen,* a mystery novel set in Charlotte and surrounding environs. I hadn't finished more than a page of this exciting read when my roommate rudely pushed it aside and climbed into my lap.

"Dmitri," I said, stroking his large orange head, "that painting is so ugly, if van Gogh saw it, he'd cut off his other ear."

"Meow."

"It's in the car, dear. If I brought it inside, our neighbors—some of whom have real van Goghs, mind you—might tar and feather me. I'll take it to the back room of the shop tomorrow and pry it from the frame."

Dmitri began kneading my stomach with his front paws. "Meow."

"Of course I'll be careful. We don't want to chip off any of that nice gesso, do we?"

"Meow."

"What I paid for it is none of your business, dear. Suffice it to say, too much."

"Meow."

"I should just barely be able to get my money back when I sell the frame. I might need to touch it up in a few spots first."

Dmitri suddenly stood and turned. I had to spit tail hairs from my mouth.

"What were you about to say, dear? Were you going to ask about the food? Well, let me tell you, it was—what the heck is that?"

But I already knew it was my car alarm. My house, like many in the Carolinas, has a carport instead of a garage, and the loudest racket this side of rapper hell was emanating from that direction.

I reached for the phone. "Don't panic, dear. It probably just went off by accident. It does that all the time. Maybe a mean old dog bumped it or something. Besides, Mama's going to call for help."

Dmitri dived beneath the couch, leaving behind claw imprints on my thighs.

I plonked my teacup on the coffee table and pushed the speed dial button for 911.

* * *

I didn't answer the doorbell until the fifth set of chimes. The racket had miraculously ceased by then, but I was paralyzed with fear. I might well have grown old on that couch, a cup of cold tea in front of me, had I not heard a familiar voice on the other side of the front door. I raced to answer it.

"Greg! What on earth are you doing here?" Trust me, I wouldn't have been more surprised to see Santa Claus standing there on the front porch, red suit and all, despite the July heat.

My once-beloved, who stands six feet tall in his stocking feet, has eyes the color of Ceylon sapphires. Tonight those eyes gazed down on me somberly, while his mouth struggled not to smile.

"You called 911, didn't you?"

"Yes, but you're a crime scene investigator. Your duties commence after a crime has been committed, not during."

"Ah, yes, but every once in a while I volunteer to do rounds, just to stay in touch. Tonight I'm paired with Sergeant Bowater, and your call was routed to him. We were just a block away when he took it."

I tried to peer around Greg but had to settle for what little I could see between his legs. "Where is Sergeant Bowater?"

"Still in the squad car, but I can call him if you like."

"That won't be necessary," I said quickly. Too quickly.

Greg's lips twitched. "So, Abby, what is the nature of your problem? The dispatcher said your car alarm was activated. I don't hear anything."

"It was activated! It was shrieking like a banshee and then—well, I don't know what happened. It just suddenly shut itself off."

"I see." The Ceylon sapphires twinkled.

"No, you don't! You're mocking me. What do you think I did, activate the alarm myself just to get you out here?"

"Well—"

"So how would I know you were riding around on patrol duty?"

Greg shrugged, but that irritating smile stayed in place. "Why don't we go out and take a look?"

"Hold your horses, buster. You need to answer my question."

"Hey, come on, Abby. I was just kidding you a little. I believe you. It's easy for a pro to deactivate a car alarm."

I glared at the man. "You're here on official police business, dear. You shouldn't be kidding."

Greg ran a large, tanned hand through thick, almost-black hair. "Okay, so maybe I get a little jealous from time to time and try to get a reaction out of you. It's only natural."

"It is?" And yes, I did mean to sound coy.

"Yeah, it's natural. You're one hell of a woman."

"I am?"

"Damn it, Abby, now you're mocking me. You'd be a catch for any man."

Since the man is an avid angler, I allowed him his fishing reference. "Am I a better catch than, say—Hooter Fawn?"

Greg's tan deepened. "That's long over, Abby, and you know it."

"Ah, but the memory lingers on. I keep asking myself, what kind of a man would date a woman named Hooter anyway?"

"A fool, Abby."

Quit when you're ahead, they always say. Well, that's easier said than done. I knew for a fact that Hooter shopped for body parts at the same plastic surgeon Tweetie did. I heard it straight from the horse's mouth, and I mean that literally. Tweetie, wouldn't you know, has taken to getting injections of horse collagen in her lips.

"Tell me one thing you like about me that Hooter doesn't have." Confidentially, I was hoping to hear words like "natural" or phrases like "more than a handful is wasted."

"Well, uh . . . uh . . . you have cuter ears."

"Ears? You can't even say that I have prettier eyes, or maybe even just a nicer personality? What kind of a man pays attention to a woman's ears?"

"A fool," Greg said meekly.

This time I quit while I was ahead. I led him through the kitchen and out to the carport. Sergeant Bowater, who had been too impatient to wait in the squad car, was already at work. A redhead, the man has more freckles than Myrtle Beach has sand.

"This big scratch on the door new?" he asked.

I gasped. "Vandals! I bet it's that Taylor boy and his friends. Last week I had to chase them out of my pool when I came home from work."

"Pity. This is really one nice car."

"It's brand-new," I wailed. The navy blue Oldsmobile Intrigue with leather seats and stereo controls on the steering wheel had been a Mother's Day present to myself. Yes, I went a little overboard, but my children are too self-absorbed to remember that holiday, and as for Mama—well, that day belongs to her, and her alone. She wears a paper crown around the house and hums the coronation theme from the Miss America pageant. God forbid you should try for equal billing.

Sergeant Bowater seemed to thrive on delivering bad news. "Look here, the window's been forced. The door is unlocked. You in the habit of keeping your car unlocked, ma'am?"

"I'm not a child," I said calmly. "I'm just short."

"Yup, no doubt about it. Somebody wanted this baby. Can't say as I blame them, though. But they weren't professionals, I can tell you that. A pro wouldn't have left all these scratches."

Sergeant Bowater was dusting for fingerprints. "You've got a lot of damage here, little lady. I hope you've got insurance."

I cringed. I don't go around calling large guys "big gentleman." And anyway, Sergeant Bowater was young enough to be my son—that is, if I'd gotten pregnant when Mama thought I would.

"Yes, I have insurance. That Taylor boy's parents better have it, too."

Sergeant Bowater cleared his throat. "Ma'am, you keep anything valuable in your car?"

"Like the crown jewels?"

"Ma'am, you'd be surprised what people keep in

their cars. Pulled over a lady once who had a diamond necklace in her glove box. Thought it was safer than the bank vault. 'Nobody robs glove boxes,' she said."

"Well, I don't even own a rhinestone necklace worth stealing. And there is nothing in my glove box except for my car registration and the owner's manual."

"What about the trunk, ma'am?"

"Just a jack and the spare tire. Oh, and as of tonight, a painting."

"How valuable is the painting, ma'am?"

"It's not. It's just a piece of junk I picked up at a church auction."

Greg smiled. He has the whitest teeth I've ever seen, although he drinks coffee by the gallon.

"Mind if I see it?"

I obligingly popped the trunk. The faux Gogh was lying there, face up, just where I'd left it. Somehow it had managed to grow even uglier in the interim.

"Oh, man," Greg said, reaching for the painting, "I love this one. *The Starry Night.* It's always been my favorite."

"The original, yes, but this is a horrible copy."

"Looks great to me."

"Nonsense. Look at this disgusting thing. Those look like real trees and houses."

"Yeah, but the stars—"

"Too real. This is supposed to be an impressionist painting."

"I like it, too," Sergeant Bowater said.

I wrinkled my nose. "Look closer, guys. One could

almost step into this painting, it's so real. That's not what Vincent van Gogh was all about."

Sergeant Bowater scratched his left armpit. "He ain't one of them fellows that makes a lot of money urinating on crosses, is he?"

"Not hardly, dear. Vincent started his career as a missionary but was dismissed when he took the Gospel teachings too literally and gave away virtually everything he owned to the poor."

"Say, I heard about him. Don't he live up near Hickory now?"

I smiled patiently. "Vincent van Gogh shot himself and died two days later on July 29, 1890."

Sergeant Bowater scratched his right armpit. "Must have been a different guy, then."

Greg winked at me. "Hey, Abby, how much will you sell this thing for?"

"One hundred and fifty dollars and ninety-nine cents."

"I thought you said it was a worthless piece of junk."

"It is. But that's how much I paid for the frame."

"Tell you what, I'll give you ten bucks for the painting, and you can keep the frame. It's too fancy for me anyway."

"Sold!"

I went inside and got a screwdriver from the kitchen all-purpose drawer, and while Sergeant Bowater worked on his report, Greg and I popped the painting loose from the frame. It took only a minute to separate canvas from gesso.

"Well, I'll be," Greg said. "This is a two-for-one."

I stared. The horrible copy of *The Starry Night* was just a loose piece of canvas. It flopped to the breezeway the moment it was freed. Still firmly attached to the wooden stretcher, however, was another painting altogether.

With trembling hands, I turned the new painting around 180 degrees. "This one is mine," I said in a small, strangled voice.

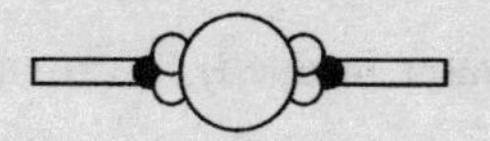

3

"You can have it," Greg said and gently picked up his ten-dollar purchase.

"You sure?"

"Positive. It's just a bunch of green blobs."

Sergeant Bowater glanced our way. "Yeah, it ain't as pretty as the other."

I willed my hands to be steady, but they were shaking like the paint mixer at Home Depot.

"Hey, Abby, something wrong?"

"I'm just a little cold, I guess."

"But it was up to a hundred today. It's got to be still in the eighties."

"Then maybe it was something I had for lunch at Bubba's China Gourmet."

Sergeant Bowater put his pen and notebook back in the shirt pocket of his navy blue uniform. "Man, I love that place. You ever have their moo goo gai grits?"

"Yes, and it's the last time." I smiled brightly. "Well, guys, I'm off to bed. It's been a long day, and an even longer evening."

"But, ma'am, I still need to interview your neighbors, and I might need to get back to you."

"Can't that last part wait until tomorrow? It's already past ten."

Sergeant Bowater nodded. "You sure you'll be all right, ma'am?"

"I'll be fine as frog's hair."

"Forgive me for saying so, ma'am, but you're looking kinda peaked."

"I already told you, it was the grits."

"Nah, them moo goo gai grits wouldn't harm my granny, not unless you put some of that Hunan hot sauce on them. You didn't do that, did you?"

"Oh, my gosh, I guess I did."

"That did it, then." He peered at me with renewed interest. "But you still got your teeth, right?"

"What kind of a question is that?"

"Granny lost hers. Swallowed them after she took a big bite of that hot sauce."

"Get out!"

"Yes, ma'am. I seen the X rays myself. You could count the teeth on Granny's dentures."

"Did they have to operate?"

"Doc said he was going to; then he noticed that them teeth was still working down in Granny's stomach. Apparently Granny had one hell—excuse me, ma'am—of a set of stomach muscles. She could make them teeth take big bites, small bites, it didn't matter. She could even chatter them things. Anyway, we got her a new pair of dentures for her mouth, so Granny, bless her little old heart, had herself two sets of teeth. Doc said having that extra pair in her stomach did wonders for her digestion."

"You mean, she chewed her cud just like a cow?"

"Yeah, kinda. Only she didn't have all them stomachs."

I glanced at Greg, who was smirking. "I see. Well, you certainly tell a good story." I wisely took a step back. "You wouldn't happen to be from Shelby, would you?"

"Yes, ma'am. How did you know?"

"Sergeant Bowater, are you by any chance related to a woman named Jane Cox? I mean, she wouldn't be your sister, would she?" "

"No, ma'am. I'm an only child."

"Any cousins by that name?"

"No, ma'am, my parents were only children, too."

I breathed a sigh of relief on behalf of humanity. But alas, I am genetically incapable of leaving well enough alone.

"You're not married, are you?" I asked, spotting a freckled and hairy, but otherwise naked, finger.

"Abby!" Greg said sternly.

I ignored him. "Would you like to meet a tall, blond woman about your own age who is also from Shelby?"

"Yes, ma'am! I've been away over a year now, and it's been kinda lonely. Charlotte girls ain't easy to meet."

"Well, have I got a girl for you."

He grinned broadly, displacing a million freckles. "Thank you, ma'am."

"Just call me Yenta."

"Ma'am?"

"Never mind, dear. Just give me your home number. I'll call you when I have it fixed up. When's your next night off?"

"Tomorrow night, ma'am." He sounded eager.

"This is highly irregular," Greg growled.

I smiled sweetly. "You, of course, don't need help getting a date, do you? I'm sure women just throw themselves at you."

"Abby, we need to talk."

I faked a decent yawn. "Been there, done that. Besides, I'm tired and want to go to bed. Alone!"

"Abby, aren't you the least little bit nervous after a scare like this? Someone breaking into your car is a serious thing."

I shook my head. "I'm fine. See, my hands aren't shaking anymore. I promise, I'll remember to set my house alarm, and I always keep a can of pepper spray on my night table. So thank you both for coming out here, and good luck tomorrow on the investigation."

Sergeant Bowater scratched both armpits simultaneously. Perhaps he had tried a new deodorant that had given him a rash.

"Ma'am, you hear anything suspicious, you call 911 again."

"I will. Good night."

Satisfied, Sergeant Bowater started to walk away. Greg was not so easy to dismiss.

"But if you need anything—anything at all—you let us know."

"Will do."

"Because we'll swing by here every hour or so, won't we, Sergeant?"

"Sure thing."

"That's awfully nice. Thanks. But I need to get up early tomorrow morning, so don't ring the bell, okay?"

Greg looked dangerously close to hugging me. "Ah, Abby—"

I snatched up the frame and the painting of green blobs and scurried back inside. I had more important things to do. Like Mama always said, there were other fish in the sea. And so what if one of the fish was short and plain? At least I was pretty sure he wasn't a shark.

I was reaching for the phone, and it rang. "Do you know what time it is?" I demanded.

"Uh . . . is Abigail Timberlake there?"

"That depends on who's calling. You're not with the prize patrol, are you? Because if you're lost, you've undoubtedly gone too far. I'm at the end of the first cul-de-sac, not the second."

"Abby, it's me, Gilbert Sweeny."

I took a deep, suspicious breath. It was Gilbert Sweeny's donation I had spread in front of me on the coffee table, and if that wasn't enough, I had my memories of shared high school years. Back then, Gilbert was a class-A jerk. He drank, smoke, and cheated, and that was just in Sunday School. In civilian life, he got my friend Debbie Lou pregnant and refused to marry her. In those days, marriage was the honorable thing to do, but it surprised no one when Gilbert left her standing—literally—at the altar.

"Gilbert, it's late. What do you want?"

"I saw you tonight at the auction."

"I saw you too, Gilbert. Now if you'll excuse me—"

"What I mean is, I saw you bid on the painting I

donated. You raised a lot of money toward the van."

"Thank you, Gilbert, but my one hundred and fifty dollars and ninety-nine cents will barely make a dent in the van fund. They're aiming for a new van, not a bucket of bolts."

"Yeah, but you got the ball rolling. After you left, things really picked up."

"They did?"

"Oh, yeah. Someone bid fifty dollars for Priscilla Hunt's flamingo night-light. Can you believe that?"

"Get out of town!"

"And you know my sister Hortense?"

"Of course." The haughty Hortense Simms was Gilbert's stepsister, and while she may not have left anyone standing at the altar, she was never on my list of favorite people. And contrary to what Mama says, I am not envious of the woman's success. Hortense had no business telling Jimmy Roush back in fifth grade that I had a crush on him, and as for the rumor she spread in seventh grade, that was a total lie. I did not stuff my bra with facial tissue! I used toilet paper.

"Anyway, Hortense donated a character from one of her books. It went for five hundred dollars."

"Come again?"

"You know that book she wrote?"

"*Of Corsets and Crowns*. What about it?"

"It's done so well, she plans to write a novel. Someone bid for the privilege of having a character named after them."

I sighed. "This world is full of idiots. What's the name of this one?"

"That would be me."

It felt like I was swallowing China. "Oh. Well, that was very generous of you, Gilbert."

"Thank you, Abby. Say, I was wondering if you could do me a big favor."

I felt like I owed him one. "Shoot."

"I want to buy my painting back."

"Uh . . . well, that wouldn't be possible."

"I'll pay you what you bid for it, of course."

"Thanks, Gilbert, but no thanks."

"Well, how about an extra fifty dollars?"

"That's very generous, but like I said, that wouldn't be possible. I gave it away."

"You what?"

"I gave it to a friend."

"Damn."

"What did you say?"

"Who did you give it to?"

"That's none of your business, Gil."

"Sorry, Abby. It's just that I had no right to give it away."

"What do you mean?"

"It belonged to my stepmother, Adele Sweeny. She's in Pine Manor nursing home now, but that awful painting hung above her fireplace for as long as I can remember. When she went into the nursing home, she took it with her. Apparently it was a favorite of hers."

"Then why did you sell it? Did she ask you to?"

"No. Adele hasn't said much of anything to me since Daddy died—in fact, we were never very close. However, I went out to see her this morning. The thing is, though, she had no idea who I was."

"So you decided to rob her?"

"It wasn't like that. You see, there were all these other ugly paintings on the walls, and . . . well . . . can I share something with you, Abby?"

"Not if it needs to be cured by penicillin."

My sling didn't seem to faze him. "Adele was one mean stepmother. I know that's sort of the stereotype, but that's how it was. I was six years old when she married my daddy. Of course, she already had a daughter—Hortense. Anyway, Adele used to beat me for the slightest infraction of her rules."

"Un-huh."

"Well, perhaps beating's not the right term. She whipped me with a wire coat hanger—and, for some reason, always a white one."

"Ouch." That sounded too inventive to be a lie.

"And do you know where she did it? Also in the living room, and always in front of the fireplace. God, how I got to hate that fireplace and the painting above it. When I saw that painting this morning—and Adele didn't know who I was—my first impulse was to rip it off the walls and stomp on it. Then I got to thinking about the church auction and how some good might come from those awful memories."

"Didn't you expect to get caught? I mean, Hortense is a member, for pete's sake."

"Yeah, but she never goes to those things. They're beneath her."

"Ain't that the truth."

"Please," he said, sounding almost desperate, "I realize now that it was wrong of me to take it."

"I see. So now you want to return it to the woman

who whipped you with coat hangers? Incidentally, Gilbert, where was your daddy when all this was happening?"

"He . . . well . . . Adele used to call him a wienie."

"A what?"

"You know, a wiener. A wuss."

"Well, I'm sorry, Gilbert, but the friend I sold it to is very fond of it as well. I can't just ask for it back."

"The friend you sold it to? I thought you said you gave it away."

"Well, I did, in a manner of speaking. I sold it for ten dollars."

Gilbert's gasp flattened my ear against the receiver. "You sold it for ten dollars?"

"I don't want to hurt your feelings," I lied, "but that painting was worthless."

"Somehow I don't think so, Abby. My stepmother liked expensive things, and like I said, as ugly as that painting was, it was her favorite."

"Are you sure? Maybe it was the frame she liked. And if that's the case, you're in luck. I'll let you have it for one hundred forty dollars and ninety-nine cents, seeing as how I made up for the extra ten by selling the painting."

During the silence that ensued, Dennis Rodman grew up, and Shirley MacLaine lived at least another life.

"Gilbert, it's getting past my bedtime," I said gently.

"Okay, I'll buy the frame. Can I come over and get it now?"

"You're joking, of course."

"No, Abby, I'm serious. I've been meaning to talk to you for a long time, anyway."

"There is nothing else for us to talk about. You hand me a check tomorrow morning, and I'll hand you the frame."

"Yeah, but I want to talk about us."

"Us? What 'us'?"

"I always had a thing for you, Abby."

"Look, Gilbert—"

"It wasn't Debbie Lou I wanted to marry. It was you. If you'll just give me a chance, I think—I know—I can get you to see that you and I belong together."

I hung up and dialed Wynnell.

Wynnell Crawford is my best friend in the whole world, which means she can say anything she wants to me and get away with it. Well, almost anything.

"No, Abby, I will not get out of bed to drive you somewhere just because you want to avoid being followed by your boyfriend. And aren't you just a little too old to be playing these kinds of games?"

"Greg and I are no longer involved," I said through gritted teeth, "and I am not playing games!"

"I still don't see why this can't wait until tomorrow." In the background, I could hear Wynnell's husband, Bob, grumble. Experience has taught me that a grumbling husband, like a snoring husband, is not altogether a bad thing. At least they are there.

"Because I am sitting on top of the biggest news to hit the art world in years."

Wynnell gasped. "Don't tell me velvet painting is

back in style. I knew it! That Elvis I bought today is worth a fortune, isn't it?"

Believe it or not, Wynnell is also an antique dealer. But our tastes, as you can see, are light-years apart.

"Sorry, dear, but velvet is still out."

Wynnell moaned. "Not those children with the big eyes? I had a chance to buy some at an estate sale Monday, but I passed. You might like them, Abby, but frankly, they remind me of starving refugee children."

"I do not like them! Wynnell, I can't discuss this on the phone, but trust me, you won't regret it. This is a major find."

Wynnell muttered something to her husband, who grumbled some more.

I waited a discreet length of time. "Well, are you going to help me or not?"

"Abby, this really isn't a good time. Call a cab."

"But you're my best friend. And besides, a cab would draw Greg's attention for sure."

"Abby—uh—remember what it was you said you hadn't had since your divorce from Buford?"

"You mean hives?"

"Think again, Abby. You know, the one exercise that's guaranteed to mess up your hair?"

"Oh gross!"

I hung up. Wynnell might be too busy doing the horizontal hootchie-cootchie to give her best friend a lift, but C. J. wouldn't turn me down. C. J., formerly known as Jane Cox but affectionately known as Calamity Jane, may be an egg short of an omelet, but she's a darn good sport. Who else would explore a haunted southern mansion with me at night or drive up to Pennsylvania with me on a moment's notice? Besides, the girl worshipped me. Yup, C. J. it would be.

But first I made another call.

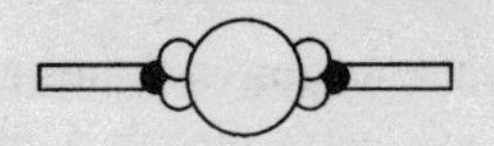

4

Much to my surprise, Hortense Simms answered on the first ring. And she answered in person. I would have thought for sure that a famous author like her would have a staff to field her calls.

"Hortense here."

"Ms. Simms?"

"Who's calling, please?"

"Ms. Simms, this is Abigail Timberlake. I hope I'm not calling too late."

"You're not a fan, are you?"

"Excuse me?"

"I'll be signing *Of Crowns and Corsets* in Pineville next week, at the new Barnes & Noble at the Arboretum Shopping Center. You can catch me there between two and four."

"Ma'am, I'm not a fan."

"Oh. Then who are you?"

"I'm the woman who bought the fake van Gogh at tonight's auction."

"Ah, yes, the pretty woman with the short, dark hair."

And folks said the woman was haughty. "Yes, that's me."

"Ms. Timberlake, what a delightful surprise to hear from you."

"It is?"

"Absolutely. In fact, I was thinking of calling you."

"You were?"

"Yes, I wanted to chat with you about the painting you bought tonight."

"As a matter of fact, that's exactly why I'm calling you, Ms. Simms."

"Please, call me Hortense. Or even Horty, if you like. That's what my friends all call me."

I bit my tongue and counted to ten. I couldn't believe a grown woman would want such a name.

"Call me Abby," I said kindly. "About my new painting, is it true it was your mother's favorite?"

I think she dropped the phone. Either that or she, too, was biting her tongue. At any rate, it took an eternity for her to answer.

"Who told you that?"

"Your brother."

"Gilbert?"

"Yes." To my knowledge, the woman had only one brother.

"Gilbert doesn't know what he's talking about."

I'm sure my sigh of relief fluttered her curtains. "Brothers seldom do."

"The painting didn't belong to Mama—it belonged to me."

"To you?"

"It was a wedding present from my stepfather."

"You poor dear," I said, and slapped my cheek on her behalf.

"Oh, I know, it was a really lousy copy, but it meant a lot. He may have been only a stepfather, but Daddy and I were very close. He showed me the painting the week before the wedding. He was so proud of it, he just couldn't wait any longer."

"Where did get it?"

"He bought it at an estate sale. I don't remember where, exactly."

"I don't mean to be too nosy, Horty, but why didn't you stop your brother from selling it?"

"Well, I didn't know he was going to bring it to the sale, and I didn't want to make a scene."

"But it was yours!"

"Yes, but I couldn't prove it. You see, Daddy died the day I was supposed to get married. Surely you remember that."

"Yes, of course." And then it hit me, and I really did remember. Of course! Mr. Sweeny had been nervous about walking Hortense down the aisle, so he went to the Rock Hill Country Club to work off some steam on the links. A stray ball landed right in his open mouth, and he choked to death. It had even made the tabloid news. MAN DIES FROM HOLE IN ONE.

"We postponed the wedding six months, but I was jinxed. The week before our wedding, he packed his bags and moved to North Dakota. Men!"

"Yeah, men!" If Buford had packed his bags and moved to North Dakota a week before our wedding, I would have been spared a whole lot of heartache and two beautiful, and sometimes loving, children.

"Anyway, Mama found the painting in Daddy's closet and just assumed it was for her because it was getting close to Christmas. I never had the heart to tell her different. I guess I thought there was really no point, since I'd eventually be getting it someday when she died. Let me tell you, it was just a bit of a shock to see it there at the auction."

"Why didn't you stop its sale?"

"Abby, please, you're not serious, are you? I'm a celebrity."

Whatever that was supposed to mean. "Of course," I said meekly.

"Besides, the money was going to a good cause."

"Then why didn't you at least bid on it?"

"That would have looked pretty silly, don't you think? Bidding on a painting my brother donated."

"Didn't he bid to be a character in your next book?"

"Yes, well, Gilbert has always shown a deficit in the decorum department. If I would have known what a fool he was going to make of himself, I wouldn't have agreed to donate that service to the auction. I would much rather have given money directly to the youth group. I was planning to do so anyway."

Two different stories so far—neither probably straight. I wasn't about to turn my painting over to Horty, and I doubted Greg would part with his, either. It was time to back out of the conversation and call C. J.

"Horty, dear, it's been very nice talking to you. I've got to go now, but next time I'm at the Bookworm, I'm buying a copy of your book. And if it's in paperback by then, I'll buy three."

"Abby, wait. I want to ask you something."

"Ask away," I said foolishly.

"You wouldn't consider selling the painting back to me, would you?"

"I'd love to, dear, but I've grown very fond of it."

"But it's a horrible rendition of *The Starry Night.* You could find a much better print at any good frame shop."

"But so could you, dear."

"Yes, but that would hardly be the same. My step-daddy gave me the one you have. Abby, I realize possession is nine-tenths of the law, and I can't prove the painting belongs to me, but it does. Maybe not legally, but rightfully."

"I understand. But here's the thing—and call me weird, if you will—I'm absolutely bowled over by the realism and technique in this version. I mean, before seeing this painting, I always thought van Gogh was kind of crude. Those sloppy brush strokes, those vibrant colors—they reminded me of finger painting. But this—well, it speaks to my soul. So I don't care if it's an obvious fake, or even a spoof. It speaks to my soul." I spoke sweetly—Mama would have been proud.

She sighed. "I must say I find this very disappointing."

"I could let you have the frame," I said generously. "At cost."

"You mean remove the painting from its frame?" She sounded alarmed.

"It's really very easy. I've done it lots of times. Those little holes left behind by the nails don't really detract from its value."

"Oh, no, you mustn't do that. That would ruin the integrity of the painting, wouldn't it? You keep the painting, dear. Forget I ever asked."

I breathed ever so much easier. Greg would not have parted with his new acquisition graciously. Once the man latches onto something, there is no prying it loose from his fingers without a fight. Besides, if he got involved, he might mention the *Field of Thistles* to Hortense. That painting for sure did not belong to her.

"Don't forget, I plan to buy your book," I said generously. "And when your novel comes out, I'll buy it, too. What's it called?"

"It's *Top Secret.*"

"Well, I'll just be patient, then, and wait."

"No, that's its name. It's a thriller about a woman who inadvertently smuggles top secret information in her breast implants."

Who said Hortense Simms was a snippy, uptight spinster? I found her to be an incredibly generous woman with a wry sense of humor. The next time one of the Rob-Bobs needed a beard for a formal occasion, I'd suggest Hortense to them.

"Your book sounds so exciting," I said. "I hope it sells well."

"Thank you. And if you change your mind about my—I mean, your—painting, let me know."

"Will do," I said cheerfully. But Wynnell Crawford would sit down and dine with Yankees at her own dinner table before that day came.

* * *

C. J. picked up on the first ring. "My house is the one with all the lights on and the arrow in the grass."

"I beg your pardon?"

"Abby, is that you?"

"Yes, dear. Who did you think I was?"

"I was hoping you were the prize patrol. Do you mind if I call you back later? Ed McMahon might be trying to get in touch with me for directions."

"Don't be silly, dear. He's a man. They only ask directions to buffet lines."

"Well, maybe you're right. And I did send them directions the last time I sent in my subscription."

"Oh? Which magazine did you buy?" I was anxious to get on with the evening, but trust me, there is no hurrying C. J. The woman is like a cat. Pushing her just makes her hunker down and dig her claws in.

"I bought all of them, silly. You don't win anything unless you buy them all."

There was no sense in making her feel bad. "C. J., can you do me a huge favor?"

She sighed. "Abby, I mopped your kitchen floor just last week."

"That's because you spilled cranberry juice all over it. This is a real favor."

"You want me to clip your toenails again?"

"No! And besides, that was during our beauty treatment night. What I need now is for you to drive a getaway car."

C. J. chortled. "Ooh, Abby, we're going to rob a bank?"

"No, dear. We're going to get away from Greg."

She chortled again. "Ooh, I love hide-and-seek."

"This isn't hide-and-seek, dear. Greg's riding patrol tonight and—well, there was this minor incident involving my car alarm, and now he hardly wants to let me out of his sight."

"So where do you want to go? I hear Maine is very nice this time of year."

"Not that far, dear. Just to the Rob-Bobs. There's something I want to show them, but I don't want Greg to follow. Do you think you could swing by in exactly twenty-two minutes?"

"No problemo. My car's already running; AC is on and everything."

"Were you going someplace?"

"Oh, no."

"Then why is it running?"

"Just in case I did go somewhere. And you see, now I am going somewhere, and we don't even have to wait for the car to cool down."

Trust me, despite the fact that C. J. is one side short of a triangle, she's nobody's fool when it comes to business. Okay, so she wastes gas, but we all have our own little areas of careless spending, don't we? My point is, C. J. has at least a few wires plugged into reality at all times, and I had no compunctions about riding with the woman.

"C. J., dear, don't even stop when you get to my house. Just slow enough so that I can jump in."

"Will do!"

5

C. J. followed my instructions to the letter. She slowed to a crawl in front of my driveway, and I was able to hop in while the car was still moving.

"Hit it," I sang. "Press the pedal to the metal."

"Gee, Abby, you're a lot of fun, you know that?"

"Thanks." I looked in the side mirror. There were no other moving vehicles on the street.

"So, what do you think of my outfit?"

I looked at C. J. for the first time. She was dressed in black from head to toe, and I mean that literally.

"Lose the ski mask, dear. It's the middle of summer. You look like a bank robber."

She peeled it off and tossed it into my lap. "It belonged to my Uncle Arnie. He was a bank robber, you know."

"You don't say. In Shelby?"

"Yup. He robbed eight banks there and never got caught."

Who knew Shelby had that many banks? "So, he retired then, did he?"

"Tried to. In fact, he tried to quit after the very first one, but he couldn't get the mask off so he robbed a second. Later he moved to California and became a full-gospel preacher. Auntie Lula Mae sent me the mask after Uncle Arnie died. She said in her note that it was one of his most prized possessions. She found it lying right next to his King James Bible."

"You don't say?" I flipped the thing to the floor with the corner of my pocketbook. "C. J., do you have any plans for this weekend?"

"Well, actually I do."

"What are they?" C. J. is like a daughter—no, make that younger sister—to me. I figured I had a right to ask.

"I'm going to string popcorn."

"Whatever for?"

She looked at me like I was pumping only one piston. "Christmas, silly."

"But Christmas is still five months away."

"I know, but I always get so excited then that I eat most of it. This year I'm starting early. Maybe by Christmas I'll have enough to wrap around the tree twice."

"Need some help?"

"Oh, Abby, I'd love it if you came to help out. But I'm planning to wear duct tape around my mouth. I won't be able to talk much."

Darn, but my timing was bad. "Unfortunately, I can't make it. But I know a nice gentleman who can."

"Abby, are you setting me up?"

"You bet I am," I said cheerily. "And he's from Shelby, too."

C. J. squealed with delight. "Ooh, Abby, you are the best friend a girl ever had. What's his name?"

"Uh . . . Bowater. Look, C. J., I don't know his first

name, but he's in the Charlotte police department now. I just call him Sergeant Bowater."

C. J. giggled. "Jane Bowater. I like it. Is he cute? Do you think we'll hit it off?"

"Trust me, dear, you two are like peas in a pod. Goobers in a shell. Now will you step on it? You're not even up to the speed limit."

"Sure thing, Abby." She drove at an acceptable speed for all of one block before slacking off again. "What's that you've got wrapped in a sheet? That isn't Dmitri, is it?"

I glanced down at my hands. "This is a pillowcase, dear. And you don't hear any meowing, do you?"

"He's dead?"

I sighed patiently. "Dmitri's at home, safe and sound under the couch. This"—I gently rocked my precious bundle—"is what's going to make me a very rich woman."

C. J.'s eye—the one that I could see at the moment—widened to the size of your average hot tub, and her gasp momentarily depleted the car of oxygen. "You had a baby?"

I may be on the short side, and I was properly buckled in, still I managed to slide my leg over and press down with my toe on the arch of C. J.'s foot. The little car shot ahead.

Rob Goldburg opened his condo door before I could even locate the bell. "You said on the phone it was extremely urgent, Abby. What's wrong?" He glanced at C. J.'s black clothes. "Somebody die?"

"It's not her cat," C. J. said helpfully. "She won't

confirm it, but I think she had a baby. Rob, did she ever look pregnant to you?"

I gave her a friendly push into the best-appointed salon this side of the Atlantic. Rob and his life-partner, Bob, are also in the business. Their shop, The Finer Things, is arguably the South's most upscale antique store. Vendors come all the way from Paris to haggle, and tourists from L.A. just to drool. The Rob-Bobs have decorated their oversize condominium with the finest from The Finer Things. Their Louis XIV furniture bears the teeth marks of Louis XV.

"Please, sit down," Rob said, ever the southern gentleman.

I selected a chair that I knew bore no impressions of royal baby teeth. This Louis XIV, upholstered in floral Genoese velvet, had a solid silver frame. It was my favorite piece in the Rob-Bob's collection but, alas, far too heavy to ever steal. C. J. settled into a companion chair that, although it looked the same, had a frame constructed of gilt over carved wood.

Rob, who was still standing, stared at my bundle. "What do you have there, the crown jewels?"

C. J. gasped. "Oh, Abby, you didn't!"

I shook my head to reassure her. "So, where's Bob?"

Rob studied his hands. They were a patrician's hands. Louis XIV must have had hands like that, only smaller.

"He's gone home."

"But this is his home," C. J. said before I could

hop off my chair and clamp my hands over her mouth.

"He's gone back to Toledo."

"Toledo?" C. J. and I chorused.

"That's where his family is. His real family."

I leaned forward. "But you're his family."

"I thought I was." He looked sad.

I wished with all my heart that C. J. would temporarily just disappear so I could speak with Rob alone. "What did you fight about?"

"Chicken."

"What?"

"Oh, that's quite common," C. J. assured us. "My cousin Lenora fights with her chickens all the time. Especially with that big Rhode Island red she calls Annabel."

Rob smiled. "We didn't fight *with* chickens; we fought *about* chicken. I like mine fried; Bob has to have his marinated in some sauce or another, and then washes that all off to get rid of the calories."

I nodded sympathetically. Rob might look patrician and have patrician taste in decor, but gastronomically he belonged, and would always belong, on the sunny side of the Mason-Dixon line. He was Jewish, of course, but southern Jewish. His mama rolled her chicken in seasoned matzo crumbs before committing it to grease. Bob, on the other hand, was a connoisseur of emu, which he thought of as just a big chicken with a lot of potential.

C. J. shook her head. "Y'all broke up over something as stupid as chicken?"

Rob blushed, and it was rather becoming. He has

classically handsome features and is just beginning to gray at the temples, even though he has passed the half-century mark.

"Well, I got tired of being his culinary guinea pig. I have rights, too, you know."

C. J. rolled her eyes. "This isn't about fighting with chickens or eating guinea pigs. Granny Ledbetter always said that behind a little fight is a little problem, and behind a big fight is a big problem."

"She's right, you know," I heard myself say. "Rob didn't go back up north just because of fried chicken. There's something else going on here."

Rob said nothing.

"All right, then, don't tell us." I counted to five under my breath, and mercifully C. J. kept mum. "Okay, do you now want to see what I brought?"

Rob shrugged. "Sure."

Slowly, and with as much drama as I could muster—which was considerable, if I do say so myself—I removed the loosely rolled canvas from the pillow case. "Voilà!"

Rob and C. J. stared mutely. It was quite apparent that they were both in shock.

"Isn't it gorgeous?" I cried.

C. J. winced. "Abby, you're not serious, are you?"

"The color," I almost shouted. "The texture! Feast your eyes on a masterpiece!"

"Ooh, Abby, I don't think so. My cousin Arvin did a picture just like that with his finger paints. Even his mama thought it was so ugly that she wanted to hold him back another year in kindergarten."

"This isn't a piece of refrigerator art," I shrieked. "This is a van Gogh!"

C. J. twittered while Rob, bless his heart, teetered. I thought the man was going to collapse at my feet.

"Where did you get that?" he rasped.

"At the Episcopal Church of Our Savior in Rock Hill. I got it tonight at a white elephant auction."

Rob extended a long, elegant finger but couldn't bring himself to touch the work of art. "It just might be, you know?"

"Of course it is! I've only seen a picture of it once—and that wasn't in color—but this most definitely is Vincent van Gogh's last study in green. The elusive *Field of Thistles*!"

"The brush strokes," Rob muttered. "The depth of feeling. The man was a genius."

"Then my cousin Arvin is a genius," C. J. snapped. The woman hardly ever gets irritable, so this was a bad sign.

Although Rob smiled, the look of condescension on his face would have made a Parisian proud. "Art appreciation is a highly personal thing."

C. J. has a lot of moxie for a twenty-four-year-old. "I suppose you like Jackson Pollack."

"Another genius," I chirped.

C. J. treated us to pitying looks. "You and Rob like these weird paintings because they're . . . they're . . . well, they're what snobby people like."

It was a good thing I was seated, because I reeled with shock. "There isn't a snobby bone in my body, C. J."

"Actually, there is," Rob said quietly.

"What?" I reeled again.

"Face it, Abby. We in the biz do tend to think we know what defines good taste. It's only natural. But like I said before, these are subjective opinions. C. J. is in the biz, too; she just happens to have different tastes."

C. J. beamed. "I like the Dutch masters. The ones before van Gogh. I like Rembrandt and Rubens."

Rob nodded. "So did van Gogh. He was particularly fond of Rubens."

"Can we get back to the subject at hand?" I wailed.

"Ah, yes, the *Field of Thistles*. Funny, but I just read an article recently that mentioned the painting."

"You did?"

Rob selected a Georges Jacob mahogany chair and finally sat. "It was an article about the Holocaust, actually. About a family in Antwerp, Belgium, who hid their artwork in a false floor in the attic only hours before being hauled off to a concentration camp. Only the father survived, and when he returned after being liberated, the house was no longer standing. Anyway, one of the paintings said to have been in his collection was the *Field of Thistles*."

I was on my feet. "What else did it say? Was there a picture?"

"I'm afraid not, Abby. Not of any paintings, just of the house—before the war, of course. The article was really about the family. Art was tangential."

"But it was mentioned!"

"Yes, Abby, but only briefly. There was another line, though, about the painting . . . hmm, let me think."

"Think!"

"Something about it being one of van Gogh's more questionable pieces. Ah, the author said the painting belonged to van Gogh's 'apocrypha.' "

I sat weakly. "Oh."

"But Abby, even if it was painted by one of van Gogh's disciples, it could still be tremendously valuable."

"How valuable?"

"Six figures, at least, for a painting that size—if we put it up for auction in New York. Could even be a lot more."

"Hot damn!" C. J. bounced on her genuine Louis XIV chair. "I'm taking a whole bunch of Cousin Arvin's paintings to the Big Banana."

I grimaced. "That's Big Apple, dear." I turned to Rob. "Who do we contact?"

"We? Abby, are you offering me a commission?"

"Yes," I said gratefully.

Rob grinned. "I just happen to have a friend who is an Impressionist expert. He owns a little gallery called Bons in midtown. I'll give him a call first thing in the morning."

I glanced at the eighteenth-century longcase clock on the floor behind Rob. It was after eleven. I had yet to negotiate a percentage with Rob, and it was possible that if I offered him fifty percent, he would call his friend at home—assuming he knew the number—and thereby undoubtedly ruin a very good working relationship. Possible, but not likely.

"Do you want me to leave the painting?"

"That would be helpful. It's easier to describe

something when I've got it right in front of me."

"Okay, but you lose it, you bought it." I said that only half in jest.

"I'll put it in my safe."

"You have one? I've never seen it."

"That's what makes it so safe. No one, except for Bob, knows its location."

"Ooh, Abby, never put something really valuable in a secret safe. Back in Shelby—"

I took pity on Rob and steered her to the door.

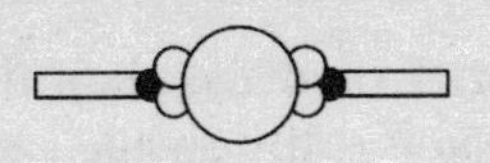

6

Some folks think that just because I'm in business for myself, I can set my own hours. That's true as long as I keep my shop open forty hours a week during prime business hours and spend another eight or ten hours attending sales. Not to mention the hours spent cleaning and organizing any subsequent purchases. I know what they mean, though. If I'm late to the shop, I may lose a valued customer, but I won't lose my job—at least not in one fell swoop.

I didn't think I'd ever get to sleep Wednesday night, and I didn't. It was well into the wee hours of Thursday morning when I stopped counting green thistles and drifted off. When my alarm beeped, I managed to turn it off in my sleep. Either that or, in my excitement, I had forgotten to set it. At any rate, the telephone woke me up at 9:30, a half hour later than the time I usually open my shop.

"Muoyo webe," Mama said cheerily.

"What?" I pushed Dmitri off my chest and sat up.

"Life to you, Abby. That's how they say 'good morning' in Tshiluba."

I glanced at the clock. "Oh, shoot! Mama, I've got to run."

"I know, dear. I tried the shop first and got the machine. Abby, you really should consider getting a professional to record your message. Someone who sounds . . . well, more cultured."

"Like Rob?" I remembered the painting. "Mama, sorry, but I really can't talk now."

"Fine," Mama said, her cheeriness deserting her. "I guess, like they say, bad news can wait."

I sighed. Mama baits her hooks with an expertise to be envied by the best fly fishermen.

"Sock it to me, Mama. But make it quick."

"Are you sitting down, Abby?"

"Mama, I'm still in bed!"

"Abby, I'm afraid I have some horrible news to tell you about one of your former boyfriends."

"Greg?" I managed to gasp after a few seconds. "Did something happen to Greg?"

"No, dear, it's Gilbert Sweeny. He's dead."

I wanted to reach through the phone line and shake Mama until her pearls rattled. "Gilbert Sweeny was never my boyfriend!"

"Abby, apparently you didn't hear what I said. Gilbert Sweeny is dead. He committed suicide. The police found him an hour ago."

"But that can't be true! I just spoke to him last night."

"It is true. I heard it from Barbara, who heard it from Dorothy, who heard it from the Queen herself."

My head spun. "Are you sure? How would Priscilla Hunt know? And so soon?"

Mama sighed. Clearly, she had failed me as a mother. Everyone knew that Priscilla Hunt was a veritable human switchboard, who not only monitored the townsfolk's movements but interfered at will. She regularly told Ben Hunter when to cut his grass and forbade Sarah Jenkins to hang purple drapes, and when that new family from Germany built a tree house in their backyard, the Queen sent a petition around asking for signatures to force the young family to tear it down. Mama says the Queen knew—and disapproved—when she switched toilet paper brands and bought that new quilted stuff. Mama also says she doesn't care and is not switching back.

"Mama, Her Majesty must be wrong this time. The police don't rule suicides this quick."

"They do if there's a note."

"There's a note?"

"Abby, did you get your hearing checked like I told you to last month?"

"My hearing is fine. Tell me about the note."

"One of Gilbert's fishing buddies found it. The men were supposed to head up to the mountains at the crack of dawn. Gilbert was on vacation, you know. He and his friend would have left last Saturday but his hemorrhoids acted up, and where they were going, the men needed to do a lot of hiking."

"I suppose that information comes from the Queen, too."

"Abby, please. Priscilla Hunt is not to be trifled with."

Actually, the woman was a paper tiger—annoying, if found wet on your lawn, but otherwise harmless. Try as she might, the Queen couldn't make Ben cut his grass or Sarah exchange her drapes. And as for the petition to tear down the tree house, not a single person in Rock Hill would sign. In fact, Hortense Simms organized a counterpetition requiring each homeowner within city limits to build a tree house. Believe it or not, that petition got eighteen signatures, Mama's included.

"Mama, what did the note say?"

"Ah, that. Abby, I was afraid you would ask."

"Mama, that's exactly why you called. Now spit it out, or I'm calling the Queen herself."

Mama cut her own gasp short, lest I follow through with my threat. "You were mentioned in the note, dear."

"Me?"

"Well, not in so many words. But it was all very clear. Gilbert said he'd been depressed lately and what he did last night was the final straw."

"But we didn't do anything," I wailed.

"Not you, dear. Him. He said he'd betrayed his stepmother by selling something that meant a lot to her. Something that didn't really belong to him. That had to be the painting you bought, Abby."

I was shaking like a paint mixer again. "Says who? The Queen?"

"Says Barbara, who heard it from Dorothy who heard it from—"

"Mama, the note didn't contain my name, right?"

"No, Abby, it didn't. I'm certain of that. Still, everyone knows you bought the painting."

"Then I'm not mentioned, Mama; I'm only implicated. There's a huge difference, you know. And I bought the painting at a church auction, Mama. It's not like I twisted his arm in private."

"No one's blaming you for anything, dear. I just wanted you to know what was going on. Besides, the man was obviously unbalanced. And so is his step-mother, if you ask me. I didn't want to say anything to you last night—it being a fund-raiser and all—but that's one ugly painting. Any woman fond of blue swirls has got to be a little bit flaky."

I gulped. I much prefer to swallow pride than to choke on words themselves.

"Mama, how did Gilbert do it?" Back in high school, the guy was really into guns. Many southern boys like to hunt, but Gilbert had his own armory. I know, because I once double-dated with him and Debbie Lou. The name of my date escapes me now, but I haven't forgotten sitting on a pine tree stump in a freshly logged woods, along with Debbie Lou, while Gilbert and my date shot bottles off other stumps. I remember this so well because I got pine sap on a brand-new skirt that I had bought with baby-sitting money.

"No gun, dear. Gilbert took pills."

It didn't ring true. "What kind of pills?"

"Abby, the Queen is not a walking encyclopedia; she's just better informed than the rest of us."

"She's nosy."

"Shhh," Mama said reflexively. "Abby, you will be at the funeral, won't you? It will look a little strange if you're not there. High school sweethearts, and now this note—"

"We were not high school sweethearts!" I glanced

at the alarm clock. "Mama, I have to go."

"Saturday, two o'clock, at the Church of Our Savior in Rock Hill."

"What?" I said crossly.

"The funeral, dear. It's all been arranged."

I shouldn't have been surprised. Quite possibly Gilbert was still warmer than sushi, but already an elaborate ritual had been planned. Leave it to we southerners, and Episcopalians in particular.

"I'll wear my black dress," I said instructively. Ever since Daddy died—killed by a kamikaze seagull—Mama refuses to wear black at funerals. She has retired the color, much like ball clubs retire the numbers on jerseys worn by team legends. While I would agree that I should stay out of my mother's business, pink is simply not an acceptable color to wear on such a solemn occasion.

"I'll wear what I want," Mama said, reading my mind. She hung up.

My shop, the Den of Antiquity, is just up the road a piece from Queens College. When I inherited the business from my Aunt Eulonia Wiggins, it was one of five antique stores clustered along the inside elbow of Selwyn Avenue. Today, more than a dozen shops line the street on either side. There are those—apart from myself—who predict that someday soon Selwyn Avenue will be the antique Mecca of the New South.

I will be the first to agree that we Selwyn Avenue dealers owe a lot to the Rob-Bobs. Their shop, The Finer Things, should more aptly be called "The Finest Things." They set the standard for which the rest of us strive. Now, having said that, permit me a smidgen of jealousy. I sell quality stuff, too, but you don't see crowds of collectors beating down my door. And no tour buses from Atlanta stop at my stoop.

"Excuse me," I murmured like a mantra as I pushed my way through knots of middle-aged women dressed in ankle-length linen dresses and Italian leather shoes. It was a calculated risk. Most folks have two elbows, and sometimes those things can be sharp. The only rock concert I ever attended left me with a horrible ringing in my ears, although I wasn't even there long enough to hear the music. And my poor dogs! Vertically enhanced people are often unaware of my presence, and my feet tend to attract their feet like magnets.

With my hands safely over my ears I dodged flailing elbows and feet the size of continents. When things are this busy, one of the Rob-Bobs hangs out near the register, and since today there was only Rob, that's where I headed.

"Abby!" a deep male voice boomed.

I whirled, at first seeing nothing but linen skirts. Hey, but this is Charlotte at the close of the twentieth century—perhaps I did know one of the wealthy older women.

"Abby, what's wrong with your ears?"

The disembodied voice was certainly familiar. Offhand, I would have said it sounded like Bob Steuben, Rob's better half, but the former was supposed to be in Toledo.

"Abby, over here."

I turned another ninety degrees. The basso profundo was indeed Bob Steuben.

"I thought you went home!" I cried, genuinely delighted to see him. I would have hugged my friend, but Bob, a full-blooded Yankee, doesn't cotton to public displays of emotion.

Bob grinned. He's skinny and has a large head, but fortunately Bob has a large heart as well and is one of the most intelligent men I've ever met.

"I got as far as West Virginia and decided to think things over."

"And?"

"And so I spent a couple of days wandering around the Mountain State, and came to the conclusion that this is my home."

"You go, boy!"

"Rob, you, the rest of my friends—that's what makes this home. Besides, Charlotte is one hell of a beautiful place to live."

"I bet Rob was happy to see you! Or was he mad? I mean, because you just took off like that."

Bob shook his head. "Someone from Rob's support group was in touch with him the entire time."

"Ah, GASPY. Gay Anorexic Southerners whose Partners are Yankees. Right?"

"That's 'Adult Southerners.' Anyway, they helped Rob understand that we unfortunate ones born north of the Mason-Dixon line are bound to act screwy sooner or later. And through understanding comes compassion, and eventually forgiveness. So, thanks to GASPY, Rob and I have another chance."

"That's wonderful!" I meant it, but it was time to

move on to more important things. "Have you seen the painting?"

Bob rubbed knobby hands together. "It's exquisite. Rob couldn't wait to show me."

"Do you think it's genuine? Did he call New York?"

"Why don't you ask me yourself?"

I turned. Rob Goldman was standing right behind me, a lottery-winning smile plastered across his face.

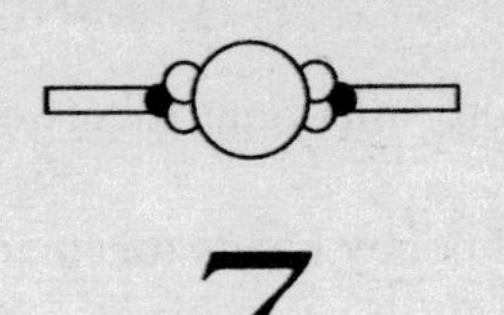

7

"It's real?" I shrieked.

Rob scooped me up in a bear hug and then set me down three feet away from where I'd been standing. "Shhh, Abby. Not here."

"Then where?"

"Bob, watch the register, please."

Bob nodded. A couple of the linen-clad matrons were fishing for their credit cards. I could tell by their finishing-school posture that they were not the type to haggle over prices. The Rob-Bobs' till would soon be merrily ringing.

While Bob rang up sales, Rob led me to the stockroom. I had been in there only once before, and it was like entering antique heaven. The savvy owners of The Finer Things do not put their finest things on the floor. They make the real collectors ask—no, beg—to enter the inner sanctum.

"What's that?" I gasped, forgetting for a moment my own treasure.

"That's an orrery."

"A what?"

"An orrery. It's a mechanical model of the solar system. They were named after the Earl of Orrery."

"No, *that*. What the orrery is sitting on. That little piano."

"Ah, that. That's a French harpsichord. Supposedly it belonged to Napoleon's mother. See the detailed painting on the lid?"

"Yes, the painting—the painting! Your friend said it's real, right?"

Rob smiled. "Fred was so excited, he actually dropped the phone. Abby, that painting of yours just might be the art find of the century."

I swayed, staggered, and finally plopped down on a damask-covered daybed. "You're not putting me on?"

Rob's dark eyes flashed. "I wouldn't kid about a thing like this. Fred said he's been hearing rumors for years that the painting was in America someplace. Only he figured it was in New York or San Francisco."

"Ah, but it was in little bitty Rock Hill, South Carolina. Not even in Charlotte. That will show those snooty big-city folks. So, Rob, what's it worth? Six figures, like you said?"

Rob glanced at the storeroom door and mumbled something.

"What?"

"I said, 'ten.' "

My hopes fell like a soufflé when the oven door has been slammed. Already I had mentally paid off my mortgage and the Oldsmobile Intrigue. And while ten thousand dollars is a lot of money, I owed that much on my credit cards alone.

"Ten thousand, eh? So what's your cut? What's Fred's?"

Rob's eyes danced. "Not ten thousand, Abby. Ten million."

I must have fainted because the next thing I knew, Rob was gently slapping my face. "Abby. Abby."

"Here, I'll make her smell this." Bob shoved a bottle beneath my nose.

I coughed and forced myself to a sitting position. "What is that vile stuff?"

"That vile stuff," Rob said archly, "is my aftershave lotion."

"He needs to shave twice a day," Bob said proudly. "And the lady customers love the smell."

"Well, it's certainly potent. It's done a number on my brain. I thought Rob said *Field of Thistles* was worth ten million dollars."

"He did."

I looked at Rob. "Y'all are teasing me, right?"

"I said I wouldn't kid about something this important."

"Tell her about the Japanese, Rob."

"Ah, the Japanese." Rob has a languid, southern way of speaking, which has its place, but at that moment in time I wanted to jump up and snatch the words from his mouth.

"What about the Japanese?"

"Fred's pretty sure that if they get in on the bidding, it could go as high as twenty."

I slapped my own face—lightly, of course, so as not to break any veins. "We're talking about twenty million dollars here again, aren't we? I mean, we're not discussing twenty egg rolls."

"Egg rolls are Chinese," Bob said. "Anyway,

Abby, you're going to be a very rich woman."

Rob laughed. "Rich enough to buy everything in this room."

"What about you? You never did tell me your cut."

"How about 10 percent? Does that sound fair?"

How quickly one's perspective can change. "Before or after taxes?" I asked wisely.

Rob seemed to anticipate the question. "Before. And I assure you, Abby, that finder's fees are usually much stiffer than that."

"Travis McGee always kept half," Bob boomed.

"I've never heard of Mr. McGee, and besides, Rob didn't find anything. I did."

I could feel the chill in the air, and it had nothing to do with the air conditioner rattling away on the back wall. "Five percent," I said generously.

The men exchanged glances, which was terribly unfair if you ask me. "I seem to have forgotten Fred's number," Rob said. "Bob, do you know it?"

"Fred who?"

"Okay, guys, if that's the game you want to play, I'm willing. I'll just hop on a plane to New York with the van Gogh under my arm, and you won't see a red cent."

Rob didn't flinch. "Hop away, Abby."

"Do you need a ride to the airport?" Bob asked. He had the nerve to sound sincere.

That did it. "What I need is for one of you to go straight home and liberate my painting. Better yet, I'm coming with you."

"I'll go," Rob said. "But Abby, you're making a big mistake."

"I thought you were a friend," Bob said, "but I guess I was wrong."

Those words cut through my heart like a knife through warm butter, but I didn't back down. A million dollars can do strange things to a woman.

When Rob returned to the living room, his face was gray. Not an attractive blue gray like the tiles beneath my chair, but a sickly yellow gray worth much more than a thousand words.

I was on my feet. "Where is it?"

"Uh, well, it's someplace."

"So is China! Where's my painting? Where's *Field of Thistles*?"

Rob looked at his hands. "I remember putting it in the safe, Abby. But it's not there. Just give me a minute, and I'll look around."

"Show me your safe!" I will admit now that I was not acting like a good southern girl. No doubt five generations of Wigginses were rolling over in their graves, including the great-great-grandmother who had served tea and lemon cake to Robert E. Lee on his visit to Rock Hill.

"Okay, Abby, but you have to promise not to tell a soul the location of this safe."

"Cross my heart and hope to die; stick a needle in your eye."

Rob sighed and led the way through the master bedroom to the master bathroom. The bathroom!

"There," he said, pointing at a bidet.

"Where?"

He pushed a button on the bidet, which swiveled a hundred and eighty degrees to reveal the top of a metal safe, replete with combination dials.

"Well, I'll be!" I knew Rob was clever, but not that clever. "What happens if someone tries to use the thing?" I asked.

Rob rolled his eyes. "Please. We buy French antiques, not French hygiene habits."

"Open it."

"Abby, please—look the other way."

I obliged, but only because I didn't have time to waste. I even hummed the tune of *La Marseillaise* while Rob turned the dials.

"Okay."

I turned. The safe was crammed with velvet boxes, the sort in which fine jewelry is stored. There was also what appeared to be a pile of paper money, held together with a thick rubber band. But alas, a white envelope on top of the pile prevented me from determining the denomination of the bills.

"There isn't any room in there for a painting."

"Yes, there is. But just barely. I left the canvas rolled, and angled it in from top to bottom."

"Did you crease it?"

He looked pained. "No, Abby. I care about that painting. I care about you."

"Well, at least one of those statements is true. So, now where will you look?"

"I'm trying to think. I put it in here just after you left. Then I took it out to show Robert. And then—oh, God, I didn't put it back!"

"That much is obvious. Where did you put it?"

"We were in the music room. I left it on the baby grand."

It was a race I managed to win, despite his long legs. "It's not in here!" I panted.

"But it has to be. I remember clearly now. I had it spread out right there on the piano. We were both looking at it, and then I looked at Bob and he looked at me and—"

"Spare me the details. What did you do with it afterward?"

Rob groaned. "There wasn't any afterward. We just went to work."

"And for that my painting is gone? My twenty million dollars?"

"Ten, Abby. Twenty only if someone gets overenthusiastic."

"You want to quibble over ten million dollars at a time like this?"

"Touché."

"I beg your pardon?" But I knew exactly what he meant.

"Abby, I swear the painting was right there, and no one has been in here since Bob and I left the room—except for Mrs. Cheng."

"Mrs. Cheng? Your cleaning lady?"

"Yes. She does the big cleaning on Monday, but on Thursdays, after Bob and I go to work, she stops by and changes the linens and towels again."

"She comes and goes as she pleases?"

"Don't worry, Abby; she's bonded and insured. I'll call her right now and see if she remembers seeing the painting, although she may not be home yet."

"But she doesn't speak English!" I wailed. "Not a word. You told me that yourself."

He extended a hand as if to calm me, but I jerked away. "But I speak Mandarin, remember?"

"Then call!"

Rob dialed his cleaning lady's number and almost immediately began chattering away in a singsong language that was quite clearly Asian. As angry at him as I was, I was impressed. I've been told that Mandarin Chinese is a very difficult language to learn because it is tonal, and a wrong voice fluctuation can result in saying something totally unintended, or possibly even nothing at all. Rob must have been saying something, because his conversation seemed to last well into the next millennium.

At last, putting his hand over the receiver, he turned to me with a grin wide enough to encompass south Charlotte. "She was just walking in the door, and yes, she has the painting!"

"What?"

"She was taking the Sunday *New York Times* home with her—I always let her have it—and she laid it down on the piano and then somehow accidentally picked up the painting with it when she left. The painting is safe and sound at her house."

Mama says my sigh of relief blew out a row of tubside candles in her bathroom in Rock Hill. "Thank God! Tell her to bring it back at once—no, tell her we'll be right there."

Rob smiled. "I already did. She wants you to come over there by yourself."

"Tell her I'm on my way. And tell her not to budge an inch. Oh, and tell her there will be a fat reward for her if the painting hasn't been damaged in any way."

Rob said something a lot longer than that. Finally he turned back to me. "She wants to know how much."

"What?"

"The reward."

"Twenty-five thousand dollars," I said off the top of my head.

Rob translated what I said. Even I could hear Mrs. Cheng laugh.

"What did she say?" I demanded.

"She said, 'The duck that strokes the camel's back is green.' "

"Huh?" I asked.

"Tell her twenty-five thousand green ducks can stroke a lot of camels, and then hurry up and get off the phone. I need directions." Suddenly I remembered that Rob had driven me over from his shop. "Oops, I don't suppose I can borrow your car?"

"Of course you can. I'll take Bob's—we rode together this morning. I'm pretty sure there's close to half a tank of gas. Just remember that I have antilock brakes—"

"I have a car of my own," I snapped. "I know how one works. What I need is directions."

Rob hung up and found a gold pen and pad of paper in the drawer of a marquetry secrétaire. The directions he wrote were clear, and the little map he drew was really quite good. I had everything I needed to get to Mrs. Cheng's house, including some more unsolicited advice.

But what Rob didn't tell me was that I needed to check my rearview mirror from time to time.

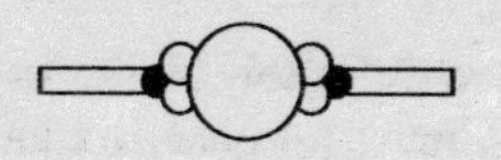

8

It was only eight blocks to Mrs. Cheng's, but it might as well have been eighty. The Rob-Bobs' condominium is just south of Myers Park, a neighborhood of stately brick homes and willow oaks. Mrs. Cheng lives in a brick home shaded by willow oaks, but her entire house could fit in the master bathroom of a Myers Park home.

I parked the car on the street and followed the cracked walk between twin rows of monkey grass to the screened porch. Fortunately, the bell was on the outside. When I pressed the button, I couldn't hear it ring, and was debating whether or not to press it a second time when the front door opened.

"May I help you?"

"Yes. My name is Abigail Timberlake. I'm here to see Mrs. Cheng."

"That's me. I'm Irene Cheng." She quickly unhooked the screen door. "Come on in. It's hotter than a well digger's ass out there, and you look a mess. You're dripping sweat."

I stared, forgetting my southern manners. Irene Cheng was a woman approximately my own age and height. She was dressed in white denim shorts, a faded green T-shirt, and flip-flops. Except for her features, which were definitely Asian in appearance, she could have been me. Her accent, like mine, was pure Dixie.

"Is there another Mrs. Cheng at this address?"

"No. Just me."

"There must be some mistake. I'm looking for a Mrs. Cheng who works for Rob Goldberg."

She smiled. "I work for Robby. I left the front door open, so come on in before I air-condition all of south Charlotte."

I followed her into a delightfully cool, if modest, living room.

"But you speak English," I said, taking the chair offered.

"So do you. And you barely have an accent."

"What? I don't have an accent at all—oh, you were just kidding, weren't you? Well, you see, Rob said you didn't speak a word of English. Besides, I heard him speaking Chinese on the phone."

"He thinks he was speaking Chinese. But his Mandarin is so awful. Not that mine is such hot shakes, either. You don't pick up that much going to Chinese school one day a week when you're a kid. And both my parents were American-born and could barely speak it themselves."

"But Mrs. Cheng—"

"Call me Irene."

"Then call me Abby."

"Abby. You're named after a monastery?"

"That's without the 'e.' It comes from Abigail."

"Ah. Well, you see, Abby without the 'e,' Robby took Mandarin in college. Chinese art was one of his interests. Anyway, when I answered his ad for a cleaning lady he just assumed I spoke Chinese. And since he was eager to practice his Chinese—well, we've never spoken in anything but. Only it's broken Chinese. I mean, just this morning he said that twenty-five million green camels were chasing Donald Duck. What the hell is that supposed to mean?"

I laughed. "I don't know. Maybe he was referring to the crowds at Disneyworld."

"Maybe. But if you ask me, Robby is a little meshugah. Say, would you like some sweet tea?"

I hadn't had anything to eat or drink all morning, and I was dying for some. Twenty-five million camels could not have been that thirsty. But she still had my painting.

"Yes, I'd love some. But could I have *Field of Thistles* first?" Just saying that used up more of my precious saliva.

"Is this another of Robby's riddles?"

"No. I want my painting."

"Oh, that! Of course." She hopped up and darted into another room.

While she was gone, I studied her decor. The furniture was better-quality Victorian. There were signed prints on the walls, and even a small original oil. All my assumptions about Irene Cheng had proved wrong.

"Here you are." Irene thrust the rolled-up van Gogh at me like it was yesterday's newspaper.

I nervously spread it across my knees. It looked all right. But wait, was that a new crack in the upper left-hand corner? How was I to tell? I had only seen the painting at night, and in artificial light.

"This painting is worth a lot, you know."

"So I heard. Although I can't imagine why."

"Why? Just look at it. See those brush strokes. And that bold, vibrant use of color."

Irene peered intently at the painting. "Frankly, Abby, this picture's as ugly as homemade sin warmed over."

A large, gray-and-white cat had appeared out of nowhere and was sniffing my ankles.

"She smells my cat, Dmitri."

"I think Esmerelda smells you."

I was about to purr with pleasure when the cat bit my left ankle. "Ouch!"

"Oh, dear, did my Essy give you a little love nip?"

"Love nip? Does she have all her shots?"

Irene nodded. "Are you bleeding? I mean, this is a brand-new carpet."

"No, I guess I'm okay." I rubbed my ankle. "She didn't break the skin or anything, but she took me by surprise. I guess she was just doing her job."

Irene giggled. "Some people say that cats are sneaky, evil, and cruel. That's all true, but they have many other fine qualities as well."

I grinned. "They're incredibly smart—much smarter than dogs. You won't find eight cats pulling a sled."

"You're right about that. People think cats are stupid because they're not obedient in the same way dogs are. Sure, dogs come when they are called, but cats take a message and get back to you later."

We both laughed.

"Dogs believe they are human," I said. "Cats believe they are God."

"Of course, dogs are cleaner."

"I beg your pardon? When's the last time you saw a dog give itself a tongue bath?"

"But that's my point. Cats aren't clean, they're just covered with cat spit."

"Oh, gross!" Despite's Irene's ignorant comment about the twentieth century's most important art find, I found myself liking the woman. She was petite and down to earth, and didn't want anything from me. Or did she? "Rob Goldman said you insisted that I pick up the painting in person. And by myself. Why is that?"

"Because I wanted to meet you."

My antennae shot up. "Me?"

"I want something from you."

I stood, clutching the painting tightly in my hot little fists. "How much did Rob say the reward was going to be?"

She wrinkled her nose. "He never mentioned a reward—unless it had something to do with all those camels. I was going to ask you for a job."

"I'm sorry, but I don't have much need for a cleaning lady. It's just me and Dmitri, and I'm gone most of the time."

Irene frowned. "I don't want to clean your house. I want a job in your shop."

"Cleaning?"

She stepped in front of me and spread her arms. "Is that all you think I can do? Clean?"

"What is it you want to do?" I wailed.

"I want to sell antiques."

"You do?"

She nodded vigorously, her short black hair rising and falling in waves. "I've learned a lot working for Robby. I observe. And I read everything I can about what he's got. Hey, I may not have his money—," she gestured at the contents of the room, "—but I do the best I can."

"You have some very nice pieces." I meant it.

"So, will you give me a job? I really need it. My husband got downsized after nineteen years with his company. He's starting a new job today, but the pay is a lot less."

Why not give the woman a job? Rob had Bob, and Wynnell had a girl to assist her on weekends, our prime time. Heck, even C. J. was considering importing a cousin or two from Shelby to help in her shop. Besides, once I sold the van Gogh, my reputation would skyrocket—and so would my business.

"I keep all my records by computer. How are your computer skills?"

Irene shrugged. "Fair."

"Well, then they're ten times better than mine. How are your people skills?"

"Fair."

"Again you've got me beat. I'd say you're hired. When can you start?"

"How about right now?"

"Tomorrow morning. Be at the shop at nine sharp. I don't open until ten, but that will give me time to show you the ropes."

"Thank you, Abby. You won't regret this."

She walked out to the porch with me. Just as I opened the screen door, a dark blue car with North Carolina plates vacated its parking spot beneath a shady oak and sped down the street. At the first cross street, it swerved and narrowly missed a pickup that was already in the intersection. The pickup driver slammed on his brakes and honked. The blue car was soon a blue dot.

"Someone's going to get killed if the city doesn't put up a stop sign," Irene said, shaking her head. "You be real careful, because I don't want my job to end before it's even begun."

"I'll be careful."

Irene Cheng need not have worried. Multimillionaires do not get run down by cars in Charlotte. They drown off yachts in the Mediterranean or choke on caviar. True, I was still only a potential multimillionaire, but already I could feel it in my bones. This time, luck was on my side.

I made a beeline home, stashed the painting in the oven, and headed back to The Finer Things to return Rob's keys. I parked Rob's car behind the shop and, finding the back door locked, walked around to the front. Just as I reached the sidewalk, another dark blue car went barreling down Selwyn Avenue, headed toward Queens College. I stared after it. Again, a North Carolina tag, but my driving glasses were already back in my purse, so I couldn't be sure of any details beyond that.

"You're going to run someone over!" I shouted,

and then clamped a hand over my mouth.

"Abby!"

I turned. Wynnell Crawford was waving madly to me from the door of her shop, the Wooden Wonders.

"Just a minute," I called. "I need to give Rob his keys first."

"Stop! Hold it right there!" Wynnell is ten years older than I, but she keeps in shape stacking the heavy wooden furniture she sells. In Wynnell's shop, the antiques are piled to the ceiling in neat rows, like library stacks. One careless move from a customer, and more than just the desired piece is history.

"How could you do that, Abby?"

"How could I do what?"

"Come inside, Abby." Wynnell grabbed the elbow of the arm holding the precious painting and hauled me into the farthest recess of her shop. On both sides, early twentieth-century veneer dressers rose in sheer walls. If it was privacy she was after, she couldn't have found a better spot in the bowels of a Roman catacomb.

"The Rob-Bobs are heartsick. They believed you were their friend."

"But I am! Next to you, Rob's my closest friend."

"You used him, Abby." Wynnell lowered brows the size of shrubs. "Shame on you."

"This is business, Wynnell."

"He wanted 10 percent. That's only fair."

"But still, a million dollars. That's a lot of money."

"That painting you bought at your mother's church auction is worth a million dollars?"

"No, it's worth ten," I said patiently. "Rob wanted a million."

"Lordy!" She took a few gulps of stale, lemon-polish-scented air. "That *is* greedy. It must be Bob's Yankee influence."

Alas, my friend is a Yankeephobe. In her mind, the War between the States (her words, not mine) is far from over. The last good Yankee died at Gettysburg, and it's a pity that more didn't join him. Of course, Wynnell is not averse to taking Yankee dollars from Yankee tourists, just as long as they leave some sand behind them at Myrtle Beach for her. The fact that Wynnell had a grandparent from north of the line is something she blatantly chooses to ignore.

"I don't think a commission should ever be more than a hundred grand; do you?"

Wynnell glanced up and down the narrow aisle. "I had an idea, Abby."

"Forget it, dear. I'm not crossing the street on my knees and begging Rob's forgiveness." For one thing, with my luck, that dark blue car would make a return pass at just the wrong moment.

"Don't be silly, Abby. You were absolutely right about Rob being greedy. Besides, with the business his shop does, he certainly doesn't need any extra money. Let's face it, the man is loaded."

"Well, I don't know if loaded is the right word, but he's certainly comfortable."

Wynnell, who makes all her own clothes, smoothed the skirt of a dress that was held together only by oversize safety pins. I'd seen that creation before. She refers to it as her "air-conditioned" dress because of all the gaps.

"What I'm getting at is that Rob doesn't need you, and you certainly don't need him."

"I don't?"

"Of course not. I'd be happy to sell the painting for you."

I willed the corners of my mouth to stay in place. "No offense, Wynnell, but mahogany furniture is your forte, not Impressionist paintings."

The hedgerows waggled in amusement. "Oh, not me, personally, Abby. But I know someone who could sell the painting for you. I'd just be the go-between."

"I see. And what would your cut be?"

With studied casualness, Wynnell opened and closed a monstrous pin. "Five hundred thousand dollars."

"Get out of town!"

"Okay, a hundred thousand."

"Not even close, Wynnell. I thought we were friends."

"We are! But you just said you'd pay a hundred grand as a brokerage fee."

"I said that would be my limit. I didn't expect my very best friend to try and fleece me as well."

"Why, I'll be! Are you sure you don't have any Yankee blood, Abby?"

I lowered my voice. "Actually, I do. I'm not supposed to breathe a word of this, but Daddy was from Cleveland. He didn't move south until he was six." There wasn't a lick of truth in that, but since Daddy died before I met Wynnell, she'd never be the wiser.

"Cleveland, Ohio, or Cleveland, Tennessee?"

"Ohio."

Wynnell staggered backward into a stack of dressers, thereby threatening both our lives. "I knew it! You've always been a little tight with your vowels, Abby. It must be genetic."

"Look who's calling the kettle black. Wasn't your grandmother originally from Chicago?"

Wynnell blanched, a startling contrast to the nearly black hedgerows. "So, tell me, Abby," she said by way of diversion, "how much will you pay your very best friend if she sells that painting of yours for ten million dollars?"

I sighed. "Wynnell, you don't even know anyone on the national, much less international, art scene. Do you?"

"I said I did, didn't I? For your information, my cousin Billy Bob works in a gallery in Greenwich Village."

"Doing what? Sweeping floors?"

"That's not all he does. They let him hang pictures sometimes."

"Well, for this job I need a professional art dealer."

"Sure you do. But let's just say Billy Bob's boss is able to sell it for ten million. How much would my cut be? You still haven't told me."

"Fifty thousand should do, shouldn't it?" I offered generously.

"Why, Abigail Louise Timberlake, you are cheap!"

"I am not!"

"You're as cheap as a nest full of sparrows. Cheap, cheap, cheap."

"I don't need to take that from you, dear. Talk about cheap! You won't even buy yourself a decent dress at Kmart. Why, just look at you. A strong magnet and a sudden gust of wind, and you'd be as naked as a baby jaybird. You may not know it, Wynnell, but you're the laughingstock of Selwyn Avenue."

"Get out of my store!"

"Gladly!" I turned and marched out of Wooden Wonders like an only slightly larger than life toy soldier.

After dropping off Rob's car keys—neither he nor Bob would speak to me—I headed for the bosom of the only friend who will never desert me. I headed home to Mama. First, however, I had another stop or two to make.

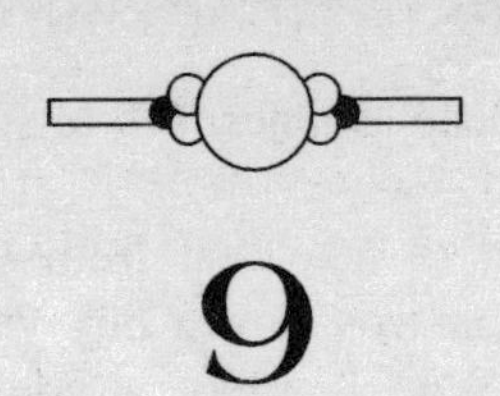

9

I much prefer back roads. During rush hour, I-77 is clogged with commuters, and at other times its still bumper-to-bumper traffic, thanks to all the tourists who try to sneak through Charlotte at "off" times. During the winter, half of Quebec passes through the city in search of a more hospitable climate. When, on those rare occasions, Quebecois wander into my shop, I insist that they speak English. I require the same from the hordes of Ohio and Pennsylvania folk headed for Myrtle Beach each summer. At any rate, on the back roads I see only Carolina plates, and the pace is much easier.

Charlotte and Rock Hill used to be separated by twenty-five miles of peach orchards, pine woods, cotton fields and the lovely little town of Fort Mill. The cotton fields are gone now, and only one orchard remains, just north of Fort Mill. But Carolina Place is as beautiful as shopping malls get, and on Route 21 there are at least three tiny bars and a wedding chapel tucked into the pine woods—just in case the mall doesn't satisfy. South of Fort Mill, the pine woods are being felled in the interest of condominiums and cookie-cutter homes, which, county officials assure us, is a sign of progress.

Only the broad Catawba River remains unchanged, give or take a few dozen dams between its origin in the North Carolina mountains and Great Falls, South Carolina, where it mysteriously becomes the Wateree. The Catawba River is named after the Catawba Indians, whose reservation is located adjacent to the city of Rock Hill and who just recently opened a high-stakes bingo parlor on Rock Hill's main drag, Cherry Road.

After crossing the Catawba, I made the first right onto Celanese Road and followed it to India Hook. Then I made the first left turn, into the neighborhood of Harlinsdale. Many of the residents of this exclusive enclave are nouveaux riches, and their homes are magnificent, if not ostentatious. The sight of these pretend palaces always leaves me panting with envy.

I knew exactly where Hortense Simms lived; everyone who was anyone in Rock Hill knew which house was hers. It was the one with the overplanted yard. Whereas most of her neighbors had four or five azalea bushes and a camellia or two, along with ubiquitous dogwood, newly rich Hortense was cultivating a jungle. She had dozens of azaleas and camellias and a forest of dogwood. Rumor had it that she'd gotten a Master Gardener's certificate from the county extension office and was planning to introduce new plant material into the mix. Even worse than that was the rumor that Hortense herself was to be seen on her hands and knees weeding her azalea bed!

A meandering drive took me to a large paved circle in front of what can charitably be described as a pseudo-Italianate villa. Plaster lions guarded a faux marble stairs that led to an enormous lead-paned door. There was no doorbell that I could see, so I rapped, using a ring that hung from a brass lion's mouth. Being a true daughter of the south, I would not have dared to show up at a bereaved person's home without bearing an edible gift, so in my left hand I balanced a cake rescued from Harris Teeter. Before you gasp and accuse me of being a Yankee imposter, let me assure you that I had carefully removed the store wrapper and replaced it with aluminum foil. Only God and myself would be the wiser—and, trust me, whoever ate the cake would be so much better off.

Hortense surprised me by answering the door herself. I hadn't expected a butler, mind you, but maybe a relative or a friend. After all, there were several other cars in the parking circle besides mine.

I thrust the cake at Hortense. "For you."

She blinked.

"Because of your brother." Okay, I will admit it. I am terrible when it comes to expressing condolences. I once—inadvertently, mind you—congratulated a neighbor when his wife died.

Hortense blinked again. The brave woman was struggling to hold back the tears.

"Thank you. Won't you come in?"

"Uh—" I peered around her, through the foyer, and into a sumptuously appointed sitting room, as curiosity briefly triumphed over common sense, "—uh, I'm sorry, I can't. Maybe next time."

Then, realizing what I'd said, I fled down the faux marble steps to my car.

* * *

Rock Hill is where I was born and raised, and even if that were not true, I would still say it is a beautiful city—with the exception of Cherry Road. Unfortunately, Cherry Road is one's first introduction to the city when coming from the north, whether by interstate or back road. Dave Lyle Boulevard, one entrance to the south, is far more attractive and has the *Civitas* statues, those four bronze ladies whose nipples were filed following a complaint from the religious right. But thanks to South Carolina zoning laws, Rock Hill is shaped like a jigsaw puzzle piece, and Cherry Road passes in and out of the city too many times to be tamed.

Fool that I am, after leaving Hortense's house I drove down the untamed backbone of Rock Hill. Mama lives on Eden Terrace, two blocks west of Cherry Road, and I could have gotten off earlier than I did, but there is something therapeutic about exposing oneself to competing signs and urban discordance and then opting for shady streets and neat homes surrounded by well-kept lawns. Besides, I felt an overwhelming urge to visit that sleazeball Vincent Dougherty at his new business, the Adult Entertainment Center. I wasn't going to tell him about *Field of Thistles,* of course. I merely intended to feel incredibly good in his presence.

Thanks to a zig in the road where Rock Hill zags, Vincent's business lies outside city limits. A blue neon sign in the shape of a voluptuous nude flaunts a glass bosom that city fathers are powerless to do anything about. I had heard that the Adult Entertainment Center rented X-rated videos and sold sex toys—

and quite possibly even sex itself—but that was all hearsay. Nonetheless, I parked so that my North Carolina plate was turned away from busy Cherry Road, and I waited for a break in traffic before darting into the tan, aluminum-sided building.

Two steps inside the inner glass door, a man with silver hair stopped me. "You a member, ma'am?"

"No, of course not!"

"Sorry, ma'am, but then you ain't allowed in. Members only."

"But I don't want to rent anything—I certainly don't want to buy anything. I'm just looking for Vincent Dougherty, the owner."

Silver eyebrows narrowed. "You his ex-wife?"

"Bite your tongue!" I said, my dander rising. "This is business."

Rheumy eyes gave me the once-over. "No offense, ma'am, but you're a little small for that position. The ad said five foot five and taller."

"I'm not here for a job, you idiot!"

Someone behind me chuckled. "You sure?"

"Vincent Doughtery!" It was him, as big as life and twice as ugly. That wild orange hair clashed horribly with a purple nylon shirt. He was wearing sunglasses again, and I noticed that this pair, at least, had green plastic frames. Clearly Vincent's ex-wife, whoever she was, had ample reason to divorce the man.

"Do I know you?"

"No. But I know you. Your picture has been in *The Herald* more times than the mayor's." Mama saves the Sunday papers for me, you see. She's convinced that someday I'll move back "home."

"Ah, but I do know you. You're the one at the auction last night."

"Guilty," I said, smiling inside. "Man, how I love that painting."

"Well, Miss . . . Miss Timberlake, isn't it?"

"Yes."

"Come on back to the office. I'll get you something cold to drink. It's still real hot out there, isn't it?"

The girl Mama thought she raised would have walked away backward, her index fingers crossed in front of her. The girl Mama actually raised decided to twist the knife a little. I followed Vincent Dougherty down a long, cinder block hall, through a set of gray swinging doors, and then left through a door marked "private." Thank God he didn't close that one behind him. Had he done so, I would have bolted, or attempted to bolt. I can be rash, and I'm sometimes stupid, but I'm not brain-dead.

"Have a seat." Vincent waved at an enormous black Italian leather couch, standing alone on a Berber carpet the color of his hair. There was no desk, no filing cabinets, not even a television.

"But where will you sit?"

"Ha! That's a good one. Now sit." He clapped his hands together like a sultan ordering his harem to dance.

I sat on the far end of the couch, on the very corner of the cushion. I kept my leg muscles tense, ready to spring into action. Even alone in the room, with the door barred, I would not have relaxed. The smell of feet and old sweat emanating from the leather made me want to retch.

"So, you're happy with your painting, are you?"

"Delirious." I wanted to shout that I had a painting worth ten million dollars, maybe more, and that despite a few alienated friends, I was happy, happy, happy!

"It would have gone good in this room, don't you think?"

I stared at the pale yellow walls. It would have at that.

"Maybe."

"So, you come here to sell it? Maybe make a little profit?"

"No."

"So, why did you come here?"

Why, indeed? I should never have entered that den of iniquity. What was I thinking? I had to have been out of my mind. Maybe I was suffering from heatstroke and didn't know it.

"Here." I reached into my brown macramé shoulder bag, the one Mama made for me when I was in college, extracted one of my business cards, and flung it at him.

He reached for it. "What's this?"

"My antique store. I also consult on decorating jobs. In case you decide you need a little work."

He said nothing and seemed to be staring at me behind the reflective shades.

"Well, I heard that you had just opened this place," I said, my voice cracking like a pubescent boy's. "I decided it was worth stopping by, on the chance you hadn't yet found a decorator."

For the longest time, he said nothing. When he finally spoke, it sounded like his vocal cords were covered with slime.

"You came all the way from Charlotte?"

"Well, yes—but not just for this. My mama lives here in town."

"I see." He slid off the armrest and settled with a soft plop on the buttery leather. "Is she a pretty little thing like you?"

I was on my feet and out of that door in less time than it took Buford to have sex. I ran smack into the pot-bellied, silver-haired doorkeeper, but it barely slowed me down. The large stomach certainly didn't hurt my head.

Once safely in my car, I didn't stop until I reached Mama's house. I know, I shouldn't have run the stop sign at Myrtle and Eden Terrace, but as for that final stop light on Cherry Road—well, everyone knows that in South Carolina, a light doesn't officially turn red until six cars have sneaked through yellow.

Mama opened the door the second I pulled up. She was wearing a frilly white apron over her full-skirted, pink gingham dress. And as she never opens the door naked, she was, of course, wearing white summer pumps and the pearls Daddy gave her on their anniversary preceding his death.

"You're right on time, Abby. I just finished setting the table. We're having fried chicken and potato salad, and there's watermelon for desert. Or would you prefer chocolate cake?"

"Chocolate." There was no point in asking how she

knew I was coming. Mama claims she can smell the future.

Mama glanced at my hands. "Where's the painting?"

"It's at home. I hid it in the oven."

"You what? Abby, everyone who knows you knows that you don't cook. That's the first place someone will look."

"Thanks, Mama. Hopefully my friends won't be trying to steal from me."

"Speaking of friends," Mama said, when we were seated, "what's this I hear about you dumping all of them?"

"Mama! Did Wynnell call you?"

"As well she should, dear. She's been your very best friend for years."

"But, Mama, she's greedy. She wants to profit big-time off my windfall."

"I see." Mama took a thimble-sized helping of potato salad before passing the bowl to me.

"Mama, are you on a diet?"

"Who, me? Oh, no, dear. I'm just practicing. Now, Abby, I suppose you think Rob was being greedy, too."

"Most definitely. He wanted a million dollars. Can you believe that?"

Mama took a single chicken wing. "But that's a million dollars of found money, dear. I mean, like you said, it was a windfall."

"But it was a windfall into my lap, Mama. They've had windfalls and never given me a second thought."

Mama barely brushed the wing against her lips before setting it down. "They're your friends, dear. *Balunda*—that's how you say 'friends' in Tshiluba. Anyway, from what I understand, even a 10 percent cut would be quite reasonable."

"You're on their side," I wailed.

Mama recoiled as if she'd been slapped. "Why, Abigail Louise, how can you say such a thing? If you only knew what I went through to bring you into this world!"

I sighed. "Thirty-six hours of excruciating labor."

"Don't be cheeky, dear. My point is, I have always been in your corner, and will always be. Even when I'm in Africa."

"Yes, but—Africa?"

"I'm going to the Congo as a missionary, dear. That's why I'm learning Tshiluba."

"Mama, you're not serious, are you?"

"Of course I am, dear." She glanced over at my piled plate. "I've been practicing in case there's a famine over there."

"You've been practicing starvation?"

"Don't be silly, dear. I'm just eating less. We in the West eat far more than we need to keep body and soul together."

That is undoubtedly true, but it was Mama's mind that needed keeping together just then. "Is this official? I mean, have you talked to the bishop?"

"The bishop?"

"You know, the man with the big hat and shepherd's crook? The guy who's in charge of such things."

Mama's face looked like a fallen soufflé. "I see no reason why I can't do it on my own."

"But who will support you? Who's going to pay your way over?"

She looked around at a house frozen in the fifties. "I could sell my things. If I have any money left, I'll give it to the poor."

"Vincent tried that, Mama. It didn't work."

"Vincent Dougherty was a missionary?"

I grimaced. "Not hardly. Mama, last year you ran off to become a nun. The year before that, you wanted to join the army. It's obvious you've been at loose ends ever since Daddy died, and while that's completely natural, it has been an awfully long time since then. You need to find yourself."

"But that's just what I'm doing, dear. And the self I'm finding wants to be a missionary."

"Talk to the bishop, Mama. Will you do that?"

"Nasha."

"What's that mean?"

Mama squirmed. "Abby, I'm old enough to make my own mistakes."

"Touché, Mama. You don't want me meddling in your business, yet—"

She was lucky the phone rang. While Mama was off answering it, I put a plump chicken breast on her plate, a proper scoop of potato salad and a homemade biscuit.

When Mama returned, her face was glowing. "You'll never guess who that was!"

"My sainted brother, Toy."

"No, he called last year. Now guess again."

"Aunt Marilyn?"

"Closer, but even better."

"Wynnell calling to apologize?"

"Wrong! And that's three guesses, so I'm going to have to tell you." She sat down and leaned across the table conspiratorially. "That was You Know Who."

"But I don't," I wailed.

Mama frowned. "Not just any you know who, but *the* You Know Who."

"You mean Priscilla Hunt? The Queen?"

Mama beamed. "None other! Oh, Abby, this is so wonderful. She's invited me to dinner Saturday night."

"As the main course?"

"Abby, don't be rude. Do you know what an honor this is?"

I nodded. Mercifully, my mouth was full of biscuit. Not only was Priscilla Hunt the wealthiest woman in the parish, but she still had a husband. Within months after becoming a widow, Mama found her stream of dinner invitations drying to a trickle, and then, shortly after the first anniversary of Daddy's death, nothing. After all, a widow is even worse than a fifth wheel. A widow is a reminder of one's mortality.

"So, Abby, you won't mind if I cancel our plans for dinner and go to Priscilla's?"

"Not at all, Mama." And then, worried that I might have sounded too happy for her, I added, "Besides, we're having lunch now."

Mama glanced down at her plate and saw the extra food. "Abby, you really do care about me, don't you?"

"Of course, Mama." I looked away so I wouldn't cry. Wet, salty biscuits do nothing for my taste buds.

"Maybe Priscilla wants me to join her book club.

It's the most prestigious one in Rock Hill, you know. That has to be it! Why else would she invite me to dinner? She never once did that the whole time your Daddy was alive." Mama's face clouded. "I won't be able to join, of course, because I'm going to Africa. Oh, Abby, what am I going to do?"

I patted Mama's arm. "That's the least of your worries. Mama, the woman is up to something."

"Are you saying that I'm not good enough to be Priscilla's friend?"

"Frankly, yes. I mean," I hastened to add, "that you are good enough, but that she doesn't see it that way."

"Go ahead, try and alienate me, too, but it isn't going to work. Mark my words, dear, someday you're going to regret speaking to your dear old mother this way."

I dropped my fork so that it clattered loudly on my plate. "Maybe you'll regret all the hurtful things you've said to me. I bet Gilbert Sweeny's mother regrets a few things she said to her son."

Mama shook her head passionately. "Adele's stepson doted on her."

"Maybe Adele Sweeny is easy to dote on," I said wickedly. "Maybe she's a sweet old lady."

Mama gasped. "And I'm not? Is that what you're saying? Well, Abby, if that's how you feel, then march on over to Pine Manor and say hello to your new mama." She stood. "I guess it's just as well you cast me aside like last year's fashion statement; I'll soon be in Africa anyway."

I stood as well. "Have a nice trip."

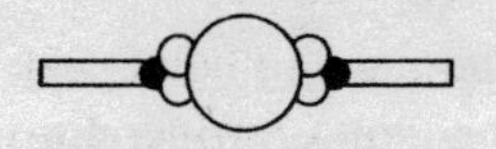

10

I drove straight to Pine Manor, which sits all by itself in the middle of a cotton field ten miles south of Rock Hill. A single Bradford pear stands as a lone sentinel on a sunburned fescue lawn. There isn't a pine tree in sight.

Part of me made the drive to spite Mama, and part of me because I really did want to see Adele Sweeny. There were a few questions that had been popping up in my mind that needed asking—although I realized this was not the appropriate time. Still, it never hurts to comfort the bereaved.

Pine Manor is one of the smallest nursing homes I know of, with only about a dozen residents, but that hardly explained the fact that there were only two vehicles in the parking lot. One was a car with the South Carolina license plate that read PINKY; the other, a van with a North Carolina plate that read TRAP. No doubt the latter was an exterminator.

I parked my car in what little shade the pear tree offered, and scurried up the short concrete walk. By the time I stepped inside the front door, I was dripping like a freshly halved watermelon. But I wasn't sweating, mind you. As a proper southern lady, born and bred, I never sweat. I merely dew. At any rate, the climate inside the nursing home was a blessed relief.

One enters this giant refrigerator through its main room, half of which serves as a lounge, the other half as a dining area. Behind a pair of scarred wooden doors adjacent to the dining area, I could hear the timpani of pots and pans. No doubt Pinky was in the kitchen, busily tidying things up after lunch.

Pine Manor lacks a reception desk, so I headed straight to the lounge where three tiny ladies sat huddled together under an orange-and-black afghan on a blue-flowered sofa. A large-screen television set was on, and I was surprised to see that they appeared to be watching *All My Children* and not some religious channel on which televangelists begged for money. The volume, however, was turned all the way down.

On second thought, perhaps they weren't even watching TV but staring in horror at the ghastly paintings that cluttered the walls of the room. They were the kind of thing one finds at "starving artist" sales: paintings so hideous and poorly executed that one can't help but wish the artists would hurry up and starve, to put us out of our misery. Compared to this collection of clunkers, Greg's faux Gogh looked positively gorgeous.

I cleared my throat. "Excuse me, dears. Could you tell me where to find Adele Sweeny?"

Only one pair of ancient eyes turned my way. "What day is it? Do you know?"

"It's Thursday, ma'am."

"Do you like my afghan?"

"It's beautiful."

"My sister made this for me. She went down on the *Titanic*, you know."

"How fascinating. But that was such a long time ago."

Perhaps she heard disbelief in my voice. "I'm eighty-nine. My sister was fourteen years older than I. What day is it?"

"It's Thursday," I said patiently. Truth be told, I was skeptical, but not about the dates. It was the polyester afghan I questioned.

"My sister's name was Sarah. She wasn't much bigger than a bird. Sang like one, too, they say. She was a professional singer, you know. She sang at President Coolidge's inauguration."

I bit my tongue. John Calvin Coolidge was elected president more than a decade after *Titanic* sank.

"You should have heard the applause afterward. They say it could be heard all the way to Georgetown."

"Isn't that Erica Kane something," I said to keep my tongue busy. "All those marriages, and she still hasn't learned a thing."

"Don't watch the show myself," she said and looked away.

"It's on now."

"Yes, but I'm not watching it."

"Ah, so you're just keeping your friends company." So far the other two women hadn't said a word.

"They're not watching it, either."

"Oh?"

"They're asleep."

I leaned forward and stared rudely at her companions. "But their eyes are open."

"That's 'cause it's too much trouble to close them."

"You're serious?" I was beginning to panic. Perhaps her friends were really dead.

"It's too much trouble for them to close their eyes. When you get to be our age, you'll see. A whole lot of things are too much trouble."

I was about to reach for the pulse of the nearest possible corpse when the woman blinked and coughed twice, before resuming her comatose state.

"You see? Margaret's just sleeping."

I shivered. "It's so cold in here. How can anyone sleep?"

"My son always says the same thing, but you get used to it." Five talons emerged from beneath the afghan to finger the left sleeve of a blue chenille bathrobe. "Gilbert gave me this robe the last time he was here. It's real pretty, isn't it? See, it matches my slippers."

"Yes, ma'am. Gilbert is your son?" My head buzzed. In a facility this small, what were the odds that more than one woman had a son by that name? Surely this woman wasn't the abusive stepmother Adele Sweeny! I mean, I'm not entirely naïve, but I couldn't imagine this mere sprite of a woman whipping even butter with a coat hanger.

"Gilbert Sweeny," she said proudly. "He's my stepson, but I love him as if he were my own. He lives in Rock Hill. Do you know him?"

"Well . . . uh—ma'am, have you had any visitors today?"

"Gilbert visits me on Sunday. This isn't Sunday, is it?"

"No, ma'am."

"Of course, not every Sunday—my Gilbert is a very busy man." She sighed, and something in her throat rattled. "I have a daughter, too, you know. Hortense Simms. She's even busier than Gilbert, I reckon. I haven't seen Hortense since—what month is it, anyway?"

"July."

"Ah. Well, I think Hortense was here at Christmas. But you know, that could have been Gilbert's ex-wife. Never did like the woman, so I can't remember her name."

I knelt beside her and put a hand lightly on her forearm. Even through the thick bathrobe it felt like a bone.

"Mrs. Sweeny, did you receive any phone calls today?"

"What day is it?"

"Thursday."

"No, no phone calls."

"You sure?"

"I'm positive. If Gilbert doesn't come, he calls, you see. But that's only on Sundays. This isn't Sunday, is it?"

"No, ma'am," I stood up. I couldn't believe no one had told Adele Sweeny that her only son was dead. Then again, maybe someone had, and she had forgotten.

I said a nervous good-bye and was about to beat a hasty retreat to the door when I noticed the skinny man in baggy overalls. Just for the record, he had the largest ears I'd ever seen on a human being, Prince Charles aside. Not that I've seen the prince in person, mind you. But I've seen enough photographs to know that if the wind ever hits Windsor from just the right direction, England's next king will become airborne.

"Sir," I said to the big-eared, baggy-clothed stranger, "are you the maintenance man?"

He couldn't have been more than twenty feet away, standing in a doorway that presumably led to the sleeping rooms, but he didn't seem to hear me. Perhaps those weren't ears after all, but mini air conditioners.

"Excuse me, sir. Would you mind turning down the air-conditioning in here? It's freezing."

The stranger stared, immobile and mute. Perhaps he was a foreigner—not that there is anything wrong with that. I'm all for hiring foreigners, even folks from Michigan. I walked toward him with a big smile.

"Cold," I shouted when I was within a few feet. "Very cold. You turn off air conditioner, okay?"

"Beg your pardon, ma'am," he said and bolted for the front door. I watched dumbfounded as he practically ran to the van with the TRAP license plate and then, with a squeal of tires and a spray of gravel, disappeared down the road.

I returned to Adele Sweeny. "Who was that man?"

"What man?"

"Mickey Mouse. Or Trap, or whatever his name is. You know, the guy who was just here."

"That wasn't my stepson Gilbert, was it?"

"No, ma'am, I'm sure it wasn't."

She nodded and gazed silently at the TV for a moment. "What day is it?"

"Thursday, ma'am."

"Ain't no use telling her nothing."

I wheeled and found myself looking up into the face of a tall young woman in a white uniform that consisted of smock, pants, and shoes with soles thick as mattresses. The amazon had the shoulders of a linebacker, the stomach of a beer drinker, and a derrière so large that one could host a small family picnic on it.

"She don't remember a thing you tell her. Short-term memory is shot to hell."

I looked helplessly to Adele, who looked away. Her eyes were filled with tears.

"Just a minute." I motioned the linebacker to follow me, and, remarkably, she did. We moved into the dining section of the room, hopefully out of earshot of the octogenarian. I have learned from watching nature shows that some birds and reptiles can make themselves seem more formidable by puffing up. I lack both feathers and an air bladder, but I put my hands on my hips, elbows akimbo. This gesture didn't increase my height in any way, but it made me wider, perhaps someone to reckon with. "How dare you speak like that in front of her?"

The linebacker looked taken aback. "Didn't mean anything by it, ma'am. Honest. She your mama?"

"Not hardly. My mama is a lot younger than that. And why hasn't anyone told her that her son is dead?"

"Ain't nobody told me, that's why."

"Where's the person in charge?"

"That be me, ma'am."

"And just who are you?"

"My name is Pinky Baxter. I work here."

"My name is Abigail Timberlake. Are you a nurse?"

Pinky smiled, revealing that somehow in her short life she had managed to lose an eyetooth. "I ain't no nurse. Nurse comes in the mornings for an hour. I just take care of these ladies."

My hands slipped to my sides. "You're here by yourself?"

"Until six. Then the night shift takes over."

"I see. Well, who was that man who was just here?"

"Don't know. Folks come and go all the time—well, mostly they don't come at all. This here ain't no regular nursing home. This here is what they call assisted living, but it's what I call a CBB. Anyway, I was in the kitchen. I didn't see no one."

"What, pray tell, is a CBB?"

"Can't be bothered. Rich folks drop their mamas off here when they can't be bothered no more. They ain't sick—least they ain't supposed to be—they're just in the way. Take Miss Adele there. I didn't even know she had a son. Ain't nobody been to see her as long as I can remember, except for the Reverend."

"How about a daughter?"

"Ain't seen one of them, either. Knew she had a child someplace, though. That's why I figured it might be you."

"We aren't related at all."

"Now, don't be getting me wrong, Miss Timberlake. I care about my ladies. They is well treated."

I smiled benignly. "I'm sure you're right, dear."

I tried to imagine Mama in a place like that. Then I tried to imagine Mama living with me and needing constant supervision. Sure, it was cold in Pine Manor—but the floor was immaculate, and there were no unpleasant smells.

"How many people live here?"

"Just six right now. All women."

"Where are the rest?"

She glanced at the sofa. "Let's see. . . . Miss Gerdy always naps right after lunch. Miss Lottie—well, sometimes I think she lives in the bathroom. Now, Miss Alma Lou—she could be doing just about anything. Likes to get into other people's things sometimes—excuse me, ma'am." She turned and trotted down a short corridor, her enormous buttocks bringing up the rear like a proper caboose.

While I waited, I walked over to the thermostat on the dining room wall. Seventy-five degrees. Not too bad. No doubt the heavy layer of dew I wore in had made it seem colder. Mama kept her thermostat at seventy-five in the summer, didn't she?

"Miss Timberlake!"

I wheeled. "I didn't touch it."

"It ain't that, ma'am. It's Miss Alma Lou. She's missing!"

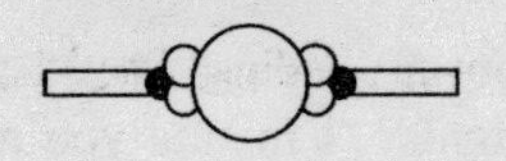

11

"Is there a back door?"

"Yes, ma'am, but we keep it locked. I know it's against the fire code, but some of the ladies—Alma Lou in particular—tend to wander. It's locked now."

"Well, maybe she slipped out the front door when I—"

"Help! Help!" They were muffled cries and seemed to be coming from down the corridor.

"Miss Alma Lou!" Despite her girth, Pinky could really move—but, to be honest, she had a little trouble turning the corner. Two-thirds of her turned to the left, but her derrière kept going straight. As a result, she nearly fell.

"You need antilock brakes, dear," I said between gasps.

"Help!" The pitiful cry went up again.

Pinky staggered but kept on her feet. "Them cries is coming from Miss Adele's room."

We charged down the hall, Pinky leading the way. Thankfully, it was a straight shot to Adele's room with only one tricky turn left: the doorway. A quick learner, Pinky applied the brakes well before the door. I, who do not claim to have quick reflexes, plowed right into her, knocking her down. For me, it was a soft landing.

"Pinky, you all right?"

"Yes, ma'am." She got to her feet, refusing my hand. "But I don't see no Miss Alma Lou."

"Is that the bathroom?"

"Yes, ma'am." Pinky hobbled over and peered inside. "Ain't nobody here neither."

"Help!"

I nearly jumped out of my skin. The cry was coming from behind a small door right beside me, a door that clearly belonged to a closet.

Pinky jerked the door open with a grunt. "Miss Alma Lou!"

"It's about time, child!"

I stared at a pixie of a woman. She could be me forty years down the line. Sure, her sparse hair was white as powdered sugar and her skin had more wrinkles than a day-old pizza, but Alma Lou's eyes sparkled with life. Her nose, however, was nothing like mine. Alma Lou had a nose like an Idaho potato, eyes and all, but one that had been stuck on her face willy-nilly, with no regard to placement. On closer inspection, I decided the unusual facial arrangement was due to a lack of teeth. Alma Lou was clearly not wearing her dentures.

"What are you looking at, child?"

I looked away. "Nothing, ma'am."

"Don't be impertinent, child. What's your name?"

"Abigail Timberlake."

"Timberlake . . . don't recognize that name. Who's your people?"

"Wiggins. Mozella Wiggins is my mama."

"Ah, Wiggins. Decent people. Not the best, but okay as it goes."

I gasped. "Excuse me?"

Pinky laughed. "Forgot to tell you, Miss Timberlake. Miss Alma here don't hold nothing back."

"Must be a Yankee somewhere in her woodpile," I muttered. I don't feel that way, honest. Chalk it up to stress and Wynnell's bad influence.

"Yankee?" Miss Alma was so livid, her enhanced color eclipsed her liver spots. "My granddaddy fought under General Braxton Bragg in Chattanooga! He died on Missionary Ridge!"

"My granddaddy died in World War I, but I don't hide in closets."

Alma Lou sputtered like a campfire in a drizzle.

Pinky clapped her hands once to get our attention. "Miss Alma, what you doing in the closet?"

"If you must know, I was looking for my teeth."

"And what your teeth be doing in Miss Adele's closet?"

"I was eating my apple from lunch. I can't be eating an apple without my teeth, can I?"

Pinky sighed. "And what your apple be doing in Miss Adele's closet?"

"Because I took it there, that's why. I'll be ninety years old next month. Do I have to explain everything I do?"

"If you're doing it in Miss Adele's closet, you do."

I shook my head. "Ninety years old and still in the closet."

Alma Lou's head jerked forward. "What was that,

child? Because, for your information, the door locked on me."

Pinky shook her head. "This here closet don't even have a lock. Now, Miss Alma Lou, you come on out of there."

Alma Lou glared at me. "What's she doing here?"

"None of your business," I mouthed.

Alma Lou spread her little legs and with withered brown arms braced herself in the closet door. "I'll stay here just as long as I please."

Pinky crossed her arms. "Fine. You just stay where you is. I'll go get your sheets and pillows. You and Miss Adele can be roommates."

Alma Lou looked from me to Pinky and back to me. "You're with him, aren't you?"

"With whom, dear?"

"With that man with the big ears!"

I took a step closer. "What about that man?"

"Don't you be playing games with me, child. You've got that same shifty look about you. My nephew sent y'all out here, didn't he?"

"Excuse me?"

"Well, I'm not signing anything. Go ahead, pull out your gun and shoot me. My nephew's not inheriting a thing."

"I don't have a gun," I said patiently.

"But he does. Go ahead, call him. Get this over with. I'm not afraid to die."

I took another step closer. I didn't even think about it.

"The man with the big ears and baggy green coveralls has a gun?"

Alma Lou dropped to her knees—more accurately, she folded like a warped wooden beach chair. "Shoot if you must this old gray head, but you can't force me to sign."

I stepped back. "Your head's white, dear, and I have no intention of shooting you."

Pinky dug strong fingers into my elbow and steered me out into the hallway. "Sorry, Miss Timberlake, but she gets that way sometimes."

"You mean paranoid?"

"Yeah, she thinks her nephew's out to get her money. But the truth is, Miss Timberlake, I don't think she even has her a nephew. I been here three years now, and there ain't never been anyone that I know of out to see her."

"Does she even have money?"

Pinky shrugged. "Her bills get paid. But, Lord, she a handful, that one. Always getting into other people's things. Always making up stories. And losing things! Third time this week she lose them teeth."

"I see. Pinky, I know you were in the kitchen just a few minutes ago, but did you ever seen a man with really big ears out here? Kind of looks like Mickey Mouse?"

"A white man?"

"Yes."

Pinky smiled. "All you white folks look the same to me."

"That's a 'no'?"

"That's what I said." She glanced up and down the short hall. "I best be getting back to Miss Alma Lou. Last time, I found them teeth of hers in the toilet."

I said good-bye to Pinky and, on my way out, said good-bye to Miss Adele. She was asleep by then, her eyes open, her mouth open as well. I tucked the afghan tighter around the trio before stepping outside into the shimmering heat.

I had a sense that someone was following me, although there wasn't a car to be seen in the rearview mirror. My friend Magdalena Yoder says that a hunch from a woman is worth two facts from a man. She's right, you know. Most of us would do well to follow our gut feelings until we've been proven wrong. Since I've always had a pretty good hunch indicator—even though I'm not blessed with a nose like Mama's—I decided to put my intuition to the test.

About a mile and a half from Pine Manor, the road curves to the right, and at the apex of the curve stands a copse of trees. Apparently it is easier for farmers to plant their cotton in straight lines. At any rate, anticipating this curve, I slowed considerably, and just past the copse I pulled over and stopped altogether.

Within a few minutes, a Harley Davidson drove by. About a quarter mile down the road, the Harley driver slowed and looked my way. At least, I thought he did. The heat dancing off the black tarmac made it hard to tell.

"Uh-oh," I said and, using the driver skills I learned as a somewhat reckless teenager, I made an abrupt U-turn and pressed the pedal to the metal. In the rearview mirror, road and cyclist shimmied and shimmered. They appeared to be getting closer.

"Better safe than sorry," I said and went to plan B.

Thank heavens that, as that somewhat reckless teenager, I had done more than just drive the back roads of York County. To be frank, I'd "parked" on a few as well, and I knew that the next road past Pine Manor in the other direction was a gravel lane that twists and turns along a streambed until it intersects with Route 901. You can bet I slowed for it, but the cyclist must have slowed as well. At any rate, I seemed to have lost him after the first turn, if indeed he was even following me at all. By the time I got to the highway, my hunch indicator was registering zero. In fact, I was feeling like a bit of a fool—but a safe fool, not a sorry one.

It was this state of mind that is to blame for the very foolish thing I did next.

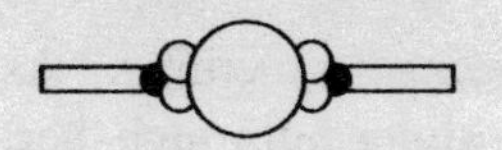

12

I drove straight to the Queen's house. She is, after all, the clearinghouse for all information in Rock Hill. If anyone knew the scoop on Gilbert Sweeny, it would be her. She doesn't have a water glass surgically attached to her ear for nothing. Okay, so that's perhaps a slight exaggeration, but you get my point. The woman knows everything.

At any rate, Her Majesty doesn't live in one of Rock Hill's newer, more posh neighborhoods; she resides in a commanding, yet unpretentious, two-story Greek Revival home in the old-money section of town. I parked in the shade of a lofty willow oak and followed a long, liriope-lined walk to the house. A lush fescue lawn at this season, plus topiary camellias up against the house, confirmed the rumor that You Know Who had a gardener in her employ.

Imagine my surprise when the grande dame herself, and not some liveried butler, opened the door. She seemed surprised as well.

"Oh."

"Hello, Mrs. Hunt. I'm Abigail Timberlake. May I have a minute of your time?"

"Well . . . uh . . . I don't really have much time this afternoon. Perhaps if you called, I could look at my schedule and arrange something." As she spoke, cool tongues of air slipped through her open door and licked at my legs.

"Mrs. Hunt, this will only take a minute. I promise."

"You're that woman from church last night, right? The one who bid such a ridiculous amount on a silly painting."

"Yes, ma'am."

"It wasn't an original, you know?"

"Yes, ma'am, I know that. But it has a decent frame."

"Oh, well, I suppose I can afford the loss better than you. All right, I'll take it off your hands for what you paid for it. Maybe I can persuade Father Foss to hang it in his office."

"Ma'am, I didn't come here to sell the painting." Priscilla Hunt was only two years older than I, but I was ma'am-ing her like a schoolgirl. I hated myself for it but was powerless to stop. I had been raised by a proper southern mother and knew my place in the pecking order by the time I was six and started school.

"Then why are you here?"

The cool air teased my thighs. "I'm here about Gilbert Sweeny."

"What about Gilbert?"

"Well, my mama—Mozella Wiggins—says she heard Gilbert is dead."

Priscilla Hunt stared at me. I had the feeling she was willing me to disappear. If she didn't invite me in, that might well happen. I've never seen it personally, but I've heard tales of folks literally melting away on Carolina sidewalks in July.

"Is this true, ma'am?"

"Yes," she said and sighed. "Come on in."

I followed her past the formal living room, which was apparently too good for me, and back to the den. There she bade me sit on a wingback chair upholstered in mauve fabric that was accented with gold crowns, while she sat on a butter-colored Italian leather recliner. Imagine that, the Queen of Rock Hill sitting on a La-Z-Boy.

"Would you care for some tea? Some cookies?"

"That would be awfully kind," I said. I was thirsty, but even if I had been sloshing with liquid, I would have said yes. Nothing would make me happier at that moment than to have the Queen of Rock Hill get off her duff to serve me stuff.

As suspected, the tea offered was iced tea, and already made, and the cookies Archway, but I got my thrills nonetheless. And of course I minded my middle-class manners and not only thanked her profusely but carried on about the victuals until I embarrassed even myself.

"Now then," she said, reclaiming the buttery recliner, "what exactly did you hear?"

"I heard that it was suicide. Is that true?"

She nodded. "As a matter of fact, I just got off the phone with Albert Singleton," she said, referring to Rock Hill's new police chief, "and he said it's official."

"Pills?"

She took a sip of tea, and I am pleased to report

that she slurps. "Yes, apparently a mixture of things. I really don't know all the details. Tell me, dear, why are you so interested?"

I took a silent sip. "I heard through the grapevine that I was implicated in the note."

Again, her face registered surprise. "Who told you that?"

"I can't reveal my sources."

She slurped like a teenager at the end of a milk shake. "Perhaps your sources are not reliable."

I regarded her evenly. "I don't think so, ma'am. The ultimate source seems to be you."

She stiffened, and the buttery recliner reclined a little. "Well, I was trying to spare you, but if you insist, I will share the details."

"Please do."

"Poor Gilbert Sweeny made a horrible mistake last night. That painting belonged to his stepmother, you see. And even though it was just a hideous copy, it had great sentimental value to her. The poor woman is devastated."

I couldn't imagine that Adele Sweeny cared a hoot about some painting. All she wanted to know was what day it was. I decided to play it cool.

"I'm sure she's even more devastated now that Gilbert's dead," I said.

Priscilla Hunt looked like a sheep that had been asked an algebra question.

"Or hasn't she been told?" Let Her Majesty squirm. It was good exercise for her back.

"Yes, I'm sure she's been told. She's Gilbert's stepmother, after all."

"Well, if she hasn't, I'd be happy to drive out there myself and tell her. She's at Pine Manor, right? I love the countryside."

My hostess used all of her facial muscles, and a few from her neck, to smile. "Perhaps I shouldn't be telling you this . . ." She paused. "Can you keep a secret?"

"My lips are sealed tighter than a clam at low tide."

"Hortense Simms owns that nursing home."

"Get out of town!"

"It's a fact. I saw the record last year when I was—well, doing some research at City Hall. Imagine buying an entire nursing home just to put your mama in."

"So she can forget her?"

"I beg your pardon?"

"Can you keep a secret?"

She leaned eagerly forward. "But of course, dear."

"From what I understand, Hortense Simms doesn't visit her mama very much. In fact, according to the staff, hardly at all."

"You don't say! And she has the nerve to put on airs."

"Don't you just hate uppity people?"

Her Majesty shuddered. "I can't abide a snob. Why take that new family who just moved in down the street—Hartz, their last name is. They plan to send their children to a private school in Charlotte and—," she lowered her voice, "—their bedsheets are 100 percent silk."

"You don't say!" I reluctantly put down my tea and stood. "Well, you've been very gracious Your Maj—I mean, Mrs. Hunt. But I really must go; duty calls."

She stood. "You have jury duty?"

"Work." No doubt it was a new word for her vocabulary list. "I closed my shop for the day, but I have lots of new inventory to sort through and price. I've hired an assistant who starts tomorrow, but I'll be so busy teaching her how to use the register and wait on customers that I won't have time for stock."

She nodded. "Well, like I said before, I'd be happy to take that hideous painting off your hands. Might give you one less thing to do."

"Oh, didn't I tell you?"

Professionally plucked brows raised inquisitively. "Tell me what, dear?"

"I already sold the painting."

"Congratulations, dear. I hope you made a tidy profit."

Trust me, that was a question, not a statement. I patiently said nothing.

"Well?"

"Frankly, ma'am, that's none of your business."

Priscilla Hunt does indeed have blue blood. She blanched, and I could see every vein in her face.

"Really!"

Perhaps I should have been born a cat. I love tuna, am litter box trained, and enjoy toying with the mice I catch.

"Let's just say I'm going to be a very wealthy woman."

Eyebrows arched again. "Oh?"

"In fact, if I were to move back to Rock Hill, then I would be the wealthiest woman."

"Surely you're joking!"

"Absolutely not."

"But that was just a silly little painting."

"Well, not to the right buyer, it wasn't." That was quite true, albeit somewhat misleading.

"And who was that?"

"I'm afraid I'm not at liberty to say."

"Why aren't you?"

"Oh, just a small thing called vendor-client confidentiality."

"Nonsense. It's not like you're a doctor or a lawyer."

"Oh, but it is. It's the same principle."

"Really! I don't suppose you would mind then, if I called the Chamber of Commerce and checked on that?"

"Call away! But I don't see why this interests you so much. In fact, I don't see why you stick your nose into half the stuff you do." Rest assured that I spoke calmly, and with my charming southern accent, so I didn't come across as nearly as rude as you might think.

"Well!"

"Face it, dear, as long as lions and tigers can't hide in Ben Hunter's grass, it's not your business how often he cuts it. It may possibly be his neighbor's business, but it's certainly not yours. You live three blocks away. And why can't Sarah Jenkins hang purple drapes in her windows? It happens to be her favorite color. And about that nice family from Germany and their tree house—what kind of welcome to America is that? And believe me, you're never going to get Mama to switch toilet paper brands. Well, maybe you could if you convinced her that they didn't have the quilted kind in 1958 and found her some really good coupons."

"Why, I never!"

"Which could be part of your problem. Then again, maybe not. I've been celibate for two years now—ever since my marriage ended—but I don't go around poking my pert nose in other people's business. Well, except for my children's, and that's allowed. And furthermore, just how do you know your new neighbors' sheets are 100 percent silk?"

"Miss Timberlake!" Her Majesty strode to the front door and yanked it open.

I ambled after her. "You know, dear, if sex isn't your bag, you could find a hobby. Perhaps you could collect Beanie Babies."

She didn't exactly throw me out. But she did put her hand on my elbow, and if an opportunistic lawyer had driven by at the right moment, we might have had a lawsuit. At any rate, I could count on not being invited to the Queen's annual tea in April. I just hoped I hadn't jeopardized Mama's dinner invitation for Saturday night.

A smart Abby would have driven straight home, locked the doors, and thought things through. A really smart Abby would have given Rob the blasted painting and washed her tiny hands of the whole thing. When you meet smart Abby, say hello from me.

This Abby drove back to Selwyn Avenue and the Den of Antiquity. I keep a stack of reference books behind the counter, and I was flipping through the index of a tome on nineteenth-century art when someone knocked on the door.

"I'm closed," I called without looking up.

"Abby, it's me, Buster!"

"Who?" It was one of those unsettling experiences, like meeting someone on the beach whom you know only from church. You can place the face but not the bulges, and of course the name escapes you.

"Buster! You know, your boyfriend from Georgetown, South Carolina."

"Georgetown!" I flew to the door. Buster is not exactly my boyfriend, but we date and have a good rapport. Because Buster and I live in cities that are four hours apart, we see each other only on weekends, and not every weekend, either. Sometimes I go down there and stay with his aunt, and sometimes he comes up here and stays in a hotel. We never see each other on Thursdays.

"Hey, Abby," he said happily after giving me a quick peck. "I know we didn't schedule anything for this weekend, but I had a consultation this morning in Charlotte. Hope you don't mind an impromptu visit. Or is this a bad time?"

I met Floyd Busterman Connelly, known to all as Buster, in his capacity as coroner of Georgetown County, South Carolina. He also happens to be a doctor, on staff at Georgetown Memorial Hospital. I have purposely withheld this second piece of information from Mama. If Mama knew I was dating an M.D., she would run out and rent a wedding hall. As things stood, Mama believed Buster to be a mere slicer and dicer of cadavers, and therefore a rung or two below Greg on the social scale.

"It's never a bad time for you to visit." I grabbed one of Buster's arms and pulled him into the shop. "You won't believe what's happened."

Buster was wearing a predominantly green polo shirt with vertical navy and white stripes. It made him look taller than the mere five feet fate had assigned him.

"Let's see, Abby . . . you won the Illinois state lottery and you're fixing to buy Tahiti as your personal playground."

"Lucky guess! Oh, well, you want to play?"

"Love to. You put on your grass skirt while I tune my ukulele."

You see what I mean? Buster has a sense of humor, something Greg doesn't even know he's missing.

I locked the door behind Buster. "I probably could buy a small island somewhere. I bought a painting last night that's worth ten million dollars. Maybe even twenty. And get this, I paid only $150.99."

Buster whistled. "Holy whiskers! How'd you get a deal like that?"

"It's an old van Gogh. It was stuck behind another painting—a very bad painting—in a rather nice frame."

"A van Gogh?"

"*Field of Thistles.* I know you've probably never even heard of it, but—"

"But I have."

My heart raced. "No kidding?"

"No kidding. I read about it in an art appreciation course."

"Art appreciation? But you're a doctor—aren't you?"

He padded the barest suggestion of a paunch. "A well-rounded doctor, I'd say. Anyway, it was my sophomore year of college, and I needed a humanities course. The professor—I forget her name—was Dutch. She claimed there was a whole slew of van Gogh paintings out there that people don't even know exist. Things he sold for a pittance just to keep body and soul together. Others, she said, have been lost to us thanks to war and natural disasters. At any rate, she said *Field of Thistles* was truly one of van Gogh's masterpieces."

"You hear that?" I grabbed Buster's other arm and practically forced him to dance a little jig. "A masterpiece! Oh, Buster, I'm going to be rich! And not just rich, stinking rich!"

He laughed. "Rich or poor, you're a lot of fun, Abby. So, where is this masterpiece?"

"At home—in a safe place. You want to see it?"

"Is rice white? Abby, this is really something. Miss . . . van Hoorne?—yes, that's what her name was—even had a photo of the painting. It was black and white, of course. But even I could see the genius. Vincent van Gogh took the ordinary and made it sublime."

I would have hugged Buster then, but the phone rang. "Hello, the Den of Antiquity."

"Abby, what are you on?"

"Mama! I'm not on anything!"

"You sound happy, Abby."

"I am," I said and giggled. Then I remembered my fiasco of a visit to the Queen. "She cancelled, didn't she?"

"What?"

"It's all my fault, Mama. No wonder you want to become a missionary to Africa—just to get away from me. Well, I'd be happy to apologize to Her Majesty if you think it would make a difference."

"What on earth are you talking about, Abby? Her Majesty—I mean, Priscilla—just called and invited you to dinner as well."

"Get out of town!"

"Promise me you won't do anything embarrassing, Abby."

"I would, Mama, but I've got other plans. Besides, the last thing she wants is to see me again. I told her where to get off not much more than an hour ago."

"But she does want to see you, dear. She made that very clear. She said you could even bring a date."

I turned to Buster, my hand over the receiver. "You ever dined with royalty before?"

"My brother's a queen in San Francisco. But that's with a small Q."

"How about dinner Saturday night with my Mama's new best friend?"

Buster grinned and nodded.

"I heard that, Abby. Priscilla is not my new best friend. But would it be so bad if she was? It doesn't hurt to expand one's horizons, dear."

"Whatever you say, Mama." I said it in the same tone of voice my kids used on me whenever I lectured. I didn't mean to sound that way; that's just how it came out.

The click of pearls against the phone was my only clue that Mama was annoyed. "Seven o'clock. And, Abby, for pity's sake, try and wear something decent. Maybe that pink chiffon thing you wore to the Leightner wedding."

"Okay, Mama." There was no point in arguing over the phone. Not with Buster standing there. But you can bet my choice of dress for Saturday night was not going to be pink, nor would it be chiffon. I'd sooner beg Wynnell's forgiveness and show up in a creation rife with pins.

"And be on time, dear."

"I'll be early," I said and hung up. I turned to Buster. "Now, where were we?"

"You were about to show me your ten-million-dollar masterpiece."

I bit my tongue.

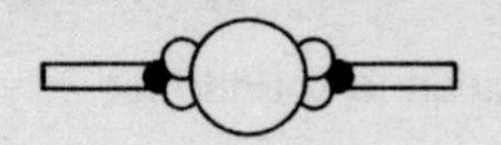

13

"That's it, all right." Buster spoke in a whisper, as if we were examining an altarpiece in some Gothic cathedral.

"You sure?"

"Well, I can't be certain. I'm not an art expert, and it's been years since I saw that painting. But that's how I remember it."

"Wow! I still can't believe it, you know?"

"Believe it. See the brush strokes there, how they imply a field of thistle plants without hitting one over the head with realism?"

"A man after my own heart," I cried. I would have offered to have Buster's baby, but I couldn't see dealing with teenagers in my sixties.

"And those smudges of blue—the thistles in flower. Pure genius."

My heart pounded with joy. "Did he paint this before or after he cut off his ear?"

"After."

"Then that little dot of reddish brown—it couldn't be, could it?"

Buster shrugged. "I could test it in my lab."

"Could you?" I caught myself. Perhaps it was better to have the picture authenticated by Sotheby's before messing with Vincent's DNA. Hmm. I might reconsider that teenager thing if it meant raising his baby.

"You bet I could test it. Hey, you hungry?"

I was starved. Unfortunately, there was nothing in the house to eat except for Cheerios and a pair of bananas that had seen better days. I suppose I could have mashed the cereal and fruit together and made banana fritters, but Buster deserved better than that.

"Yes, but let's go out to eat. My treat. I'm the millionaire, remember?"

"Fine by me."

You see, that's another reason I liked Buster. Greg claims he's not a chauvinist, but he wouldn't let a woman pay her own bribes.

"What sort of food are you in the mood for?" I asked, feeling unusually adventurous.

"You like surprises?"

"Love them." Especially if they were a ten on the Mohs' scale of hardiness.

"Well, since you're buying, how about I drive? Several of the doctors I consult with have been raving about this little place down in Pineville."

"Sounds great! Do I need to change?"

Buster smiled politely. He was, of course, wearing a suit and tie. I, on the other hand, was wearing white shorts and a T-shirt from Cracker Barrel that said GRITS, Girls Raised in the South.

"Be right back," I said and dashed off to the bedroom. Five minutes later, I was wearing my little black dress and a double strand of pearls. Unlike

Mama's, my pearls are faux, but so good they may as well be real.

"You look like a princess," Buster said.

I'm sure I beamed. If only Greg would say things like that. I would have been Mrs. Gregory Washburn a long time ago and would never have met Buster. I might even be happy.

"Bubba's China Gourmet!"

"It's supposed to be the best."

I bit my tongue again. Hot sauce and open wounds don't mix.

Buster insisted on opening my car door for me but then made no effort to stop me from opening the restaurant door for him. I liked that. It showed give and take.

Bubba himself showed us to our seats. That was a first. Bubba is usually in the kitchen cooking, when he's not swearing at the staff.

"Got me a real chef," he said as if reading my mind.

"What? No more iceberg lettuce in the salad bar?"

Bubba shook his massive head. The man is 90 percent jowls.

"This here is a real, authentic Chinese restaurant now. I took the salad bar out."

"Since yesterday?"

"Here," he said, handing us a pair of handwritten and photocopied menus. "They're laminated and everything. I've been planning this changeover for months. It was time to get with the trend, you know.

Lucky for me, a real Chinese cook answered my ad in the paper."

I studied the offerings. Szechwan, Hunan, Fujian . . . there was even a small Thai section.

"Where's the moo goo gai grits?"

Bubba regarded me coldly. "Like I said, we don't do that no more. Now we cater to the 'in crowd.' "

I glanced around. The room was as empty as Buford's heart the day he told me he was trading me in for a younger model.

"Where is that crowd?"

Bubba frowned. "Folks been coming and going all day."

"So business has been brisk, has it?"

"No, ma'am. I said they'd been coming and going, but they ain't been staying to eat. You don't suppose it's these handwritten menus, do you? I mean, 'cause we'll be getting store-bought ones next week."

"I don't think it's the menu, dear. Tell me something, are these fickle folk the same customers you used to have?"

"Yes, ma'am. Most of them."

"I see. Well, Bubba, it could be that they just don't like the change. I mean, there already is a traditional Chinese restaurant right down the road. If your customers wanted that, they would have eaten there all along. My guess is, they liked your salad bar with the iceberg lettuce and Jell-O squares, and Lord knows there's not a soul who has tasted your Beijing barbecue and not loved it."

"You think so?"

"Which is not to say it loved them," I said remembering my lunch the day before. "Too bad you hired this chef, Bubba, because my advice would be to go back to how things were."

"Heck, that don't matter. This cook I hired ain't a real chef. He's just between jobs. We both know he ain't going be around for long."

"But he can make all these things on the menu?"

Bubba blushed. "Maybe not all, but he can read. I got him a pile of cookbooks from the library."

"How clever. But you know what they say, Bubba. If it ain't broke, don't fix it."

Bubba nodded, and his jowls flapped like twin dewlaps. "Maybe you got a point. Was that what y'all were wanting? My Beijing barbecue?"

I looked at Buster.

"Don't look at me, Abby. You're the expert; you order."

"Beijing barbecue it is, then, and two orders of moo goo gai grits. Oh, and we'll have one order of eggs foo Benedict to share."

"Coming right up," Bubba burbled happily.

"Why, Abby, that was right nice of you," Buster said after Bubba disappeared into the kitchen.

"Thank you, Bus—" My mouth hung open like a nightjar catching mosquitoes.

"Abby, what is it? You look like you've seen a ghost."

"It's him," I managed to finally say. "And he's with her."

"Him who?"

"My ex-boyfriend, Greg."

"Good-looking guy. Who's the babe?"

"Hooter Fawn!"

"Aptly named. Although, speaking as a professional, I'd say she has a surgeon to thank for that."

"Aha! I thought so! And Greg tried to convince me they were real."

"You sound like you're carrying a torch for this guy."

"I am not!"

"You want to make him jealous?"

"Of course not!" I swallowed. "How?"

"Well, we could neck like teenagers."

For some reason, that made me laugh. Which made Buster laugh. Together we laughed like two teenagers at a pajama party to which someone had smuggled a bottle of cheap wine—not that I would know about such things. At any rate, it was much easier for two vertically challenged people to laugh across a sharp-edged formica table than it would have been to neck.

"Man," Buster finally gasped, "is he ever looking our way!"

I turned slightly, still laughing. Greg looked like I feel at least five days out of the month. Hooter, thank heavens, was minding her own business.

"You know, he's eating his heart out," Buster said.

"You really think so?"

"Got to hurt like hell catching you with a stud-muffin like me."

I laughed even harder.

"He's up and coming this way."

I jerked around in my seat. Greg was approaching with that long, loose stride of his. Cary Grant with a purpose. I willed him not to, but Buster stood.

Caught, I had no choice but to make introductions. I did them my way, however.

"Tall, dark and handsome, meet witty and urbane. Investigator Gregory Washburn, this is Dr. Floyd Busterman Connelly."

A look of genuine concern crossed Greg's face. "You all right, Abby?"

"Of course I'm all right! Buster is my date, not my physician."

"Oh."

"I see you have a date as well," Buster said mischievously. "Would you two care to join us?"

I tried to kick Buster under the table, but it was pointless. Unless I slid all the way down and kicked like a swimmer doing the backstroke, I wasn't going to reach him.

"I'm sure Heidi would rather you two ate alone," I said gaily. Ever since my divorce, forced gaiety has been my forte.

Greg has a dazzling smile, and he proceeded to blind us. "Her name is Hooter, and, actually, we'd love to join you."

"Maybe you should ask her," I wailed.

"No problem."

He was back in no time with the bottled blonde in tow. Greg introduced us all around. Although I had seen Hooter before, I had never met her. It was a pleasure I would gladly have forgone. On the plus side, however, Greg directed his bundle of silicone joy to sit next to Buster, while he slid into the booth next to me. The aroma of "Greg scent" sent my defensives crashing.

"I spoke to C. J.," I said, for want of anything better to say. "She'd love to be fixed up with Sergeant Bowater."

Greg nodded. "That was very nice of you, Abby, but I was thinking Hooter here might enjoy meeting Ed."

"Ed who?"

"Sergeant Ed Bowater."

"You didn't—I mean, you wouldn't! How could you fix her up with Sergeant Bowater when she's your . . . your . . ."

"Friend?" Hooter had a soft, melodic voice, like water through a bamboo pipe.

"Girlfriend," I snarled.

Hooter made a face. "Gregory and I are not involved."

"And I'm the Pope."

"Honest. I would never be involved with a man as besotted with someone else as he is."

Besotted? What kind of person used "besotted" in everyday conversation? Could it be? Did a brain lurk under that lustrous mane?

"And just who is he besotted with?" Perhaps Greg had a whole stable of ladies with silicon-compound parts.

Hooter turned impossibly blue eyes on me. "Why, you, of course."

"Tell me another."

"The man worships you," she said, without blinking a fake eyelash. "You are all he ever talks—all he has ever talked about. I never even stood a chance."

"He paid you to say this, didn't he?"

"I wish. Seems all the good ones are taken."

"Maybe not all," Buster said with a wink.

"Buster," I wailed, "are you jumping ship?"

"You tell me, Abby. Is there room on board?"

Before I could answer, Greg's hand found my thigh under the table. He gave it a gentle squeeze.

"I guess this cruise is booked solid," I heard myself say. It was as if I were a ventriloquist's dummy. Well, a dummy at any rate.

Greg squeezed again. "Good girl," he said, just loud enough for me to hear.

Buster turned to Hooter. "Ever been snorkeling in the Bahamas?"

"Yes, and I love it!"

"Puerto Rico?"

"Culebra or Vieques?"

While the two of them chatted on about coral reefs and angelfish, Greg proceeded to tell me how much he missed me. It was all very precious, and I was wishing I had a cassette recorder with me. In fact, I was about to ask him to repeat everything so I could write it down, when the front door to Bubba's China Gourmet opened.

I gasped involuntarily.

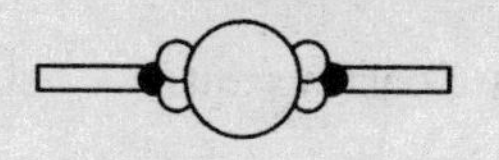

14

"Abby, what is it?"

"That woman!"

"What about her?"

"She was at my church last night."

"And?"

"Well, don't you think that's odd?"

"Just because she's black?" He stared at the beautiful woman with the cornrows and swan neck. She was wearing a long denim dress with an exquisitely embroidered bodice. The frock was tied in the back and emphasized her figure, but she would have been a knockout in a gunnysack.

"No, silly. I mean, isn't it odd that we're here at Bubba's at the same time? She's not a member of Our Savior, you know. She was just there for the auction. And now she's here. What are the odds?"

He shrugged. "What are the odds that I'd be here as well?"

"Exactly! But you live in Charlotte. You know this place."

"What makes you think she's not from around here?"

"Intuition."

He laughed.

"And a West Coast accent."

"You sure?"

"Well, I'm not positive, but she's not from around here."

"Maybe she's a Yankee transplant. Isn't Rock Hill growing by leaps and bounds?"

"Yes, and to Mama's dismay. But that would only prove my point. If she's new to Rock Hill, then how does she know about this place? And if she's new to Charlotte, how does she know about the auction down in Rock Hill?"

"You want me to get up and ask her? Maybe stick out my belly, flash my badge, and drawl?"

If Buster had said that, I would have died laughing. With Greg, it sounded lame.

"No, I don't. I just think it's weird. That's all."

Greg slid one arm around me just as Bubba appeared with our orders. I casually shrugged it off. I was open to reexamining our relationship, but I wanted to take it slow. Real slow. Let what had just transpired percolate, so to speak. In the meantime, I wanted to enjoy my dinner. For the record, Bubba outdid himself.

I had come to Bubba's with Buster, but I agreed to let Greg drive me home. Buster, after all, now had his hands full. I politely refused Greg's request to come inside but allowed him to kiss me. Fortunately, the man had the sense to just peck me on the lips.

After another long, loving look at *Field of Thistles*, I headed for the phone. Wynnell, bless her, answered on the third ring.

"It's Abby," I said. It's hard to sound contrite in

two words, unless one of them is "sorry," but I needed to ease into an apology.

Wynnell was silent.

"Whatcha doing?"

Nothing. But I could hear her breathing, so I knew she was still on the line.

"Wynnell, I called to say I'm sorry."

"Oh, so you didn't call to laugh?"

"No, of course not."

"Why not? I'm the laughingstock of Selwyn Avenue, aren't I?"

"But you're not. That was a total lie. I just said that because I was angry."

"Angry? Try mad, Abigail. Mad as in crazy. It was like talking to a stranger."

"I know, and that's why I'm calling. To say I'm sorry."

She sighed but said nothing.

"So, will you forgive me? Please, pretty please, with sugar on top?"

"Oh, all right. But only because you're my best friend and I hate being angry at you."

"And I hate having you mad at me. So, what are you doing?"

"Watching a rerun of *North and South.*" Wynnell hates the miniseries, thinks it's Yankee propaganda, but watches it every time it's aired.

"It's not going to change, you know. The South is always going to lose."

"I know. It's just wishful thinking. Hey, you want to come over and watch with me? Ed's in the bedroom watching some international soccer match."

"Thanks, I'm kind of tired. It's been a long day, what with getting back with Greg and all."

"Yeah, it's been a long day for me—what do you mean getting back with Greg?"

I told my friend about our reunion in Bubba's.

"Abby, I'm so glad for you. I didn't want to say this before, but I just couldn't see you and Buster as a couple."

"He has an excellent sense of humor, dear."

"That may be, but the two of you together were just too cute."

"Because we're both short?"

"Face it, Abby, your children would be munchkins."

"I'm not having any more children!"

I could hear Wynnell smile. "So now that you're back with Greg, you're going to drop your other boyfriend?"

"I already told you that. He's with Hooter as we speak."

"I mean your *other* boyfriend. The one you won't tell even your best friend about."

"What on earth are you talking about?"

"Peter Fonda."

"Wynnell, did you open a new bottle of Livingston Cellars?" Watching the South lose has driven her to drink before.

"You really don't know who I'm talking about?"

"I haven't the foggiest."

She hesitated, obviously not sure she believed me. "Young man, maybe mid-thirties. About five feet ten, medium build, with a slight paunch. Light brown hair. Hazel eyes."

"Are you reading this off a wanted poster?"

"And he rides a Harley, Abby. Who do you know like that who rides a Harley?"

My blood may not literally have run cold, but it was cool enough for Wynnell's wine.

"What time was this?"

"This morning. Not long after you left here."

"You talked to this man?"

"Of course. You know I'm not the judgmental type. He came into my shop asking for you, so I sent him down to your mama's."

"You what?"

"Well, that's where you went, wasn't it?"

"How did you know?"

"Abby, that's where you always go when you piss off your friends."

I would have hung my head in shame, except that I was lying on my back. "He asked for me by name?"

"Yes."

"Did he call me Abigail or Abby?"

"I forget. But he made it clear that he knew you."

"How so?"

"Abby, what is this, the third degree? He seemed like a very nice guy, that's all."

"He's following me."

"Like a groupie?"

That was a new and exciting concept. Antique groupies that followed me around from shop to estate sale.

"No, not like a groupie."

"Then what?"

"I don't know. But after I left Mama's, I drove out to a nursing home south of Rock Hill, and he followed me there."

"You sure?"

"Positive. And what's more, a woman's been following me, too."

"Another biker? You know what C. J. would say, don't you? She'd say this biker and his chick have picked you to be the third side of their ménage à trois. No doubt the same thing happened to her up in Shelby."

I couldn't help but laugh. "No, this chick is no biker. She drives a dark blue car. And both of them were at the auction last night."

"Hmm. I don't mean to scare you, Abby, but you don't suppose they're after your painting."

"I don't see how. The painting they saw at the auction wasn't worth the ten bucks Greg paid for it."

"You made him pay?"

We both laughed. "Seriously," I said, "what do you think I should do?"

"Well, you're back to dating a detective. Why don't you ask him?"

"I did. About the woman, anyway. Greg thinks there's nothing to it. Thinks I'm jumping to conclusions."

"Men! They're all so innocent."

"Just little boys with big penises. Makes you want to mother them, doesn't it?"

"I'd love to mother Greg," Wynnell whispered.

"Hey, watch it!"

"I was just kidding, of course. Do you think Hooter has really fallen for your doc friend?"

"Hook, line, and floaters."

"I can't figure that out. No offense, Abby, but what would a tall, voluptuous thing like Hooter want with Buster?"

"Free maintenance on her body parts?"

"Oh, you're bad. So, Abby, are you going to let me broker the painting?"

Boy, did that take me off guard. "I haven't figured out what I'm going to do about the painting."

"What's that supposed to mean?"

"Exactly how it sounded. In fact, I don't know if it's even mine to sell."

"You're kidding!"

"No, unfortunately, I'm not. Gilbert Sweeny called me last night to tell me the painting belonged to his mother, and that he had no right to sell it at the church auction."

"Well, you tell him—"

"He's dead, Wynnell. Gilbert supposedly killed himself this morning."

"Oh, gosh, Abby, that's awful. I suppose this wouldn't be a good time to straighten things out with his mother."

"Unfortunately, no time is. His mother doesn't seem to be all there."

"Alzheimer's?"

"Probably. At any rate, my plans are kind of on hold." That was only a partial lie, mind you.

"I understand totally. But if the painting does belong to you, give me first crack at brokering, okay?"

"Well—"

"At least think about it."

"Will do, dear."

Wynnell and I chatted for few minutes more—until her wine glass needed refilling. Apparently something horrible was about to happen to the South. Something called Gettysburg.

I called Rob next. Unfortunately, Bob answered.

"We're not buying tonight," he said tartly.

"This is Abigail."

Click.

I tried again. "I just want to say—"

Click.

"Sorry!" I screamed the second he picked up the third time.

"Go on."

"Go on what?"

Click.

"Okay! I'm sorry I treated y'all so shabbily. Y'all are two of my dearest friends in the whole world."

Bob harrumphed. "And?"

"And what?" I wailed.

"And you want us to broker *Field of Thistles,* right?"

I gave Bob the same story I'd given Wynnell. Unfortunately, he was not such an easy sell. Perhaps my theory on men was all wrong. Or was it just that gay men are different? Maybe only Greg was a little boy with—not that I've ever seen it, mind you.

"Where did you buy the painting, Abby?"

"You know," I said annoyed. "At a church auction."

"Were you the only one there?"

"Of course not. There were a hundred others. Maybe two hundred. I've never been good at estimating crowds."

"My point is that dozens of people saw you purchase it from a church sale. It was open bidding, and you paid a fair price for what you thought you were getting. Possession is nine-tenths of the law, Abby. The painting is yours."

"You're not a lawyer, dear."

I swear I felt the receiver turn cold against my ear. Perhaps it was just the extraordinarily long pause on Bob's side.

"What's that supposed to mean?" he finally asked.

"It means I need to get my legal ducks in a row before I make a major move. I wouldn't want to"—I chuckled pleasantly—"be arrested for fencing stolen property."

"You certainly wouldn't want to do anything rash like benefit your friends."

"Let me speak to Rob," I said patiently.

"He's sleeping."

"Give me a break. Rob never goes to bed this early."

"He has a migraine."

"Since when does Rob get migraines?" I've known Rob a lot longer than Bob has, although of course not as intimately. Still, I would have known if my friend got migraine headaches.

"Since you've been acting like such a jerk," Bob said.

I hung up and called Mama.

* * *

"Abby, I really can't talk now."

"I'm sorry, Mama. I shouldn't have been so rude at lunch."

"Think nothing of it, dear. It's a mother's job to forgive, and I forgave you before you were out of the driveway."

Perhaps so, but she hadn't forgotten. I could bet my business on that. Mama has a memory that elephants envy.

"So, Mama, now that that's out of the way, I've got some really good news."

"That's nice, dear, but like I said, I really can't talk now."

"Mama, you don't go to bed until ten, and it's not even nine-thirty."

"It's not that, dear. I have company."

"You Know Who?"

"Of course not, dear." That's all she said.

"Then who?" I prompted gently. You would be right to think it was none of my business, but Mama was given a different script than most folks, and, besides, if it was one of her regular friends, she would have told me.

"Her name is Marina, dear. Isn't that a beautiful name?"

"It's lovely—particularly if you're a boat. Is this woman in your book club?" All right, I was being nosy, but it was only fair. In high school, Mama hadn't let me date anyone until she'd examined their bloodlines. In Rock Hill, it isn't *what* you know but *who* you know, and Mama was not about to waste her only daughter on some nobody. Mama has more connections than a box full of Tinkertoys, although a fat lot of good it's done me.

"Don't be silly, dear; she's from Oregon."

"Come again?"

"She's a tourist. She stopped to ask for directions, and I invited her in for some tea."

"What? You have some perfect stranger sitting there in your house?"

"She isn't a perfect stranger, dear. We had a nice long chat outside first. I was watering the garden after supper—it was too hot during the day—and she pulled up. Did you know that folks come all the way to Rock Hill to see the *Civitas* statues?"

"Think how many would come if religious fanatics hadn't insisted that the city file off the statues' nipples."

"We'd be inundated, dear. Marina says she's been to Paris, Rome, and Athens, and none of those cities have anything quite like our *Civitas* statues. Although I'm sure the statues in those places have nipples."

"Hmm. Paris, Rome, Athens, Rock Hill—she's certainly well traveled. Retired, eh? I take it she's about your age?" Mama was in fairly decent shape and had, in fact, been talking about taking karate. A tea-sipping little old lady was not a serious threat.

"Oh, no, dear, she's younger than you. And she's very well groomed, Abby. You could take a page or two from her book."

"Thanks, Mama. Why don't you just adopt her? Better yet, just tell folks that she's the long-lost daughter you forgot you had."

"Don't think I'm not tempted, Abby, although they'd never believe me. Marina is black."

"I beg your pardon?"

"African-American," Mama said, still whispering. "I didn't know any lived in Oregon."

It's a good thing I have short hair, because it was standing on end. Since I was lying on my bed, I sat up to keep my hair company. Thank heavens the South is integrated now, but you still don't find many black tourists roaming the byways of small towns, not predominantly white byways like Mama's neighborhood.

"Does she have cornrows?"

"Yes, and they're beautiful. I want my hair done up like that before I leave for Africa."

"That's nice, Mama. What is Marina wearing?"

"A denim dress with a beautifully embroidered bodice. Frankly, it looks more like it's from India than Africa."

"Mama, stay right where you are."

"Of course, dear. Now if you'll excuse me, I have a guest to attend to."

"Mama, keep her there, too. I'm coming right down."

"That's very nice of you, dear. She'll be impressed with our southern hospitality."

"But don't tell her I'm coming, Mama. I want it to be a surprise."

"Yes, but—"

"Keep her there, Mama!"

My hair and I made a beeline to Rock Hill.

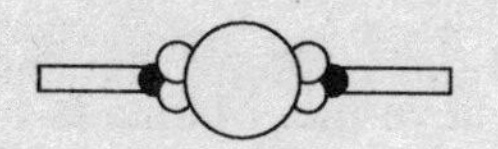

15

I got on Eden Terrace at Sullivan Middle School and was just a block from Mama's house when I saw the car pull out of her driveway and head south toward Winthrop. In the streetlight, it appeared blue. I couldn't see the driver, but she was accelerating awfully fast.

For a split second, I struggled with the choice of chasing the blue car or checking on Mama. What if Mama was perfectly all right, but the blue car got away? On the other hand, what good would a license plate number do if, while I was obtaining it, Mama breathed her last breath? The choice was obvious. I swerved into Mama's driveway like a teenager on a joyride and, before my headlights dimmed, was ringing the bell with my right hand while pounding the door with my left.

"For heaven's sake!" It had taken Mama all of five seconds to open the door. She appeared to be in one piece, and there was no visible blood.

"Mama! Are you all right?"

"Of course I'm all right, dear, which is more than I can say for you. Perhaps I'm having another senior moment, Abby, but did I raise you in a barn?"

I stepped inside and closed the door behind me.

There was no point in giving the Queen grist for her rumor mills.

"Sarcasm does not become you, Mama."

Mama recoiled as if she'd been slapped. "Why, I never! I can't imagine having talked to my mama like that."

"Your mama probably never invited death in for tea."

"Death?" The fingers of Mama's right hand played across her pearls. "I don't have to go to Africa as a missionary. I suppose I could stay here and nurse you through your convalescence."

"Convalescence?"

Mama nodded somberly. "Your nervous breakdown, dear."

"I'm not having a breakdown," I wailed and threw myself on an overstuffed gingham sofa.

Mama sat demurely on a plump armchair on the opposite side of the room. Although she had been working in the garden earlier, she was wearing a dress, and her crinolines puffed around her like the crust of a bubbling pot pie. Her white pumps didn't come close to touching the floor.

"It's all right, Abby. It happens in the best of families."

"Mama! I'm not having a breakdown!"

"Yes, you are, dear. My cousin Betty—I think she died before you were born—had one, and I remember the signs. First she—"

"Mama, I just want to know about your guest."

"What guest?"

"The one who just left!"

"Oh, Marina. Well, she wasn't really a guest, dear, she was company. There is a difference, you know."

"Yes, Mama. A guest is always invited; with company, it's not necessarily so. Why didn't you make her stay until I got here? I asked you to!"

"You're beginning to sound like company, dear."

I sighed. "Tell me about Marina."

As Mama settled back in her chair, her crinolines puffed higher. "Such a lovely girl. And considerate, too. Some folks like to do all the talking, but Marina made sure I had a chance to say something, too."

"I bet she did. So what worked, sodium pentathol or bamboo slivers under the nails?"

"Now who is being sarcastic, dear? She even asked about you, you know."

"What did she ask?"

"The usual."

"What does that mean?"

Mama shrugged. "You know, what you do for a living. Were you married. Did you have any children."

"Mama, did you tell her where I lived?"

"Of course not, dear, I'm not stupid."

"But you told her about my shop, right?"

"She loves antiques, dear. She made that very clear."

"I bet she did. So, Mama, what part of Oregon is she from? Portland? Eugene?"

Mama shrugged again. "I never asked."

"What does she do for a living?"

"Abby, I didn't interrogate the poor woman."

"But you answered all her questions about me!"

"Not all, dear. She asked if you were involved with anyone, and I said you were dating Greg."

"Well, as a matter of—"

"I know, I know, you've had your head temporarily turned by that coroner down in Georgetown, but—"

"I'm back with Greg."

Mama glowed. "I'm so happy for you, dear. You know how fond I am of Greg."

"Thank you, Mama. And I do know how fond you are of him. I was just hoping you could be fond of a doctor as well."

"Greg's going to medical school?" Mama looked positively rapturous.

"No, Mama, but Buster already is a doctor."

Mama stiffened. "Why didn't you tell me that before?"

"Because it was my trump card, only now I don't need it anymore. I'm back with Greg, and Buster has Hooter. So, you see, I traded a doctor for a detective. Mama, you got your wish."

Mama looked like a child in Miami who has just been given a new sled for Christmas. "So, you're sure about Greg?"

"Pretty sure. But you know how life is. Maybe Buster's brains will lose their appeal, and she'll angle for Greg again. But I sort of doubt it, seeing as how Buster's brains are backed by big bucks. And I mean big bucks. He comes from old money."

"But this isn't fair," Mama wailed. "You withheld vital information."

"Don't worry, Mama; I'll sell the painting, and then I'll have big bucks. In a couple of generations—if my kids don't squander it—it will be old money, too."

Mama wrung her hands in anguish. She and Daddy were both teachers, a respected profession in their day, and they both descended from practical pioneer stock, but she has always longed to be part of the gentry.

"Speaking of your children, dear, do you know what they're up to?"

"Of course. Charlie and his best friend are touring Europe on a rail pass. I keep his itinerary on the fridge. If I'm not mistaken, they're in Belgium today—no, that was Tuesday. Today they're in Denmark. At any rate, you know how kids are. They might have gotten tired of northern Europe and headed straight for Spain. I'm just glad the running of the bulls is over for this year."

"I'm talking specifically about your daughter, Susan."

"Well, that's easy. Susan is sharing an apartment here in Rock Hill and taking a summer class at Winthrop before taking off to graduate school next fall. Oh, and she works part-time on the serving line at Jackson's Cafeteria."

"That's right, but do you know what she does in her spare time?"

"Goes to the beach?" Susan is determined to become a prune before the age of thirty.

"Yes, but who does she hang out with?"

"Well, let's see . . . could it possibly be her roommate, Jinna?"

"I mean who of the male persuasion."

My daughter, Susan, is very pretty, if I do say so

myself, and she has more personality than Bill Clinton. I wish I could say she had a bevy of suitable beaux waiting in line. The truth is, Susan had always liked boys—and now men—who were a bit on the wild side. Rest assured, my daughter has no designs on the gentry.

"Mama, unlike some mothers I know, I don't pry."

"Well!"

"If the pump fits, Mama. I mean, you have to admit, I involve myself a lot less in my children's affairs than you do in mine, and I'm almost fifty!"

"Be that as it may, Susan is not keeping proper company."

"Is it that Thompson boy again?"

"No. This one has a motorcycle. Abby, it may not be against North Carolina law to ride without a helmet, but it's downright stupid to do so. Edwina Rankin's son split his head open like a cantaloupe. They say he'll never walk, and when he talks now, even Edwina can't understand him."

"Susan was riding without a helmet?"

Mama nodded with satisfaction. She would never think of herself as a tattletale, but that's exactly what she was. My children knew it, too. As much as they loved their grandmother, they resented her for all the times she turned them in for smoking, drinking, what have you.

"Well, then, I'll just have to go straight over there and have a little chat with her." But that is exactly what it would be: a chat, not a lecture. Susan is twenty-one, after all, and basically self-supporting.

"Be careful, Abby, you're no match for a motorcycle gang."

"Come again?"

"Well, I don't know that this man belongs to a gang, but I'd say it was a safe bet."

I tried to smile patiently. "And who used to always give me lectures about not stereotyping?"

"Yes, Abby, but this man looks the part."

"The part?"

"His vest," Mama said irritably, as if I could read her mind. "It had more studs on it than Myrtle Beach the year the war ended."

I gasped. "You mean he had a vest like the one that man had on at church last night?"

Mama crossed her arms and smiled. "Of course I didn't know it then, dear—I only saw them together this afternoon—but that man is Susan's boyfriend."

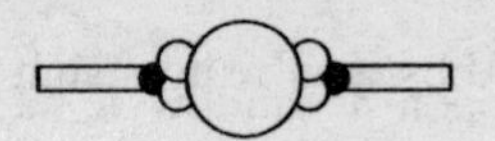

16

Magdalena Yoder was wrong. I had a lot of hunches, but no facts to back them up. Just one fact from a man would have been very useful right then. I couldn't very well tell Mama to barricade herself in the house simply because a black woman in braids and a flashy biker kept popping up. But I could feel that something was wrong, something undoubtedly connected to my fabulous new acquisition.

Alas, there are folks in Rock Hill who still don't lock their doors, and Mama is one of them. On the pretext of getting a glass of water, I locked the kitchen door, and I almost got away with surreptitiously locking the front door behind me on the way out. Unfortunately, Mama has eyes like one of the bald eagles that nest along the Catawba River.

"I'm not a baby, you know," she said, twisting the knob so that the button popped to the unlocked position.

"I know you're not a baby. But, Mama, Rock Hill isn't the same place it was thirty years ago. Or even twenty."

"Don't be silly, Abby. No one is going to know if my door is unlocked unless they try the knob. And anyone who tries the knob—well, what's to stop them from forcing open a window if the door is locked? This is a big old house, and with the air conditioner going, I can't hear from one end to the other."

"There's no point in making it easy for a burglar, is there?"

"It's the principle of the thing, dear. I refuse to live my life in fear. In Africa—where I'm going—they don't even *have* locks on their doors."

"That's because they have nothing to steal!"

"Exactly. I've been thinking a lot about that, lately. Things. Possessions are like chains, you see. We tie ourselves to places because of things."

"Is this going to be a lecture, Mama?" I was, after all, in the business of selling things.

"Oh, no, dear. This doesn't have anything to do with you. It's about me." She waved her arm at the room behind her. "I've decided to get rid of everything. Who knows, maybe after I'm done being a missionary to Africa, I'll volunteer for the Peace Corps. Or maybe I'll get on a tramp steamer and sail the South Pacific. I could work in the galley. You always said I was a good cook."

"That you are. But you're not serious about selling everything."

"Indeed, I am. You know, why bother with the time it would take to sell things? I could put a sign on the porch that reads 'Come on in and help yourself.' That way I could even sleep with the door open."

"What about your personal safety?"

"What about it? We all die, sooner or later."

"Later is preferable, Mama. And I bet there are

some things worse than death. But—I see your point. And since I'm here, can I take the pearls? You won't be needing them where you're going."

Mama's hands flew to her throat. "Abby, how could you? They were a gift from your daddy."

"Then isn't it better I have them, than some stranger?"

"These pearls aren't going anywhere. I'd feel naked without them."

"How about those silver candlesticks on the mantel? You won't be wearing those to Africa."

"Those were a wedding present from my parents."

"That carriage clock, then. It doesn't work, and you bought it yourself. Or how about that little table under the window?"

"But I always get so many compliments on the carriage clock. And that little table—don't you just love its lines?"

"Then lock your door, Mama. Double-lock it. Turn the dead bolt when I leave."

Mama nodded. There were tears in her eyes. Perhaps I'd been too hard on her.

"I love you, Mama."

"I love you, too, dear. *Yaya bimpe.*"

"What?"

"That's Tshiluba for 'good-bye.' "

"*Yaya bimpe,*" I said.

"Actually, you would say *shalla bimpe,* which literally means 'stay well.' "

I hugged Mama. If she ever did go to Africa, joined the Peace Corps, or sailed the South Pacific, I was going to miss her. But right now, my daughter needed me more than my mother.

"Remember to turn the bolt," I said and hurried down the walk to my car.

Jackson's Cafeteria was closed at that hour, and Susan, bless her well-tanned hide, was actually at home. Much to my relief, she didn't seem the least bit upset to see me. Apparently there were no reefers to hide, no condoms to stash back in the drawer, and no boyfriend to shove in the closet.

"Come in. We're just watching *Ally McBeal.*"

"Ally is on Thursday now?"

"We taped it. What's up, Mama?"

I glanced at Jinna, Susan's roommate. Jinna, bless her pasty hide, could read my mind.

"Hey, why don't y'all talk in here? I've got a phone call to make in the bedroom. Besides, I've seen this episode before. It's the one where Ally transports a prisoner's sperm donation in a see-through food container. It's really gross."

Susan blushed. "Jinna!"

"Hey, sorry," Jinna said and scurried off to the bedroom.

Susan turned off the VCR, and I picked a reasonably clean spot on the secondhand sofa. The girls live in Gardenway Apartments, just a scalpel toss from Piedmont Medical Center, where Jinna is a first-year nurse. It isn't the lap of luxury, but it sure beats at least one of the places Susan has found herself in since leaving the nest.

"So, Mama, what gives?"

"You know how I don't like to interfere in your life, right?"

Susan smiled. Thanks to Buford's bucks, she has perfect teeth.

"I love you anyway, Mama. You know that."

"But I don't interfere," I wailed. "Not like your grandmother!"

"That's true. Grandma is in a class of her own. But there are those"—she winked—"who might argue that you've been a pretty good apprentice."

"What?"

"Just kidding, Mama. So what is it you disapprove of now?"

She wasn't kidding, of course, and that hurt me to the quick. But trust me, all my so-called interference has been well intended. I've lived longer than my daughter, after all, and I've learned more lessons. If I can't pass on my wisdom, than what's the point?

"I hear you have a new boyfriend," I said, without sounding the least bit judgmental.

"No, I don't."

"The guy with the motorcycle."

Susan cocked her head. "I know lots of guys with motorcycles, but I'm not dating any of them."

"But your grandmother said—"

Susan laughed. "Grandma must have seen me with Freddy. He gave me a ride to work this afternoon."

"Freddy who?" At last, a name. Now I was getting somewhere.

"I don't know his last name, Mama." She looked me in the eye. "And grilling me isn't going to do any good. I just met him this afternoon in the parking lot."

"And you rode with him? Without a helmet?" It was easy for me to forget that she was a grown woman.

"Yeah, without a helmet. It's too damn hot. Look, Mama, I know you think I'm still a baby, but I'm not. I've made some stupid mistakes—I know that—but at least I didn't go out with Mouse."

"Mouse?"

"Oh, some creep who came through the line at the cafeteria. He kept coming back through the line just to talk to me. That can get me fired, you know."

"Was Mouse his real name?"

She shrugged. "Who knows? But he looked like a mouse, that's for sure. Great big ears, and teeth a mile long. Like I'd date him—not!"

My head spun. Mouse . . . TRAP . . . they both had to do with rodents, didn't they? Could this be the same man I'd seen at Pine Manor? The exterminator? If so, were there three people tailing me and/or my loved ones? Life was turning into a Martin Scorsese movie.

"Was Mouse wearing green coveralls?"

"You know him?"

There was no point in worrying Susan. On the other hand, she deserved to know if there was even the slightest possibility she was in danger.

"I bought a painting at a church auction last night. It has suddenly made me very popular. Unfortunately, it seems to have made you and Grandma popular as well."

"Mouse hit on Grandma?"

"No.

"Oh." Susan sounded disappointed.

"But a woman who was at the auction just paid her a visit. Freddy was at the auction, too. I didn't see Mouse there, but he showed up at a nursing home today where the former owner of the painting resides."

"I don't get it. What's the connection?"

"I sighed. Beats me. But it gets even worse. Gilbert Sweeny, who donated the painting to the auction, killed himself this morning."

"In the nursing home?"

"No, the nursing home resident is his mother. It's a long story."

"Spill it," Susan said. "I don't have anything better to do."

That was a compliment if I ever heard one. My daughter wanted me to stick around.

"You have anything cold to drink?"

"Sure. What would you like—juice, cola, beer?"

I was tempted to choose beer. The very fact that Susan offered me alcohol was a sign that she had begun to see me as a fellow adult and not just as an oppressive parent.

"Juice," I said. We didn't need booze to bond.

"It's the kind with grass in it."

"Excuse me?"

"You know, all the pulp."

I breathed a sigh of relief. "That's fine."

While Susan got the juice, I studied my surroundings. It was definitely an adult's apartment. No psychedelic posters and black light—nor today's equivalent, as far as I could tell. Jinna held the lease, so there were more of her things there, but I noticed touches of Susan. The framed and signed Robert Booth print titled *Palmetto Sunset* that I gave her for Christmas was on the wall behind me. On top of the TV was a photograph of Mama and me on Mama's seventieth birthday. There was even a snapshot of Susan's brother, Charlie. Notably missing, however, was anything to do with her daddy, Buford.

"So out with it," Susan said, returning with a plastic tumbler full to overflowing.

I took a big slurp. "This will have to stay between you and me, okay?"

"Of course." Susan pushed aside a wobbly coffee table and sat on the floor in front of me, her legs crossed.

"The painting I bought could be worth a lot of money."

"How much?"

I smiled at her candor. "A lot. More money than I ever dreamed I'd have."

"Ten thousand?"

"Try ten million."

Susan's mouth popped open. "You're shitting me, aren't you?"

I slurped again.

"Sorry about the language, Mama, but I thought you said ten million."

"I did."

"Geez! You're rich!"

"Well, not yet. First I have to get the painting appraised, and then put it up for auction."

"How do you do that?"

"Well, that's the tricky part. I don't have the right contacts, but Rob Goldburg does. Unfortunately, we're not speaking at the moment. So I may end up taking the painting to New York myself."

"When will that be?"

"I don't know. You anxious to get your hands on some of that money?" All right, I know it. That was an uncalled-for remark. But I said it, and I can't unsay it.

Susan's face clouded. "I don't want your money."

"Well, not all of it, of course, but—"

"Mama, I don't want a damn cent!"

"You're serious?"

"Mama, I want to make it on my own. Sure, Daddy paid for college and is going to help me with graduate school, but I plan to pay it all back. Well, the money for graduate school, anyway."

"Oh, don't worry about that. Your daddy has so much money, I'm sure he doesn't miss it."

"That isn't the point, Mama. I want to feel like this is *my* accomplishment."

I stared at Susan. Where had the sneaky, conniving, irresponsible girl gone? What alien species had appropriated her body, and when did it happen?

"Damn, but I'm proud of you," I said.

Susan blushed. "Let's not get all mushy."

I stood. It was time to go before I ruined the moment by inserting tab A into slot B. A size-four shoe may be small by most people's standards, but so is my mouth.

"Be extra careful, okay? I don't know what these people are up to, but it can't be good."

"Have you told Greg?"

"I'm calling him as soon as I get home. Oh, and by the way, we're together again."

"You go, girl!" Susan was on her feet and, before she could help herself, had given me a tight hug.

I kissed Susan good-bye, and while she made a great show of wiping her cheek, I knew she didn't mind. It would have been polite, not to mention wise, of me to say good-bye to Jinna. Unfortunately, I had forgotten all about her.

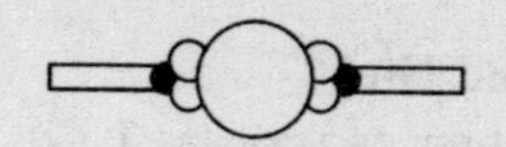

17

Greg wasn't in when I got home, so I left a garbled message. Then I crashed. I must have slept right through the act of shutting off my alarm, because when I awoke it was twenty after ten, and Dmitri, who often sleeps on my chest, had his paw in my open mouth.

I spit out cat hairs. "Dmitri, dear, you were supposed to wake me an hour ago."

My big, yellow lug of a cat, who does nothing but sleep, yawned. A cloud of stale fish breath settled across my face and pillow.

"Off," I said. "Get me off me." If Dmitri didn't immediately move, it would be a sign from above that I should sleep in.

Heaven must have had other plans, because the phone rang and Dmitri, who still has his back claws, used my chest as a springboard. I was through cursing by the time I found the phone, buried under my clothes from the day before.

"Hello!" I squawked

"Abby? It's me, Irene Cheng."

"Oh, my God! Where are you?" I had forgotten all about my new employee.

"In your shop."

"But you can't be. It's locked."

"Rob gave me his key."

"What?"

"You know, the spare he keeps for you. I told him you were expecting me, and he said no problem."

"He did?"

"Okay, let's see. I dusted everything and swept the floor. By the way, you need a new bottle of toilet bowl cleaner for the bathroom."

"I do? I mean—what's that noise I hear in the background? You don't have customers in there, do you?"

"Of course. We're a business, aren't we?"

"We?" If I could have reached through the phone wire, I would have wrung her scrawny neck.

"Please don't be mad, Abby. I really need this job. My husband got fired last night."

"Oh. Why? Where?"

"I told you he was downsized after working nineteen years as an engineer, right?"

"Right."

"So after almost a year of job-hunting, he finally gave up and took a job as a chef."

"He cooks?"

"He's the best—his parents owned a Chinese restaurant in San Francisco. Anyway, he found a job as a chef at this greasy spoon down in Pineville called—"

"Bubba's China Gourmet?"

"You know the place?"

"I've heard of it," I said lamely.

"Well, never eat there. The so-called Chinese food

they serve is a real laugh. So guess what happens? Everything's going fine—Mike was able to find all the right ingredients for some authentic dishes—and then some idiot customer complains and says she wants the old menu. Boom! Just like that, Mike is out of a job."

"That's awful!" I guess I owed her something, if only a chance to prove herself. "Irene, if anyone wants to buy anything, try and stall them. I'll be right there."

"Oh, no hurry. Everything's under control."

"What does that mean?"

"Look, Abby, I sold that oak hutch for its listed price, but—"

"You've been selling my merchandise?" I shrieked. "How can you do that? Even Rob doesn't have a key to my register."

"I made the customer pay cash. There's a bank just down the street. I've got the money right here in my pocket. Oh, another customer wants to know about those two Federal-style sofas with the hideous plaid fabric—"

"Dump them. Give the customer a 30 percent discount." I'd had those two monstrosities for weeks and had been meaning to get them reupholstered, but just hadn't found the time.

"I sold them already—full price. The customer wants to know where she can buy more of that fabric to make drapes."

"Probably Mary Jo's in Gastonia. She has the largest selection of fabric in the Southeast, possibly even in the world. She was written up in *Southern Living,* you know."

"That's nice, Abby, but I don't have time to chat. I've got work to do."

"What?"

I heard her say something to someone who was part of the background noise. Finally she turned her attention back to me.

"Look, Irene—"

"It's Captain Rich Keffert and his wife, Terry. They're from Belmont."

"I know who they are! They're two of my best customers. Don't you dare say or do anything to put them off."

"Oh, no, to the contrary. They want to buy the Louis XIV bed and want to know if it comes with a guarantee."

"Well," I said, a bit miffed because the Kefferts should know by now that I stand behind my merchandise's authenticity, "tell them if they learn elsewhere that it's not a genuine Louis XIV, I'll cheerfully refund their money."

"I'm afraid that's not the sort of guarantee they want, Abby. They're concerned about the bed breaking during—," she paused, and then whispered, "—sex."

I laughed. "Tell them the bed didn't break under Louis, but that's what insurance is for."

"Will do. About your files—"

"Don't you touch them!"

"I won't, Abby, I promise. There's no need to, anyway. I got here a little early, so I organized them."

"You what?" Even if I could stick my arm into the phone in an attempt to strangle her, it wouldn't reach much past the receiver.

"I took all those uncashed checks and put them in a new file I created called 'Urgent Bank Business.' "

I tried taking deep, slow breaths. "What uncashed checks?"

"Well, there was one for $285 under Z, and . . ."

Z! So that's where it was. A customer bought a Victorian side chair the day I planned to see the movie *Zorro,* and—well, to be honest, I seemed to have lost it. Up until now!

"How many checks did you say, dear?"

"Five. They total up to more than a thousand. If you'll sign them, I'll run them over to the bank after work. Oops—Rob's here!" she hissed. I heard her say something in Chinese, but she didn't hang up.

A moment later, Rob got on the line. "Abby?"

"Rob! What's going on?"

"I thought I better check on Mrs. Cheng. What with her language difficulties and all."

"She seems to be doing all right," I said. There was no need to put an end to Irene's little charade. Let Rob think he was fluent in one of the world's most difficult languages.

"Say, Abby—"

"Rob, I need to say something."

He could read my miniature mind. "You don't need to say anything."

"Yes, I do. I'm sorry. I've been acting like a jerk. I could really use your help in authenticating—not to mention selling—the painting, and 10 percent is a reasonable fee."

"Yes, but I see your point. A million dollars is a lot of money to pay someone for a commission."

"Granted, but it needs to be kept in perspective—something I've never been very good at. There are nine other million dollars coming my way, maybe twice that if we find the right buyer."

"Good for you, Abby. That's the attitude to have. Now if only you can keep perspective when Uncle Sam hits you up for half."

"What?"

"You'd forgotten about taxes, haven't you?"

"Why can't we have a flat rate?" I wailed. "Maybe 10 percent."

Rob laughed. "Perspective, Abby, remember. Half of nine million is still a lot of money."

"I could finally afford to get those spider veins on my legs zapped with a laser."

"Hell, you could afford a new pair of legs—not that you need a new pair. I mean, your legs are very nice as they are."

"Not that you would notice, dear, but thank you anyway."

"Say, Abby, if you're feeling okay about the commission and all, I have a little confession to make."

"Confess away!" I said breezily.

"Well, my contact in New York—Reginald Perry—is coming to Charlotte."

"What? When?"

"Sunday."

"You invited him down here?"

"Guilty. But, Abby, in my opinion he really is the world's foremost authority on van Gogh. If he authenticates this painting, you can skip Sotheby's and Christie's. You'll have offers coming out of the woodwork, and no auction commissions, either."

"Wow, in that case—"

"But there is a possible downside, Abby."

"I'm all ears."

"There is always a chance the painting will prove not to be authentic. There are some damn good forgers out there."

My heart pounded. How easily one can adapt to wealth, even wealth that is hypothetical.

"And if he says it's not the real McCoy?"

"Well, there are other experts. But, to be honest, we would need a team of them to oppose Reginald Perry. The man is a legend."

"So why did he agree to come here. What's his cut?"

"Don't you worry about that, Abby—"

"But I do."

Rob sighed. "I'm splitting my fee with Reggie. Although frankly, once I told him the scoop, he was so eager to see your painting, he almost called you. It was all I could do to stop him. I think he'd almost be willing to pay you just to look at it."

I briefly considered allowing Reggie to do just that. In fact, why not turn my shop into a private museum? Surely there were hundreds, if not thousands, of people who would pay to see such a masterpiece. Would fifty bucks a peek be unreasonable?

"Abby, are you there?"

"Yeah," I mumbled. "I had something in my eyes for a minute."

"Dollar signs?"

"You know me too well!"

"So, Abby, his plane comes in at five-fifteen. How about dinner at my place at seven?"

"Will he examine it before or after we eat?" Bob does the cooking in that alternative family and is heavily into exotic foods. Perhaps that's putting it too kindly. The last time I ate with the Rob-Bobs, I was served curried tripe with kiwi chutney. How was I to stomach a supper of stomach while waiting for a verdict on my financial freedom?

"Well, he'll want to look at it first—can you blame him? But the actual examination will have to wait until after we eat. Rob's making caramelized quail, and they get tough if you don't eat them right away."

I shuddered. I was going to have to down a bottle of antacid before dinner and sneak a heavyweight plastic bag to the table. Hopefully, whatever I couldn't drop into the bag—hidden by my napkin, of course—would be neutralized.

"Terrific," I said. I should have ignored Mama and become the actress I always wanted to be.

"Great. Well, got to go, Abby. If you have any problems with Mrs. Cheng, just let me know. And by the way, Reggie says to say hello."

"Will do, and hello back at him," I said and hung up. So Mohammed was coming to the mountain! It wasn't a bad way to start the day.

* * *

Irene Cheng certainly didn't need me to tell her what to do. She was a born saleswoman, and when she wasn't busy bringing in the bucks, she cleaned, straightened, and organized. That woman couldn't sit still with an elephant on her lap. I showed her my system of filing—which was vastly inferior to hers—and how to use my register, a machine she was already quite familiar with. After hovering superfluously for several hours, I came to the conclusion that I was finally free to do exactly what I wanted to do in this business, and that was to attend sales and buy, buy, buy. First, however, I had something else to do.

"Can you hold down the fort if I take off for a little while?"

Irene had the grace to smile. "I'll lock up and give Rob back his key. I already had an extra made. I'll be coming in early tomorrow, if that's all right. I thought we might run a sale on the Fenton glass. It's cluttering up the place."

"By all means, run a sale. Sell my firstborn, while you're at it."

"I beg your pardon?"

"Nothing. Sure you'll be all right?" That was like Pat Robertson asking the Pope if he was "saved."

"I'll be fine," she said, dismissing me with a curt nod. I couldn't blame her, though. A wealthy Charlotte matron whom I privately refer to as Mrs. Money Bags had just walked in.

I left the moolah matron in Irene's capable hands and set about my errand. The Charlotte whites pages, which were to serve as my travel guide, had a number of Trapp listings, but only two for Trap with a single *P*. I jotted down both addresses. One was over in west Charlotte; the other, all the way up by UNCC. I followed my gut instinct.

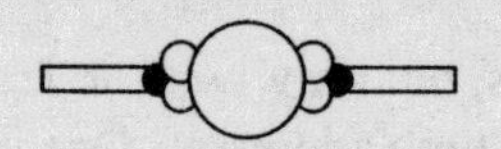

18

Queens Road just happens to be the most beautiful stretch of urban roadway in the United States, and I took it to Morehead and followed that to John Belk Freeway. Then it was Freedom Drive all the way west to Moore's Chapel. In the neighborhood of Paw Creek Christian Academy, I found the modest brick home with the striped awnings. A single Bradford pear punctuated the parched lawn. Unfortunately, the carport was as empty as Mother Hubbard's cupboard.

Still, I rang the doorbell. I may not have a silver tongue, but I can sweet-talk my way out of most ugly situations, and besides, few adults would dare hit a woman who is four foot nine. Children, however, are another story.

The man who answered the doorbell had the same enormous ears and buck teeth as the man in the green overalls, but that's where the resemblance stopped. This man was a good one hundred pounds heavier than the other. He grimaced when he saw me.

"I'm looking for a Jonathan Trap," I said, perhaps sounding a bit confused.

"Are you a Jehovah's Witness?"

"No."

"Baptist?"

"No."

"Well, you're not Mormon because there's only one of you, and you're obviously female."

"I'm Episcopalian, but we don't do door-to-door soul-saving."

"Then you're not selling something, right?"

I shook my head.

"In that case, I'm Johnny Trap."

"I'm Abigail Timberlake. You wouldn't happen to own a white van, would you?"

"Nope." He sounded cagey.

"With a vanity plate that says 'Trap'?"

"Do you see a van?"

"No, it's just that—"

"And how did you know my name?"

"I looked you up in the telephone book. There were only two Traps listed. I'm trying to find the owner of the white van."

"What's my brother done now?"

Sweat was streaming down Jonathan Trap's face and collecting in one huge, viscous drop under his front chin. Just looking at him made me hotter.

"Well, I'm not sure. It's kind of complicated. Could we possibly talk inside?"

He looked me up and down, which, considering my size, didn't take but a few seconds. Still, it was a waste of his time. He could have laid a hand on me—I mean that literally—and I wouldn't have had the strength to push it off.

"Okay," he said, "but I work at home. You're disturbing my work."

I followed Johnny into the house and was shown to a brown leather couch that had depressions the size of bathtubs in it.

"Have a seat," he said, sitting opposite me on a brown leather armchair. It, too, had a tub-size depression in it, but Johnny's behind fit it perfectly. No sooner were we both seated than Johnny remembered his southern manners.

"Care for some tea?"

"Sweet?"

"Is there any other kind?"

"I'd love some."

While Johnny was off being a good host, I studied my surroundings. Besides the leather suite, there were some good used pieces but no antiques. The most interesting things were the framed posters on the wall behind me. They looked like enlarged book covers, and they all had the name Johnny Trap on the cover. Except for one. It was the cover of Hortense Simms's dreadful tome, *Of Corsets and Crowns.*

Johnny caught me studying them when he returned with the tea. "Those are my book jackets."

"You're a writer?"

"Guilty."

"What kind of writer."

"A very good one. But alas, I'm underpaid. Vastly underpaid."

"I meant what genre?"

"Ah, a reader! I write mysteries."

"I see. But what about that book on royal underwear? What's Hortense Simm's book jacket doing on your wall?"

"Can you keep a secret?"

"I'm as mum as a mummy."

"I ghostwrote *Of Corsets and Crowns.* Hell, I did even more than that—I did half the research. Sure, it doesn't have my name on the jacket, but it's mine."

"Is the title yours?"

"Yeah. Do you like it?"

"It's clever. In fact, all your titles are clever. But, to be honest, I've never heard of you."

"That's no surprise. Over six hundred mysteries get published a year, but you can find me in virtually any bookstore."

"Well, I'll have to try one of yours. Tell me, though, do you use a lot of dialogue?"

"Well—"

"Because I don't like books that are mostly dialogue. I always feel cheated, you know. Give me a book with nice, long descriptive passages I can sink my teeth into."

"Like *War and Peace*?"

"There you go." I was deadly serious. "And what about humor? Too much of it distracts from the story, don't you think?"

"Not if it's done well."

"Which you do?"

"Absolutely. Of course, my books will never win any awards—the funnier it is, the less likely a book is to win anything. Good writing is most often equated with serious writing."

"Mr. Trap, do you mind if we get back to the subject of your brother? He wouldn't happen to be named Mouse, would he?"

"Yeah, that's his name. Our parents, go figure."

I nodded sympathetically. "I have a brother named Toy."

"What's Mouse done now?"

"Like I said, I don't really know—except that he asked my daughter out."

"Is she good-looking like you?"

"Flattery will get you nowhere. I've already got a boyfriend."

"That's a real shame. He's a very lucky man."

I could actually feel myself blush.

"Or," he continued, "are you just making that up, because you can't be bothered by a fat man?"

"Of course not! Some of my best friends are fat!"

"Is your boyfriend fat?"

"No, not that's it any of your business."

Johnny smiled, his point made. "So, Mouse asked your daughter out. Is she underage?"

"She's twenty-one."

"How refreshing. Most mothers of adult women don't do background checks on their daughter's boyfriends."

"Your brother isn't her boyfriend. But he's up to something. I ran into him at a nursing home this morning, and the next thing I know he's asking Susan out." I clamped my hand over my mouth. I hadn't meant to mention Susan's name.

"That's all right. I won't be passing any details on. Mouse and I don't talk."

"Oh."

"And it's not because I'm fat. Or poor. Or even a

writer. Mouse is okay with all of that. I happen not to approve of him."

"Oh?"

"Like you, Miss Timberlake, I can be as mum as a mummy. Let's just say that my brother does not incorporate compassion into his lifestyle."

"So, he isn't likely to be visiting the elderly in nursing homes?"

He cleared his throat. "Not hardly."

"Can you tell me what he does for a living? Does he deliver things?"

Johnny shrugged, causing an avalanche of quivers that began with his face and ended with his belly. "The last time I spoke with Mouse, he said he was starting a new job. Something about the import/export business. As long as he doesn't ask for money, I don't ask about his professional life. As for his personal life—well, that's a matter of public record. I read about him in the paper just like everyone else."

"Excuse me?"

"Minor brushes with the law. Marriages. Divorces. That sort of thing. Mouse gets a lot of newsprint. I think the folks at the *Observer* are in love with his name. Mouse Trap. Can you blame them? Anyway, like I said, I don't gossip. You want the scoop on Mouse, go to the paper."

"Will do. Would you advise me against talking to Mouse myself?"

Johnny stared at me. At least, I think he was staring at me. The man's eyes were mere slits, but they seemed to be glinting with extraordinary intensity.

"I wouldn't, if I were you," he said at last. "Look, it's a matter of public record—oh, what the hell. Mouse spent three years in juvenile detention for killing a man."

"That's all a life is worth these days? Three years?"

"It was a black man, and don't get me started."

"Well—"

"Because if it had been a white man—maybe a doctor or lawyer—Mouse would still be behind bars, juvenile offender or not. Anyway, our parents never could get over the shame. They moved to Florida and left us behind."

"I'm sorry."

"For what? Because I'm fat and poor and have a murderer for a brother?"

"No, because you are obviously in pain."

"Is that pity, Ms. Timberlake? Because I don't do pity well."

"It isn't pity, dear. Life sucks; there's no doubt about it. But it's all we've got."

"Yeah? Well, what would you know about pain?"

I tried to jump to my feet, but the leather bowl in which I was sitting made that impossible. Finally, after the third hard rock, I was able to spill out onto the floor.

"Do you think it's easy being called 'dwarf' and 'midget' your whole life?" I yelled. "Don't get me started! Because my daddy's dead, and my mama's a sandwich short of a picnic! Oh, and did I mention that I was married to a megalomaniac who took my home and children away from me?"

"I'm sorry," he said quietly.

We both grinned.

"Look, I'd better go now and let you get back to work. Did you say your books were available everywhere?"

"Yeah, just about. I'd give you a copy, but my publisher isn't very generous with freebies."

"No problem. If I buy one, will you sign it?"

"Be glad to. Try *The Sting and I.* It's about a man who uses killer bees to commit murder. It's my current favorite."

"Mind if I ask you something personal?"

"Go ahead."

"How can you write funny books when you're in pain?"

"Humor comes from pain."

"Then I should be a standup comedienne."

"Maybe you should—but you'd need a podium."

"Very funny. But thanks for sharing with me."

Johnny walked me slowly to the door. "About Mouse—stay away from him, Ms. Timberlake. I can't emphasize that enough. My brother is really bad news."

"I'll keep that in mind," I said.

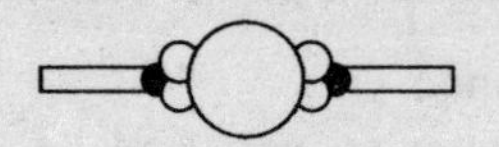

19

There is no use having connections if one doesn't use them. I drove straight to the supercooled comfort of my home and called Greg. He was "away from his desk" but not out on assignment. I fed Dmitri, waited ten minutes, and called again.

"Hey, Abby!" Greg sounded cheery, so I knew the trip away from his desk had been successful.

"Well, I was wondering what you were doing tonight."

"Tonight? Well, I signed up for another ride-along with Bowater. In fact, I was just about to head on home for a little shut-eye. What gives?"

"Oh, nothing. I just thought—"

"No need to say more. I feel the same way. How about tomorrow night?"

I told Greg about my dinner obligation with Mama and Her Majesty, Queen Priscilla Hunt. I took the liberty of inviting him along, knowing he would refuse. Greg has the social skills of an armadillo, but that doesn't bother him. What holds him back are the cloying looks and roaming hands of mature women. Incidentally, younger women—those of an age to drool over Leonardo DiCaprio and Matt Damon—ignore my Cary Grant look-alike.

"Sunday?" he asked. I imagined those luscious lips pouting.

"Sorry, but Sunday's no good. How about Monday for sure?"

"What are you doing Sunday, Abby?"

"I'm washing my hair."

"Right. While the Fonz and I tune my hot rod. Abby, you have a date don't you?"

"It's a business meeting."

"With who? It's not with Buster, is it?"

"Gregory!"

"Sorry, Abby. So who is it?"

"It's none of your business, but if you must know, it's the Rob-Bobs."

"Oh. Well, why the hell didn't you say so?"

"Because even they make you jealous."

"They do not."

"Greg, you'd be jealous of my daddy if he were alive. The one time you met my brother, Toy, you nearly tore his hand off shaking it."

"That's because I didn't believe he was your brother, for pete's sake. The man is blond and six feet tall."

"He's six foot two. And you should trust me more."

"Yeah, you're right. So, Monday night, then?"

"For sure." I swallowed and shifted gears. "Say, Greg, ever heard of a guy named Mouse Trap?"

"I know this one. Just give me a minute and I'll think of the punch line."

"What?"

"It's got something to do with cheese, right?"

"This isn't a joke," I wailed. "I'm dead serious. I

need information on a man whose name is Mouse Trap. Mouse is his real first name."

"What kind of information?"

I could sense Greg's antennae going up, and I knew I needed to back off. If he didn't know about Mouse's priors, then Johnny had lied. There isn't a crime that goes on in Charlotte that Greg hasn't either dealt with personally or known someone who has.

"Just general," I said casually. "Like where he works and stuff."

"Abby, do I look like a credit bureau to you?"

"Of course not, dear."

"Listen, I'd be careful about hiring a man to help you out in your shop. I mean, there could be some awkward moments, like when you're reaching for something that's up high or have to get on a stepladder. Besides, lots of men don't like working for a female boss. Oh, they'll say they do on their application, but taking orders is another thing. And personally, I prefer to be waited on by an attractive woman when I shop."

"Oh, so she has to be attractive, does she?"

"Well—"

"Well, for your information, I've been interviewing several people, and I'm leaning toward Mouse. He's a real studmuffin, you know."

"A what?"

"A hunk."

During the ensuing silence, we southerners gave up eating fried foods and the NRA membership all became Mennonites. "You're just trying to get a rise out of me, aren't you?" he asked at last. "I mean, he's probably some wizened old geezer who can barely stand anymore. Right?"

"Wrong."

"Abby, are you trying to make me jealous? Because if you are, it's working."

I sighed. "You've got no reason to be jealous of Mouse, I assure you. He lives up to his name."

"Yeah? Say, Abby, I know I said I was riding around with Bowater tonight, but you don't suppose I could drop by anyway?"

"Well—"

"You could have C. J. over, and the two of them could meet. We'd make it very casual-like."

I'd totally forgotten about fixing C. J. up with the sergeant, but that gave me an idea. "Sounds like a good idea, but just so I know—so I can be sure to have C. J. there—let's decide now on a time."

"Well, Bowater's shift starts at eight. How about ten?"

"Ten it is. But don't be early, because we might take in a movie first."

"Okay, but make sure it's just you and C. J."

"Good-bye, Gregory," I said and blew a kiss into the phone before I hung up.

I called C. J. at her shop.

"Ooh, Abby, didn't you get my message?"

"What message?"

"Some hunk came in here asking about you."

"Greg?"

"No, silly, a real hunk. This guy had a leather

jacket with studs. I mean lots of studs. You know what that means, don't you?"

I refrained from asking. "Was he driving a motorcycle, dear?"

"How did you know?"

My heart sank. "What did you tell him?"

"I sent him over to you, only you weren't there. He said your assistant told him to butt out and mind his own business. So he came back here. Abby, I didn't know you had an assistant. Why didn't you tell me?"

"I only hired her yesterday. So then what did you tell him?"

"I told him to butt out and mind his own business, of course. But ooh, Abby, I hated to because he was so cute."

"Good girl. You did the right thing. Say, C. J., would you like to hang out with me this evening?" That was a no-brainer. The girl adores me.

"No can do, Abby."

"What?"

"Sorry, Abby, but I need to stay in tonight and string popcorn."

"Whatever for?"

"For my Christmas tree, silly."

"But it's only July!"

"I know," C. J. moaned, "but it takes me so long to string it. Those kernels are very hard, and I keep breaking needles."

"C. J., you big doofus, you're supposed to pop it first!"

"Now you tell me."

"Look, C. J., I know you want to string popcorn, but remember the sergeant from Shelby I was telling you about? Well, Greg is dropping by with him and—"

"Ooh, Abby, I'd love to meet my new dreamboat, but like I said, I can't tonight."

"What if I help you string popcorn some other time?"

"It's not the popcorn, silly, it's the moon."

"Come again?"

"I plum forgot about it the other night, Abby, but tonight is the full moon!"

"Huh? Is that prime popcorn-stringing time?"

"Actually, it isn't, so I thought I might do something else instead. My household cleaners need reorganizing."

"C. J., dear, don't do this to me. I finally got you a live one, and you're going to line up your Lime Away?"

"Abby, I appreciate what you've done, but I can't afford to take any chances."

"What do you mean?"

"The change, silly. Folks from Shelby can't go outside when there's a full moon or they're subject to the change."

"Of life? Of sex? C. J., make sense!"

"Werewolves," she whispered.

"Tell me you're not serious!" I, Wynnell, the Rob-Bobs, even Mama—we have all worried about C. J.'s sanity. Once we even managed to drag her to a see a psychiatrist, Dr. Fleischman. Unfortunately, the good doctor was himself as nutty as a pecan pie. There is an upside to C. J.'s illness, however; she makes Mama seem normal by comparison.

"I'm very serious, Abby. It happened to my granny all the time."

"Granny Ledbetter?"

"Granny Cox. The poor dear would start to itch something awful every time there was a full moon. If she rubbed calamine lotion all over her body and stayed inside, she'd be all right, but if she stuck as much as one toe out the door, she'd turn as hairy as a Frenchwoman's legs."

"Get out of town!"

"It's true, Abby."

"You saw this?"

"No, but we lived only a block away. The howling was something awful."

"C. J., maybe it was a dog," I said patiently. "I mean, who told you it was your granny baying at the moon?"

"My brother Kyle."

"The same brother who told you baby oil was made from babies?"

"So Kyle was wrong once, Abby. I know what I know."

"Have you ever been outside during a full moon?"

"Not if I can help it."

"But you have, haven't you? And nothing happened, did it?"

"No, but—"

"But nothing. You get your butt over here right after work. We'll grab ourselves some supper at Southpark Mall, and then we're going hunting."

"Ooh, that sounds like fun Abby. What are we hunting?"

She suddenly sounded too eager to join me. I would have to keep an eye on her hair follicles.

"The world's largest mouse, dear."

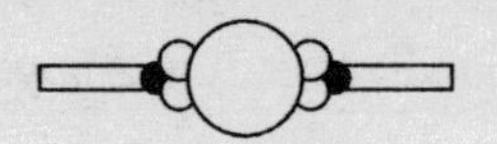

20

Southpark Mall has a Cinnabon shop, and I practically overdosed on warm buns. If I had to choose one food only for the rest of my life—provided that food was nutritiously complete—I'd choose cinnamon rolls. With cream cheese icing, of course. Biting into one of those is heaven to my taste buds, and that soft, slightly doughy center is—well, better than sex.

I may be a small person, but I have a large appetite, and I polished off two large rolls while C. J. nibbled at a chicken sandwich. At the start of our meal, I'd made the mistake of informing her that birds were descended from dinosaurs. C. J. balked at eating Barney on a bun until I threatened to put a hex on her. Fortunately, C. J. is as superstitious as a room full of professional ball players and finally deigned to dine on dino, rather than risk my wrath.

After supper we window-shopped for a bit before heading out to visit Mouse. A closer inspection of my Charlotte map revealed that the man lived well to the northeast of UNCC and, in fact, within whizzing distant of the Charlotte Motor Speedway. We took I-77 to I-85 and got off on Mallard Creek Road. It was dark by then, and we had trouble finding Mouse's house, which was set back from the road. I mean way back.

When we finally saw the house, we both gasped. It was immediately clear to me that Mouse made a lot more money than his brother the writer. And there was a Lamborghini parked in the circular drive, not a van. I convinced C. J. to ring the doorbell, just in case I had made a mistake.

I couldn't see what all transpired, but C. J. was back in a New York minute, and she was as white as cottage cheese.

"Well?" I demanded.

"It's him!"

"Mouse?"

"I don't know about your mouse, Abby. All I know is that that's Albert in there."

"Albert?"

"Albert Westerman. We went to high school together in Shelby."

"C. J., are you sure?"

"Positive."

I firmly believe that genuine coincidences are few and far between. "Does Albert Westerman have enormous ears that stick straight out and buck teeth?"

"Ooh, Abby, you know him?"

A goose walked over my grave. "I know him as Mouse Trap. But I thought that name was too eccentric even for a southerner!"

C. J. slammed her car door shut and locked it. "Step on it, Abby. We have to get out of here."

I turned the car around and drove reluctantly back up the lane, stopping just before it met Mallard Creek

Road. Even though it was still stifling outside, I turned off the ignition so that my automatic headlights wouldn't give me away.

"Spill it, C. J. Tell me what you know."

"I know that man in there is dangerous," she said, a quaver to her voice. "In high school, he used to brag about how he and his brother killed their parents. They were just kids—maybe nine or ten, I think, and besides, the state couldn't prove it, so they got off scot-free."

"That happened in Shelby?"

"No, ma'am. Folks don't kill their parents in Shelby. They move there from someplace else. Wilmington, I think."

I glanced in my rearview mirror. The Lamborghini was still in place. The same lights were on in the house.

"Did you know his brother? Was he overweight?"

"Is the Pope Dutch?" C. J. has always been metaphorically challenged.

"I don't understand," I wailed. "It couldn't possibly be the same pair of brothers. One fat, the other skinny, both with huge rodent ears. C. J., tell me everything you know about these guys."

C. J. scratched her head and stared at me. She has enormous blue-gray peepers, but they invariably lack emotion. It's like looking into the eyes of a Scandinavian cow.

"Well, the brother is a writer."

"A writer?"

"At least in high school he was. Johnny Westerman wrote the best stories for English. He always said he was going to be rich and famous someday. Ooh, Abby, maybe Albert decided to become a writer, too."

"I can't believe this," I wailed.

"Oh, but it's true, Abby. One of Johnny's stories was so good that our English teacher cried when he read it."

"I believe you! What I mean is, I can't believe the amount of trouble I seem to run into. Boy murderers, yet! You'd think I was Angela Lansbury."

"Oh, no, Abby, you're much older than she."

"Thanks, dear." I turned on the ignition and stomped on the gas pedal.

Perhaps it was a foolish thing, calling from a pay phone in front of a convenience store. But at the time it seemed safer than calling from home, thanks to that modern horror, caller identification. C. J., who is quite good at sound effects, helped set a trap for Johnny Trap.

"Mr. Westerman?" I was speaking through a facial tissue and using my best British accent.

"Sorry, ma'am, but you have a wrong number." Still, he didn't hang up.

"Mr. Westerman, this is Christy Marple calling from London, England."

"Look, I said—"

In the background, C. J. wailed like a foghorn on the Thames.

"Mr. Westerman, I represent Dorfman, Marple, and Daily, one of England's most respected law firms."

"What does that have to do with me?"

"It seems you have quite a large inheritance coming your way."

"Yeah?"

"Yes. According to our records, your great-great-grandfather was the youngest son of Lord Angus Westerman, the famous English industrialist. Is that so?"

"Well, it could be. I think my mama did have some English ancestors."

"This would have to have been your father."

"Oh, him, too. Daddy was definitely English."

"So he was a Westerman?"

"Born and bred."

"Of the Wilmington, North Carolina, Westermans?"

"Yes, ma'am."

C. J. tooted like the horn of a London cab.

"Great. Now we're getting somewhere. You see, your great-uncle Louis Westerman—not a lord, alas—died without any heirs on our side of the pond and—"

"How much is the inheritance?"

"Oh, millions."

"Pounds or dollars?"

C. J. brayed like a British ambulance.

"Uh . . . Euro-dollars. But it's still millions. Now, Mr. Westerman, according to our records, you have a brother. Is that so?"

"No, ma'am."

"But you do. It says so right here. Albert Westerman."

"Uh, yeah. It's been a long day."

"Mr. Westerman, does your brother also live in Charlotte?"

"Well, ma'am, the truth is, I don't know where Albert is these days. He was always kind of a free spirit, you know. Kind of roamed from one city to the next. Hell, he could be out in California for all I know. Maybe even Alaska."

"That's a shame, Mr. Westerman, because according to British law—"

"Ma'am, I just remembered—"

Unfortunately, C. J. picked that very moment to bong like a clock. That happens to be her worst imitation.

Johnny Westerman didn't have enormous ears for nothing. "What's that?"

"Oh, that's just Big Ben. It chimes on the hour, you know."

"That's funny, because it's not the hour here. What time is it there?"

"It chimes on the half hour, too," I said, grasping at straws.

"But it's exactly ten after. I just reset my watch this morning."

"Uh, Big Ben is slow today."

"Miss Timberlake, is that you?"

I hung up and turned on C. J. "Now you've done it! He knows it was me."

C. J. blinked, but her face remained placid. "It isn't my fault you can't clip your vowels."

"I clipped my vowels," I wailed. "I clipped them back to the cuticle. It was your pitiful Big Ben and your abominable timing."

"Well, Abby, if that's the way you're going to be, then just take me home. I'd have an inch of popcorn strung by now—maybe more if that popping idea of yours works."

"C. J., I'm sorry. It's just that I'm scared. Albert Westerman knows I'm onto him, and if he and his brother really did kill their parents—how did they do it?"

"Bonked them on their heads with baseball bats while they slept. The parents were sleeping, I mean, not the boys."

I shuddered. "You're sure?"

"They showed me baseball bats just like the ones they used. Like I said, they bragged about it all the time."

I glanced around me. A skinny blonde in platform shoes was pumping gas, and an elderly man was just walking out with a paper under his arm. The convenience store parking lot seemed as safe a place as any.

"I think the Westerman boys might just be the ones who tried to break into my car the other night."

"Did they hit it with baseball bats?"

"No. But Mouse has definitely been following me. First to the nursing home, and then there was that business with Susan. Oh, and the motorcyclist—and that black woman from church. C. J., do you ever feel paranoid?"

C. J. rolled her bovine eyes. "Of course not. I just tune those voices out."

"Thanks, dear. You're always a big help."

She grinned happily. "I try. Hey, Abby, maybe you should tell all this stuff to Greg."

"Maybe I should."

But I wouldn't. Not all of it, at any rate. I would fish for bits of information, but I wouldn't lay my cards on the table, for fear that Greg would force me out of the game. Greg can be as cautious as a chicken at a fox crossing. I wasn't about to sit back and do nothing while he took his sweet time going through channels and following procedures. Mama claims that I was born running—ran right off the delivery table. Of course, that isn't true, but you get the picture. I was born to do. And I would get to the bottom of this puzzle, just not tonight. Now it was time to take C. J. home to meet the new love of her life.

C. J. and I strung eight feet of popcorn by the time Greg and Sergeant Bowater showed up, a full hour late. We would have strung a lot more, but C. J. was ravenous. She polished off two ham sandwiches—after making me sign an affidavit that pigs were not descended from dinosaurs—and three luscious Carolina peaches. The bowl of popcorn became her second dessert.

"Well, well, look what the cat dragged in," I said sourly to Greg. I'd had it with C. J. by then. One more Shelby story, and I was going to explode like a popcorn kernel.

"Couldn't help it, Abby. We got called to assist Officers Massey and Kurtz. There was an attempted holdup of a convenience mart."

"Where? Up by the Charlotte Motorway?"

Greg gave me a funny look. "That's way out of our jurisdiction. This was over on Providence."

"Well, you could have called."

Sergeant Bowater stepped forward. "Pardon me, ma'am, but Investigator Washburn—" Bowater stopped midsentence. His mouth hung open, and his eyes bulged. He had seen C. J.

C. J. had seen him. "Ooh," she squealed, "is this the hunk you were telling me about?"

Sergeant Bowater's myriad freckles connected, forming one vast blotch. He was still apparently incapable of speech.

"Ooh, Abby," C. J. said, turning to me, "he's even cuter than you said."

"And he's from Shelby."

C. J. moaned, sounding remarkably like Mama does when she bites into chocolate fudge cake.

"Love at first sight," I said.

Greg snickered. "Give me a break, Abby. The man hasn't even said one word."

"Classic symptoms, dear. And she couldn't hear him if he did, what with all the violins playing in her head. In fact, knowing C. J., I'd say she had the Vienna Boys' Choir in there, too."

"What should we do?"

"Do? Why, nothing, of course. Except leave them alone." I grabbed him by one tanned elbow and steered him to the kitchen. "You hungry? There might be a piece of ham left."

"Naw." He glanced toward the living room. "You sure they'll be all right?"

"They'll be fine as frog's hair split three ways. It was a match made in heaven. Say, Greg, you ever hear of a pair of brothers by the name of Westerman?"

Broad shoulders shrugged.

"Albert and Johnny."

"Isn't that a singing team?"

"That's Eddy Albert, and he's one person. I'm talking about two men."

"They singers, too?"

I sighed. "Yeah. They're coming to Charlotte. They'll be at the Oven's Auditorium next Friday. I thought we might go."

"Whatever you say, babe." Greg put his arms around me. "I like it when the woman does the asking. I like it when the woman—"

I slid deftly away from his embrace. It was still silent in the other room, and while some silence was good, too much was definitely not. I had just had my upholstery shampooed.

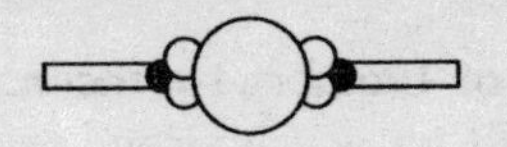

21

Thanks to Irene, I could afford to sleep in. I woke about ten, because of light sneaking through the blinds, but I lolled about decadently. Friday is sheet-changing day in this house, and I'd remembered to do so before going to bed. There is nothing quite as delicious—except for maybe a cinnamon bun—as lolling about on clean sheets. I lolled, yawned, and stretched, and lolled again. Dmitri, who weighs a good ten pounds, lolled, yawned, and stretched as well, but on my chest. It was a wonder I could breathe.

When the phone rang, close to eleven, I picked it up languidly. "Hello," I purred.

"Abby? Rob here. You busy?"

"I'm lolling, dear. You, however, are at work, right?" There was no point in suppressing the glee in my voice.

"Actually, I'm not. I'm at Charlotte Douglas International Airport."

"I'm here, too," I heard Bob boom in the background.

I pushed Dmitri off and sat up. "Are you going to New York? I thought that art expert friend of yours was coming here tomorrow."

"That art expert friend has a name, Abby. It's Reginald Perry, and he just happens to be the world's foremost authority on van Gogh. And his apocrypha."

"What?"

"Works attributed to van Gogh that weren't really his."

"Well, this one is!"

"I'm sure it is. Anyway, Reginald has never been south before, and he expressed a desire to come early and then spend a couple days at Myrtle Beach."

"You're joking!"

"No, I'm not. If this works out—I mean, if the painting proves to be real, Bob and I will drive him there ourselves. We could use a few days off."

"I can't believe that a van Gogh authority from New York City would want to visit the Grand Strand. Besides, I'm pretty sure I read in the paper that if you're not a native Carolinian, you have to show an Ohio birth certificate at the city limits."

"So, Abby, can we come right over?"

"Now? But I have a funeral to go to this afternoon, and tonight I'm busy as well."

"What time is the funeral?"

"Two, but—"

"No problem. I'm calling from my cell phone, and I'm already out of the parking lot. We'll be there in twenty minutes." Rob hung up.

"What? What?" I slapped the receiver with the heel of my hand. It was, of course, only a useless gesture. And it was useless to try and call the Rob-Bobs back because I didn't know their cell phone number.

Left with no choice but to cooperate, I decided to

put my best foot forward. I had planned to wear shorts and a T-shirt until it was time to change for the funeral, but clearly that would no longer do. I took the shortest shower in history and had just pulled my black, floral print funeral dress over my head when the doorbell rang.

I dashed to the door, pushed wet clumps of hair behind my ears, and opened it serenely—yes, I know, I should have first peeked through my specially installed peephole. At any rate, I had expected Reginald Perry to be a dapper little man, perhaps with a Maurice Chevalier mustache and a silk ascot. The man accompanying the Rob-Bobs was dressed in Madras shorts and a pink I LOVE NEW YORK T-shirt. Judging from his belly, he was nine months pregnant, and instead of wearing proper shoes, he was wearing thongs! What was the world coming to? If Mama really wanted to serve mankind, she should skip going to Africa as a missionary and join the fashion police instead.

Rob proudly made the introductions while I shook a hand that was as hot as a freshly served bowl of chili and every bit as wet.

"I can't tell you how excited I am to be here," Reginald said. He didn't sound to me at all like a New Yorker. Perhaps he had immigrated from the hinterlands.

I surreptitiously wiped my hand on my skirt and ushered the men in. "I'm so glad you could come, Mr. Perry."

"Please, call me Reggie. All my friends do."

I smiled graciously. "You may call me Abby. Care for some tea?"

Only Reginald laughed. "That's a joke, right? Tea in this heat?"

"She means sweet tea," Rob said, and then quickly added, "iced tea."

"Sounds good, but you got any beer?"

"I might be able to scare one up. You want that in a mug, or is the can all right?"

"Abby!" Rob gasped.

Reggie laughed. "Can is fine. But I need to use the john first."

I pointed to the hallway. "First door on your left."

"Abby," Rob said sternly, the bathroom door having barely closed, "do you know who you were just talking to?"

"A potbellied man who sweats like a pig? I'm sorry, but that's no way to dress on a plane. Every year, airline passengers are taking more liberties with their clothes. Soon you won't be able to tell them from the folks down at the bus depot."

"Reginald Perry can dress any way he damn pleases! The man is a world expert in his field."

"And besides," Bob whispered, his voice barely below a boom, "who are you to talk? Your hair is all greasy."

"Oh, the conditioner," I wailed. "I forgot to rinse it out."

"Don't worry, Abby," Rob said kindly, "I'm sure he didn't notice. Not with your dress being inside out."

"What?" I glanced down. Sure enough, the frayed

rayon seams on the outside of my dress were a dead giveaway. The floral design was only barely visible on the reverse side of the material. My dress looked merely smudged.

"Turn your backs," I snapped.

They obediently did so, and I turned the dress inside out. In the process, however, I got white deodorant streaks on the outside front. I barely had time to dab at them with a wet paper towel before Reggie returned. As soon as he did, I shoved a cold, sweating beer into his hand. Maybe he wouldn't notice the water spots or the shredded bits of towel.

"You ready to go back to the guest bedroom and see my masterpiece?" I asked brightly.

There was absolutely no innuendo intended. Nonetheless, both Rob-Bobs gasped, and Bob put a warning finger to his lips.

Reggie smiled. "I've been waiting for this moment my entire professional life, Abby. If what you have really is the *Field of Thistles,* I will die a happy man.

Reggie stared at the painting, his mouth open wide enough to catch a frog catching flies. Perhaps he was dead. I knew for sure that Rob and Bob weren't breathing. That's all I needed—three corpses in the guest room. It was going to take me every bit of my ten million dollars to get me out of that one.

"Well," I demanded after an eternity, "is it, or isn't it?"

Reggie's mouth closed and opened several times before the first syllable squeaked out. "Yes."

"Yes, what?"

"It's her, all right."

"Her?" Were paintings assigned the feminine gender, like ships and cars?

"It's *Field of Thistles.*"

"By Vincent van Gogh?" I shrieked.

Reggie gave me a pained look. "There is no mistaking the master's hand on this one. Those brush strokes—pure genius."

Rob must have resumed breathing. "You're absolutely positive? I mean, don't you have to scrape off some paint samples and run a few tests?"

I all but threw myself across the canvas. "Scrape this baby, and you die!"

"Easy, Abby," Rob said. "The man knows what he's doing."

I eyeballed Reggie, who regarded me calmly. "I do need to take some paint samples," he said, "but I won't really be scraping them off. A painting this old will flake naturally with just a light brushing. If it doesn't, I have a very sharp razor that will allow me to shave a layer so thin you won't even notice it. I will, of course, be collecting a few canvas fibers, but those will be taken from the back. Trust me, even an expert like myself would not be able to tell that samples had been taken."

"Be careful," I wailed. "This is my early retirement."

"You want your kit in from the car?" Bob asked.

Reggie nodded. He couldn't tear his eyes from the van Gogh. I'm proud to say that Buford had that exact same look on our wedding night.

While Bob ran back to the car and Reggie stared,

Rob steered me to a far corner of the room.

"You do realize, don't you, that it could still turn out not to be the genuine article?"

"What? But—"

Rob placed a well-manicured hand on my shoulder. "I'm just saying, it isn't over until the fat lady sings. I don't want you to get your hopes up too high. Just in case."

"There is no just in case," I hissed. I ducked loose from Rob's hand and grabbed Reggie's pink sleeve. "You are positive, aren't you?"

Reggie wiped his eyes on his other sleeve. "I'd stake my reputation on it. The art world is very fortunate, Abby, that this masterpiece"—he chuckled—"fell into your hands. But don't worry, I've decided to scratch my little jaunt to Myrtle Beach. I'll be catching the first plane back to the city that I can get a seat on."

"Really?"

"And to think I remembered to bring my Ohio birth certificate."

"You mean I was right?" I had just made up that birth certificate thing, but you never knew these days. It had been years since I'd been down there, and it seems to me like we were mostly Carolinians back then. Now, I've been told, every other car is from Ohio.

"He's only teasing about the birth certificate," Rob said. "I told him what you said on the way over here. But he really is from Ohio."

Reggie nodded. "Cincinnati. Fine arts degree from UC and then three years at the Sorbonne. Of course,

I live in the Big Apple now. Everyone does."

"Rob doesn't," I said wickedly.

"Well, almost everyone."

Bob panted into the room. "Here's the kit. Did I miss anything?"

Rob grinned. "Our Abby's still standing. You lose the bet."

I whirled. "What bet?"

Bob blushed. "I bet fifty bucks you'd faint if Reggie told you it was real."

"Well, I never!"

"Shhh." Rob snapped his fingers. "The man needs to concentrate."

I can't stand to watch surgery performed on TV. Once I made the mistake of watching a liposuction on the Oprah show, and consequently lost my cookies. While barfing on my La-Z-Boy was no big deal, gagging on a van Gogh is quite another story.

Call me a wimp, but I staggered out of the guest room and threw myself on one of my white cotton sofas. Bob, bless his Yankee heart, followed suit on the other. Between you and me, he didn't have the stomach for it, either.

"So, Abby, what are you going to do with all that money?"

"You mean if the painting is real?"

"Oh, it is. Reginald Perry never makes mistakes. So, you going to sell your shop and retire?"

"I don't know. I've been too busy to do any actual planning. How about you? What would you do? What are you going to do with Rob's commission?"

"Yes, the commission. We're thinking maybe we'll

build a house in one of those gated communities. Something with high ceilings and lots of room for antiques."

"And if you had it all? Would you move someplace else?"

He read my mind. "You mean, like San Francisco or Key West?"

"Yeah."

"I don't think so. Rob and I love it here."

"I do, too, but I saw this ad in one of those real estate magazines you can buy at the supermarket. You know, those real upscale, glossy things that showcase mansions in Miami and Atlanta. This ad was for a twenty-five-acre private island in the Bahamas. It had a mansion and a caretaker's house. But it cost twelve-point-five million dollars." I sighed, suddenly feeling poor. "If I sell the painting for only ten million dollars, I won't be able to afford this place. Even if I sell it for twenty, I might not be able to afford to keep it going. What if I can't pay the taxes? Lordy, I don't want to end up in a Bahamian jail. They probably aren't air-conditioned, are they?"

Bob laughed. "That's our Abby! Always borrowing trouble. You're the only woman I know who would go bankrupt in her daydreams!"

I was about to defend my foibles when Rob and Reggie emerged, their faces triumphant.

"Ta-da!" Rob held up a small plastic bag.

I was on my feet. "And?"

"The patient—I mean, the painting—survived beautifully."

I dashed into the guest room and saw that it was

so. I dashed out again. "How long will the lab work take?"

All eyes turned to Reggie.

"Well," he said, obviously enjoying the limelight, "a mere matter of minutes."

"Minutes?" we chorused.

"Well, normally, it would take a lot longer, but I have paint samples from *The Starry Night* and six other van Gogh paintings in my files. So, to answer your real question, you should find out tonight. That is, if Rob can get my ticket changed."

"I'll do my best," Rob said.

"But I have dinner plans for tonight!" I wailed.

"Sure you can't change them?" Bob asked sympathetically.

"It's the Queen. A command performance."

Reggie looked at me with new interest. "Her Majesty, Elizabeth II? I've authenticated a number of her paintings."

"Her Bossiness, Priscilla I."

"A maven friend of her mother's," Rob explained. He turned to me. "Don't worry, Abby. I'll call you there when I hear something. I have Mrs. Hunt's phone number."

"You do?"

"She's a good customer of ours," Bob boomed. "Bought a fauteuil from us just last week."

I wanted to chide my friends for doing business with the enemy, but in retail, like in love and war, anything goes. "So where do I do keep the painting in the meantime?"

Reggie frowned. "Where have you been keeping it?"

"Well, the first night I kept it in Rob's safe, and the second, right there where it is now."

The Rob-Bobs turned as white as Mama's best lace tablecloth. "Oh, Abby," they moaned in unison.

"But I was in the next room!" The fact that I had gone gallivanting off during the day was none of their concern.

"Actually," Reggie said, "a bed is a good place to keep a painting. Especially one that is off its frame."

The Rob-bobs wheeled. "It is?"

"Not on top, of course. Under the sheets. A friend of mine who likes to play fast and loose with the law—never mind. Just put it on the bed and pull the sheet, blanket, and spread up over it. It's less likely to be found there than in a safe. No matter how cleverly a safe is hidden, a good thief knows where to look."

"Even in a bidet?" I clamped my hand over my mouth.

The Rob-Bobs scowled, but Reggie smiled. "Even there. One of my clients had a safe made that resembled a cat litter box. You know the kind with the cover?"

"Boy, do I! Half my life is spent sifting that darn thing."

"Well, a cat burglar—no pun intended—found that safe in five minutes. Another two minutes, and he had it opened. Made off with a diamond necklace worth well over a million dollars. The whole time, my client was in the shower shampooing her hair."

"Diamonds," I said, primarily to Bob. "I never thought about that."

"Abby, be careful not to sit on the bed after you make it," Rob said anxiously.

"Or let Dmitri sit on it," Bob added.

We all laughed nervously. We had good reason to be nervous. By bedtime, if all went well, I would be a confirmed multimillionaire, Rob at least a millionaire, and Reggie would have his reputation permanently made.

If all went well.

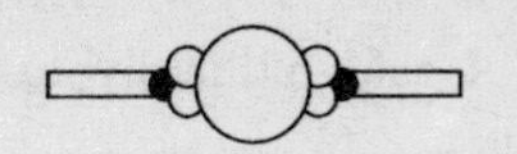

22

Time got away from me. I had to iron another dress—alas, not black—rinse the conditioner out of my hair, and of course eat something. I hadn't had a bite since the cinnamon buns, and I was ravenous.

Folks assume that just because I'm petite, I don't need to eat. On the contrary, think of me as a hummingbird. I may have a tiny tummy, but I burn up energy at an incredible rate. Forget three squares. I need seven or eight mini-meals throughout the day. So you can see why it was absolutely imperative that I stop by the IHOP in Pineville on my way down to Rock Hill. Two poached eggs, some bacon, and a pancake or two later, I was feeling much better. Unfortunately, I was also late for the funeral.

"For shame," Mama said when I slid into the pew and sat next to her. "This is the last hymn. See, they're getting ready to push the coffin out."

Indeed they were. As is the custom in the Episcopal Church, the casket was covered with a heavy drape, called a pall. Two men, presumably from the funeral home, had lifted the pall and were folding it. In a minute, they would expertly wheel the casket down the center aisle, where the pallbearers would take over, lifting the coffin into the hearse and out again when it reached the cemetery.

"You coming to the cemetery?" Mama asked. She sang the words to the tune of the hymn.

"I hadn't planned on it."

"Oh, but you have to. It wouldn't look right for you to just pop in and go. This isn't one of those drive-in funeral parlors I've been hearing about so much lately."

"Okay, Mama," I said glumly. "I'll go with you to the cemetery."

I glanced around. Thanks to the Sweeny family's connections—mainly the famous Hortense Simms—the place was packed. No one was going to miss my being there, least of all the forgetful Adele Sweeny.

"I thought you were going to wear your black dress," Mama sang. As usual, she was off-key. Mama sings in the church choir and is what the choir director calls a "mercy member." When folks hear her sing, they like as not say, "Oh, mercy!"

"Had a little accident," I said.

"Notice anything about me?"

I looked at Mama, really seeing her for the first time that day. Thank heavens we were singing the last stanza, because I dropped the hymnal.

"You're wearing black!"

"Of course. Gilbert Sweeny was Hortense Simms's half-brother, and—"

"And Hortense Simms is the Queen's archrival!" My timing was off, and every word but the "and" was spoken after the hymn ended and before the benediction.

Folks in all directions turned and stared.

"Abby!" Mama was truly mortified.

What could I possibly say to dig myself out of that hole? Thinking of nothing, I flung myself to the kneeler and began praying.

"You can stop it now," Mama said after a few minutes. "Just about everyone has left. If we don't get a move on, we'll miss out on riding in the procession."

I looked up. Only a few stragglers—no doubt gossiping about me—remained. We hustled our bustles to the parking lot. Rock Hill has only recently discontinued the practice of having the police escort funeral corteges, but, nonetheless, funerals command great respect here. More often than not, oncoming motorists will stop wherever they are and wait patiently until the cortege has passed them by.

At any rate, we took Mama's car because it was parked much closer than mine. I drove, because Mama knows only two speeds—pedal to the metal and dead stop. Since we both knew where the cemetery was, we didn't need to keep up with the group, although we pretty much did. Three blocks from the church, we halted at a red light.

"You could have put some makeup on, Abby."

"I'll be damned!" I said, pounding the steering wheel with my fist. Fortunately, the horn is hard to find in Mama's car.

"Why, Abigail, that was just an innocent observation. If you want to look like death warmed over, that's your business."

"Sorry, Mama. It isn't what you said. It's that woman behind me."

"She's not talking on a cell phone, is she? I hate it when drivers talk on their cell phones. It's so—"

"Mama! She's not talking on a phone. It's Marina."

"Who, dear?"

"The woman who paid you a visit the other evening. The so-called tourist."

Mama tried to turn, but the shoulder strap restrained her. "But that's silly, dear. Marina was just passing through. If she was going to spend the night, I would have offered her a room. Besides, how do you know it's her? You never met her."

I bit my tongue, wondering how much to tell. "I've seen this woman around, Mama. I know it's her."

"Then describe her, dear."

"Well, she's a black woman in a dark blue car."

"Is that it?"

"Well—"

"Why, Abigail Louise Wiggins Timberlake! Didn't I raise you any better than that?"

The light turned green and I floored the accelerator, turned right on Main, left on Hampton, and right again on West Black. Then I quite cleverly pulled into the public parking garage that is opposite the police station. I waited for five minutes and, not seeing the now-familiar blue car, continued to the cemetery. In the meantime, Mama gave me a lecture on the fallacies of prejudice and how, if we could all choose our bodies at birth, the world would be populated by six billion Mel Gibsons. I listened respectfully, although I may have rolled my eyes a few times. Believe me, if the world was populated by six billion Mel Gibsons, and I was an unborn soul about to choose, I'd go for something a little different—like maybe Mrs. Mel Gibson.

"I don't care about her race, Mama," I said as we turned in at the cemetery. "It's just a concise description. You didn't see many people of color at the funeral, did you?"

Mama sniffed and patted her pearls. "I don't count colors."

"I am not prejudiced, and I didn't notice any African-Americans. Gilbert Sweeny was not known for his tolerance, after all. My point is that the woman back there has been following me."

Mama shook her head. "The trick, I hear, is finding a really good therapist. A mediocre one might just make things worse."

"Is that the pot calling the kettle black?" I wailed. "I know that's the same woman I saw at the auction Wednesday night, and, like I said, I recognized the car."

"All cars look alike," Mama said pompously. "And there are plenty of blue cars. Yours is blue."

We pulled into the cemetery. Now we were late. We had to park practically near the gate, and interment was on a knoll at the opposite end.

"You go ahead," I said to Mama.

"Why, dear? Are you mad at me?"

"Just mildly irked, and that's got nothing to do with it."

"Oh, I get it. You want to sit here and keep a lookout for secret agents."

If you can't beat them, join them. I patted my purse.

"That's exactly right. Thank heavens I remembered to bring my secret decoder ring. Now, you better get, Mama. It looks like they're fixing to start."

Mama got, grumbling the whole way, I'm sure. Meanwhile, I slumped down and made myself inconspicuous. One of the few perks that come with being my height is that I don't have to slump far to hide in a car. All I have to do is slide my booster cushion out from under me and relax. You can bet I left the car running, with the AC cranked to the max.

Perhaps it was the sound of the fan at high speed that prevented me from hearing the car pull up right behind mine. But the slamming of the car door was practically loud enough to wake the dead. I popped up to see Marina striding to the knoll. Already she had covered a good deal of ground.

I hoofed after the woman, not something I would recommend when both the temperature and humidity are hovering near one hundred. "Miss," I called. "Miss."

Marina stopped and turned. She was halfway between her car and the graveside mourners. Evergreen Cemetery has only a small number of large monuments, and there is a dearth of shrubs. There was really no place for her to hide. She appeared to wait calmly while I trotted right up to her. By that time, however, I was dewing like the target of a Kenneth Starr investigation.

"You," I gasped. "I need to talk to you."

Marina nodded. "I guess it's for the best."

I blinked away drops of stinging sweat. I didn't like what I saw: flawless chocolate complexion; perfect, symmetrical features. To add insult to injury, her legs reached halfway to the sun.

"Perhaps we should talk in the shade." Marina gestured to a nearby tree. She was impeccably dressed in a pearl-gray silk suit and didn't look the least bit hot.

We moved to the dense shade of a limbed-up magnolia. The thick, dry leaves of yesteryear crunched beneath our feet.

"You've been following me, haven't you?" I demanded.

"Guilty."

"Why?"

"I needed to know more about you."

I folded my arms, but it was too hot to keep them that way. "Why?"

Marina smiled. It was obvious her Mama hadn't weaned her on gooey desserts.

"Ms. Timberlake, right?"

"You tell me!"

"Ms. Timberlake, my name is Marina Weiss."

"I'll bet it is. And you're a tourist from Oregon, right?"

"That, too. But primarily I'm an art investigator."

"Come again?"

"I track down the provenance of artworks. Upon occasion, I search for missing pieces of art."

"And that brings you to Rock Hill? No doubt you're trying to track down the missing *Civitas* nipples. Well, you won't find them, Ms. Weiss. The fundamentalists threw them away."

Marina couldn't help but smile again. "Ms. Timberlake, have you ever heard of a painting by Vincent van Gogh called *Field of Thistles*?"

My knees buckled, and I had to steady myself against the magnolia trunk. "I don't go to museums much."

"Oh, you won't find that in any museum. It was stolen by the Nazis during World War II and hasn't been seen since."

I licked my salty lips but said nothing.

"It wasn't stolen from a museum, of course. It was stolen from a Jewish family. My family."

"Your family?"

"Don't look so surprised, Miss Timberlake. Judaism is a religion, not a race. But yes, I married into the family. The Harry and Selma Weiss family of Long Island. They're my husband's grandparents. *Field of Thistles* belongs to them."

"This is all very interesting, Mrs. Weiss, but what does it have to do with me?"

Marina casually smoothed a wrinkle from the pearl-gray skirt. "We believe that the painting is now in your possession."

I wanted to faint. "Don't be ridiculous. I don't buy stolen art."

"Perhaps not intentionally. But you purchased a painting at the auction Wednesday evening—"

"That was a fake. *The Starry Night* indeed!"

"Of course it was a fake, Miss Timberlake. But I believe that it may have been painted over *Field of*

Thistles. Perhaps with a water-based paint that is easily removed."

My knees felt stronger. I moved away from the tree trunk.

"I can assure you, Mrs. Weiss, that that is not the case. That so-called *Starry Night* is the only painting on the canvas. The colors show through to the other side. In fact, the painting looks much better on that side."

Marina smiled. "Might I have a look at it?"

"I'm afraid that's out of my say."

For the first time, Marina looked ruffled. "Did you sell it?"

"As a matter of fact, yes."

The woman's beautiful chocolate complexion turned ash-gray. "So soon? To whom?"

"I sold it that night. To another investigator. A police investigator."

"For how much?" She sounded incredulous. "Ms. Timberlake, law enforcement officers don't make that kind of money."

"This one does. I sold it for ten dollars. I think Greg can afford that."

"Ten dollars?"

"But that was without the frame. He couldn't have afforded that. Greg's always strapped for cash on account of his fishing trips—"

"Ms. Timberlake." She took a step forward, and I took one back. "Ms. Timberlake, am I to believe that you sold one of the greatest masterpieces of all time—property that belongs to my husband's family—for just ten dollars?"

"Oops, I forgot to add tax. You wouldn't happen to work for the IRS as well, would you?"

"Ms. Timberlake—"

I felt emboldened by my joke. When it came down to it, I didn't know who the woman who called herself Marina Weiss really was. Maybe she did work for the IRS. Maybe she was just out to get the *Field of Thistles* for herself.

"How about you prove who you are, Mrs. Weiss. Do you have something that says you're an art investigator?"

"As a matter of fact, I do." She reached into a pearl-gray purse and withdrew a slim, gold card holder. As she was handing me a card, another fell to the ground.

I took the proffered card. Marina K. Weiss, it read, art investigator.

"That's very nice, dear. It's even embossed. But you can have something like this made up at any printer."

Marina flinched, and it took a second for me to figure out that it wasn't necessarily what I'd said. Apparently the interment was over, because the crowd was headed our way.

"Abby!" Mama called. "Marina! Marina, is that you?"

"I'm staying at the Hampton Inn," Marina said quickly. "Call me."

By the time Mama reached me, Marina was already in her car.

"So, you were right, Abby," Mama said grudgingly. "It is the same woman. But she's not a secret agent, is she?"

"Not exactly."

"I told you. So, Abby, what did you think of the way Hortense carried on up there?"

"I don't know, Mama. I never made it that far."

Mama clutched her pearls and staggered. I moved out of the way so she could slump gracefully against the tree. She is my mother, after all, and I must accommodate her quirks.

"Oh, Abby, how rude! First you skip the funeral, and now this?"

"What can I say, Mama? You failed miserably. Your daughter is nothing but a boor."

"Don't mock me, Abby. There's something up between you and Marina, isn't there? I knew it by the look on your face just now."

"What does that mean?"

"Come on, dear, you can tell me. You can tell me anything. I watch those talk shows. I know what goes on in this world."

"What?"

"So that's why she came to see me! She was checking me out, wasn't she? Well, you tell her you come from good stock, Abby. You tell her—"

"Mama!"

"I got used to the Rob-Bobs; I can get used to this. Thank heavens you've already raised a family—oh, Abby, you're not thinking of having a family together, are you?"

"Mama, don't be ridiculous."

I snatched up the card Marina had dropped. "Here.

This will tell you who Marina really is."

Mama read the card and handed it back. "It's the heat, isn't it, dear? Even as a little girl, the heat bothered you. Well, some ice-cold tea when we get home will do the trick. And there's still plenty of time for you to lie down before dinner."

"Mama, you're not making a lick of sense."

"And you are, dear? You honestly expect me to believe that's Marina's card?"

I read the card. Twice. Then I screamed.

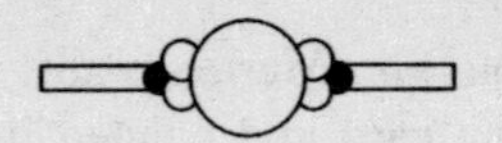

23

Actually, it was more of a shriek, but I've got to hand it to the good folks of Rock Hill. No one even turned. Perhaps they were used to shrieks emanating from the nether reaches of cemeteries. Perhaps they were just used to the Wiggins clan.

"That's Vincent Dougherty's card!"

"I'm glad you've come to your senses, dear. It would be awfully hard for Marina to impersonate Vincent. She's a good two inches taller than he."

"But how did that card—wait a minute, I bet the two of them are in cahoots."

Mama grabbed my elbow. "The tea, dear. It's all made. It will just take me a second to pour it."

I shrugged off her hand. It was too hot even to be Mama-handled.

"Tea sounds great, Mama," I said once I had her safely in the car. "But first we're going to make a little detour."

"Oh, Abby, you wouldn't!"

"It'll just be a short visit, Mama. In the meantime, you can do your part."

"What part?"

"Tell me everything you know about Vincent Dougherty."

"Me? He was one of your boyfriends, Abby. Just like Gilbert."

"He was not my boyfriend! And I'm asking you because you still live in town and hang out with his cronies."

"I most certainly do not!"

"Doesn't Vincent's mama belong to your club?"

"I belong to lots of clubs, Abby. I don't know everyone's children."

"Yes, but this is the club you joined just last year. The one you wanted to join so bad, you could taste it. What was it now—ah, yes, the Apostates' Club."

"That's Apathia Club, not Apostates'!"

"And Eudora Dougherty belongs to Apathia, does she not?"

Mama sighed. "You've got to promise me you won't breathe a word of this to anyone."

I steered with my right hand and crossed with my left. "I promise."

"Well, we usually meet at the Rock Hill Country Club, but sometimes if there is a special luncheon, we meet at a member's home. This past April—or was it May?—Eudora had us all to her home on the river. Anyway, I stayed after to help her clean up, and we got to talking."

"What about?"

"Mostly our kids. How we have to look past the disappointments and heartaches they bring us, and concentrate on their positive points."

"She did most of the talking, of course."

"Actually, I did."

"Boy, I bet Toy's ears were burning!"

Mama stroked her pearls. "I'm not sure I even mentioned him."

"What? Well, you couldn't have been talking about me, that's for sure."

"But I was."

"Mama! I went to college like you wanted. And I married well—at least on the surface. Sure, I'm divorced now, but I was married. And I'm self-supporting. Oh, don't forget the two beautiful grandchildren I gave you!"

"Yes, well, there is that." Mama sounded every bit as enthusiastic as I did the day Buford suggested oral sex.

"Mama, what are you driving at? Have I been a disappointment?"

"Well, frankly, dear, you have."

I couldn't believe my ears. I do plenty for Mama. And it's not like she's helpless. Daddy didn't leave her rich, but Buford—and it's one of the truly good things he did—invested wisely on her behalf. Now, eighteen years after Daddy's death, Mama lives quite comfortably.

"Mama, I call you almost every day and have dinner with you at least once a month. That's a whole lot more than some daughters do for their mamas."

"You don't talk to me."

"That's ridiculous!"

"I mean like a friend. You don't share the kind of stuff with me that you do with Wynnell."

"Yes, but you're my mama!"

"Toy does. Toy respects me as a person, not just as his mama."

"What? Toy hardly ever calls. You said so just recently."

"Your brother may not call often, but when he does we talk."

This was too much for me. In a minute, I was going to start resenting a brother I had hitherto considered unworthy of resentment.

"So what did Eudora Dougherty have to say about her Vincent? Was she able to find words to describe how disappointed she must be?"

"To the contrary, dear. Eudora is very proud of her son."

"Is Vincent an only child?"

"He is. Eudora said they're best friends."

"Oh, come on!"

"He tells her everything."

"So, he's a mama's boy with loose lips. It has got to break her heart that he runs the Adult Entertainment Center on Cherry Road."

"Oh, I've always wanted to go there."

"You have not!"

"You see? I can't even share my thoughts with you."

"Not those kinds of thoughts, Mama. Don't you have a nice recipe you want to share?"

Mama snorted. "You are such a prude, dear. I just wanted to take a quick peek inside. I'm curious about what actually goes on in there."

"What goes on is disgusting. And if Eudora Dougherty had any pride, she'd disown Vincent and move out of state." The truth is, I had no idea what went on behind the Adult Entertainment Center's closed doors. For all I knew, they played board games and drank lemonade.

"Eudora said Vincent has a heart of gold."

"Gold plate, maybe. Ten-karat, at that."

Mama looked meaningfully at me. "He gives a lot of money to charities, dear."

"Guilt money."

"The homeless don't care. I doubt if the orphans care much, either. Perhaps it bothers the cancer researchers."

"You're being facetious," I said angrily. I swerved across three lanes and into the large parking lot that was just ahead on the left. "Well, here it is, Mama. Vincent Dougherty's Adult Entertainment Center. Come on in and gawk a little bit, and then we'll have a nice heart-to-heart talk. Maybe we'll bond."

"Now who's being facetious?"

"I learned at the foot of the master," I said.

Mama smiled and patted her pearls. "At least you give credit where credit is due."

The silver-haired man with the acne scars was still at his post. He recognized me immediately.

"Mr. Dougherty's in his office. The door will most likely be partly open—he has this thing about closed spaces. Anyway, knock before you go in."

"So I don't break up any love fests?"

"Abby!" Mama chided, but her eyes were glowing with excitement.

"Who is she?" the previously pimpled pimp demanded.

"She's my mother. She's with me."

"You a member?" he asked Mama.

Mama giggled.

"Of course she's not!"

The silver pocks ignored me. "You care for a tour, ma'am?"

"She most certainly does not!"

Mama's eyes narrowed. "Speak for yourself, dear." She turned to the doorman. "I'd love a tour."

"Mama!"

He had the nerve to let Mama take his arm. "Room on the end," he said to me. "Remember to knock."

"But—"

Mama wagged a finger at me. "Believe it or not, I'm a grown woman, Abby. As long as we're not sharing, I'll mind my business, and you mind yours."

There was no use in arguing further. I watched in disbelief as my mama—a choir member, to boot—left for her guided tour of sin city. As soon as she disappeared through some swinging doors, I ran down the hall to Vincent's office. To be honest, I forgot to knock.

"What the hell?" Vincent shouted.

I jumped. I couldn't believe my eyes. Vincent Doughtery was lying flat on his back, his legs propped up against the wall. He was fully clothed, I might add, and quite alone. The ubiquitous sunglasses were still in place.

"Uh . . . uh . . ."

"Oh, it's you, Ms. Timberlake. Have a seat."

"I prefer to stand, thank you."

"As you wish. I hope you don't mind if I don't stand."

I couldn't help but stare. "What are you doing, yoga?"

"No, ma'am. I'm giving my veins a break."

"Excuse me?"

"Varicose veins are more common in women, but many men have them as well. It feels good to get your feet up above the level of your heart every now and then. Helps stop the throbbing."

"Oh."

"Now, what can I do for you this time?"

"It's about Marina. Marina Weiss."

Vincent slung his legs down and around. In one smooth move, he was on his feet. His bright red hair, however, defied gravity. It stuck out in all directions like a clown's wig.

"So, you've met Marina."

I spread my legs slightly. It was a stance that could be modified into flight or fight, depending on the circumstances.

"Aha! You know her!"

"Yes, of course. What did she tell you?"

"That she was an art investigator."

"Go on."

I wasn't about to spread that cockamamy story about my painting's being stolen. Not until I had more facts.

"There's nothing else to say, except that she had your card."

"I'm a businessman. Lots of people have my card."

"Yeah, I'll bet. You really wanted that painting, Mr. Dougherty, and then this so-called art investigator shows up, and she has your business card. What gives?"

"Well—"

"And what's with those creepy sunglasses? Are you in the Mafia or something? Or is it just plain old run-of-the-mill drug abuse?"

He gingerly removed the dark glasses. I gasped.

"It's just a little plastic surgery," he said and then laughed. "I turned fifty last week. For years, my friends have been telling me that I could pack for a two-week vacation in those bags. So I decided to get rid of them. What the hell, I thought, plastic surgery isn't just for women anymore."

"Did it hurt?" I asked, forgetting my mission.

"You bet. But I'm glad I did it. I've talked Ed out there into signing up for laser resurfacing. He's a little nervous, I think, but if I can do what I did—" he pointed to the bruises, "—anyone can. It will do wonders for his self-esteem, don't you think?"

"I suppose it will. Look, this is all very nice, Mr. Dougherty, but I didn't come here to discuss cosmetic changes."

"What exactly do you want to discuss?"

"I want you to explain Marina! What was she doing with your business card?"

"My exchange with Ms. Weiss seems to be very important to you, Ms. Timberlake."

"You're darned tooting it is."

He smiled and then winced. "Well, if you must know, Ms. Weiss observed me bidding at the auction.

You know—against you. She wanted to know why I seemed so intent on getting such a bad painting."

"Good question. Why were you?"

"Because I liked the painting." He blushed, and his bruises momentarily faded. "I know now it was only a lousy copy—she already told me that—but I thought it was beautiful. I thought it would look really great in one of the workout rooms."

"Workout rooms," I sneered. "Is that the euphemism of choice these days?"

"Yes, I suppose it is. It might be hard for a classy lady like you to believe, but I've always been interested in art. Did lots of drawing back when I was a kid. Always wanted to paint, but didn't have the money. Now that I do, I don't have the time. Anyway, I would still like to get some nice paintings to hang on the walls around here. Hey, you're in the biz, aren't you? Maybe you could help me out."

"I don't buy and sell pornography," I said archly.

Vincent recoiled in a clever display of mock surprise. "I think I've been very patient with you, Ms. Timberlake. Now I must ask you to leave. I have work to do."

"I'll bet."

"Abby, how rude."

I whirled. Mama was standing in the doorway, her arm still casually draped through the doorman's.

"Mama!"

"Put a zip on it, Abby, and quit pestering this nice man."

"Mama, do you know what kind of place this 'nice man' is running here?"

"Indeed I do. And if you weren't such a stick in the mud, you'd sign up this instant."

I glared at the woman who had endured thirty-six hours of agonizing labor. "And you want to be a missionary! What would the bishop say if he saw you here?"

"He'd probably ask for a membership, dear. Their annual fees are really quite reasonable. Although just between you and me," she lowered her voice, "they could supply larger towels."

I clapped my hands over my ears. I couldn't bear to hear her make a fool of herself. As an Episcopalian, I can handle a bit of irreverence, but this was going too far. Our church has a dicey enough reputation without Mama adding to it.

Mama snatched my right hand free, nearly taking my ear with it. She literally dragged me to the far corner of Vincent's palatial office.

"Abigail Louise Wiggins Timberlake, whatever is your problem?"

"Mama, please," I said through gritted teeth, "I just want to get out of this . . . this . . . den of iniquity! It makes me feel filthy just to be here."

Mama laughed. "Oh, Abby, you are so funny. I guess there is no accounting for personal taste, is there?"

"Taste?"

"I know, dear, I brought you up as a proper southern lady, to believe that there are only two places one should perspire—the garden and bed—but times have changed, and . . . well, this seems as good a place as any. Vincent Doughtery has some magnificent equipment, and this week he's offering a 20 percent discount."

I pulled loose from her grip. "That's disgusting! Mama, I'm out of here."

"Have it your way, dear, but I'm going to join. The health club on the other side of town charges almost double, and I don't like its rowing machines nearly as much. Mr. Dougherty's machines are inside real little boats, and they look just like the one your daddy died in." She sighed. "Of course, you realize this is only an introductory offer. Next year the rate will go up."

"Rowing machine?"

"Oh, Abby, and the treadmills! Vincent has eight of them, and each one has its own large-screen TV. With cable!"

I gave myself a good, hard mental slap. "This is a health club?"

"The very best. Sylvester Stallone will be here at the dedication next month."

"But . . . but . . . what about that naked fluorescent woman on the sign out front?"

"She's not naked, dear. She's wearing a leotard."

"You don't say." I hung my head in shame.

"You know, dear, if you sign up with me we'll get even another 10 percent off. We could row together—in different boats, of course, but side by side. Your daddy would have liked that."

I was dumbfounded. "But you're going to Africa!"

"Oh, Abby, do you honestly think the good Lord wants me to miss out on Sly? Besides, the bishop turned me down."

"He did?" My voice may have sounded gleeful, but my eyes were properly subdued.

"The bishop said he thought I needed to pray about my decision a little more, so I did, and now there's this." She waved her arms.

"Okay, Mama, I'll join," I heard myself say. After all, I was going to be very rich in just a matter of days—and when that time came, I'd buy Mama her own little rowboat, and possibly Sly Stallone as well.

"That's my girl," Mama said happily. "Now you trot right on over there and apologize to that nice Mr. Dougherty."

I trotted obediently over but fudged on the apology. Varicose veins or not, Vincent Dougherty needed to know with whom he was dealing.

"Remember, I wasn't born yesterday," I said, wagging my finger.

"I can see that."

"And if you're running such an innocent health club, why is your bouncer here keeping an eye out for tall women?"

Vincent and Ed exchanged glances and then laughed. "I told Ed to keep an eye out for the job applicants."

"Voluptuous women who will look good in scanty outfits with bunny tails?"

"I don't care what they look like, Ms. Timberlake, but when they're leading aerobic exercises in the five-foot pool, it might be helpful if more than just their heads showed."

"Your aerobics pool is five feet deep? Well, that's height discrimination."

"Give it a rest, dear," Mama said quietly.

That was easy for her to say. At least she could stand on her tiptoes and tilt her head back to breathe. Five feet for me was a watery grave. Still, perhaps it was time to change the subject.

"Well, tell your friend Marina to stop following me," I snapped in desperation.

Then I wrote a huge check that covered memberships for both Mama and myself.

24

I had barely enough time, and not nearly enough energy, to drive to Charlotte and back for my command performance at Her Majesty's. A more generous person would say that Mama came to the rescue when she offered me her rose-colored taffeta dress, but Mama is substantially taller than I, and the cinched waist of the fifties-style garment aligned with my hips and wouldn't close properly. Mama solved the problem with a large safety pin and a belt so wide it flattened the bottoms of my breasts and chafed my armpits. The starched crinolines that she insisted I wear under the skirt made me feel like a walking tent. It is for occasions such as this that God invented high heels, and I teetered and staggered my way back to the car like a little girl playing dress-up. I drove while Mama lectured.

"Always start from the outside and work in."

"Of course, Mama. It's hard to gnaw chicken bones without getting through the meat first."

"I was talking about the silverware. You may have as many as four forks. That funny little one that looks like a trident is for shrimp. Now remember, if there's a little bowl of water by your place, it might be a finger bowl."

"Or a very weak consommé."

"Did you learn how to curtsy?" Mama asked anxiously. Just the year before, we'd had the privilege of meeting an English countess and had, with the best intentions, genuflected.

"I am not curtsying to Priscilla Hunt."

"Oh, dear. Will you at least bow your head?"

"Maybe—if she says grace."

Mama sighed. "Whatever you do, Abby, don't take a bite until she does. And when she lays down her fork, you do, too. Just follow her lead, dear, and you can't go wrong."

"What if she burps?"

"Please, Abby, this is very serious. Our social position in Rock Hill could hinge on your behavior tonight."

"Then we're in big trouble, Mama, because I plan to just be myself. If Her Majesty doesn't like it, she can lump it."

Mama trotted out the biggest gun in her arsenal. "Your brother, Toy, always had impeccable manners."

"Toy ate like an animal."

"Abby!"

"It's true, Mama. Toy chewed with his mouth wide open and had both elbows permanently glued to the table. When he moved to California, didn't he have to take the table with him?"

"Toy had a lot on his mind, dear. He took your father's death very hard. He was younger than you, after all."

"That's true, but Daddy died thirty years ago. The

last time I saw Toy—two years ago this Thanksgiving—he still ate like that. But, if you insist, I'll do my level best to be just like him."

My passenger stiffened but wisely said nothing the rest of the way.

Mama tapped her watch. "We must be early. What time do you have?"

"Six o'clock on the button, Mama."

"But there aren't any other cars."

"Maybe we're the only guests invited."

"Don't be ridiculous, Abby. The crème de la crème of Rock Hill society will be here. You can count on that."

We waited ten fashionable minutes, but no other cars as much as turned down the cul-de-sac. "Maybe you're one crème and I'm the other," I finally said.

Mama tapped her watch crystal furiously. Then she tapped my watch, then the digital car clock. "When does the time change? It wasn't last night, was it?"

"That's not until October, Mama. No, I'd say we were the only guests."

"But we can't be! I mean, if no one else is here, how will they know we were?"

"Oh, they'll know, all right. Besides, think of it as an honor. Queen Priscilla doesn't want to share us with anyone. Frankly, I'm flattered."

"You are?"

"Absolutely. When those ladies in your Apoplexy Club hear that you were the only one of their number invited to this dinner, they'll eat their hearts out with envy."

"That's Apathia Club, dear. But do you really think so?"

"Have good manners been on a decline since *Father Knows Best* went off the air?"

Mama rolled her eyes. It was such a no-brainer question.

"Of course."

"Well, I bet Mer Majesty is trying to make a statement that good manners are in again. And what better example of good manners could she find in this city than you?"

That managed to cheer her up considerably, and she was fairly bouncing by the time we reached the front door of Priscilla Hunt's house. I half expected Her Majesty to slam the door in our faces when she saw me standing next to Mama, but instead she flung it wide open.

"How delightful to see you," she said, positively beaming.

Mama looked expectantly behind her and, seeing no one, curtsied hastily. "Oh. Yes. And it's so good to see you, Mrs. Hunt."

"Good evening, ma'am," I said and bobbed my head foolishly.

"Call me Priscilla, please," our hostess purred.

"Call me Mozella," Mama murmured. One would think she'd just been handed the key to the city.

"Call me anything you'd like," I said, "just say it with respect."

Mama glared at me. Then she handed Priscilla a bottle of wine.

Priscilla handled the bottle like I did the pair of

panties I found in Buford's and my bed, and which weren't mine. "Thank you. This looks very interesting."

"It's from Bolivia," Mama said proudly.

"Were you on a tour there?"

"Oh, no. I picked this up at Harris Teeter. It was on sale. Who knew you could buy a good bottle of wine for just $3.99?"

"Who knew Bolivia produced wine?" I muttered.

Priscilla twittered politely. "William—my husband—is a connoisseur of wines. I'm sure he will find this fascinating. Unfortunately, he will be unable to join us tonight and sends his regrets. He was called away on business just this afternoon. Oh, well, you know how the corporate game is played."

"Do we ever," I said. At least, I did. Buford often left town on a moment's notice, and even when he was in town, many was the night when he worked straight through. That's what he claimed, at any rate. Frankly, I think it odd that Mama spotted him in downtown Charlotte on a Wednesday, when on both Tuesday and Thursday he called me from Japan.

Priscilla smiled, revealing the benefits of braces at an early age. To be honest, she was quite an attractive woman with regular features; a long, slender neck; and shoulder-length brown hair that was just beginning to gray. She was dressed in an off-white linen dress which, as I might have expected, didn't dare wrinkle.

"Please come in."

The second she stepped over the threshold, Mama began oohing and aahing like a teenage boy in a used car lot. You would think she had never been out of her house.

Not that Priscilla minded. "Well," she said, sounding quite pleased, "one does what one can with what is available."

"To some, more is available than to others," I said, hoping to sound like a Chinese fortune cookie.

"Abby!" Mama said sharply.

Priscilla displayed her perfect teeth again. "Right this way. I thought we might have hors d'oeuvres in the drawing room."

We followed her into a large room with high ceilings, pale peach walls, and white crown moldings. The furniture was French, light but ornate, with lots of gilt and ormolu. Everything was in disgustingly good taste.

Priscilla clapped her hands. "Please, sit."

I looked around for a throne and, finding none, opted to sit on a bergère, a chair somewhat lower than a fauteuil and with padded arms. The fabric, not original, was nonetheless a high-quality satin brocade in blue and gold stripes.

"Would y'all care for some wine?" she asked. She glanced at the bottle she was holding. "Let's see—we have a nice merlot here with a lingering fruity taste, or I have a crisp sauvignon blanc with herbal undertones chilling in the refrigerator."

"Would you happen to have any tea?" Mama asked. No doubt she wanted to keep her wits about her.

Priscilla Hunt blinked. "Tea? Oh, yes, it will just take a minute." She turned to me. "Would you care for tea as well? Or would you prefer a glass of milk?"

On Mama's behalf, I restrained myself. "I normally drink only yak's milk. But since you don't have that, I believe that tonight I'll have the crisp wine with herbal undertones."

Mama glared at me. Priscilla, however, seemed unfazed by my rudeness.

"I'm going to try the Bolivian merlot," she announced.

Mama beamed.

"Manipulator," I mumbled. I said it so softly, even my guardian angel couldn't hear.

"Well, if you'll excuse me, then." Priscilla disappeared into another room.

The second she did so, Mama was all over me like white on rice. "Abby, how could you?"

"How could I what?"

"Mock her like that. And yak's milk, indeed!"

"But I do like yak's milk." Okay, I didn't, but I had tasted it. Bob does the Rob-Bobs' cooking and is forever experimenting with strange and imported foods.

Mama snorted. "That woman is the epitome of graciousness. You would be wise to tear a page from her book."

"Gracious, smacious, the woman is a big phony."

"Abby, dear, the woman is elegance personified."

"Mama, like I said. This is all an act. This—," I waved at the room, "—isn't where she normally hangs out. She's got a den, just like you or me. She sits in a La-Z-Boy recliner."

"Nonsense, dear."

"Mama, I saw it."

"You what? You mean you've been here before?"

One should never lie, and lying to your mama is the worst kind of lying. On the other hand, it is wrong to hurt a mother's feelings.

"Well, I didn't really see it, but C. J. did. You Know Who bought a Tiffany floor lamp from her, and C. J. delivered it."

"Our C. J.? The one who's an egg short of an omelet?"

"Please don't mention it to either of them," I begged. "From what I heard, it was a horrible experience for them both."

"Oh, Abby, tell me more!" Mama's eyes were glistening with excitement.

The web I was weaving was getting more tangled than my collection of pantyhose with runs in one leg. It was time to put a stop to it.

Fortunately, I didn't have to. Her Majesty materialized, bearing a silver tray that held our drinks. The paper cocktail napkins, by the way, were the soft, expensive kind.

"If y'all will just excuse me for another minute, I'll get the hors d'oeuvres. I hope y'all like seafood."

"Love it," we chimed.

Poof! Our hostess was gone. The woman had a knack for dramatic entrances and departures.

"This tea's from a mix," Mama hissed, as soon as she realized we were alone. "You might be right about the recliner."

"Oh, go on." I took a sip of wine. It was all I could

do to swallow it. "I think the wine is from a mix, too."

"Too dry?"

"It could strip paint off a door, and those herbal undertones go all the way down to China."

Mama giggled nervously. "Oh, Abby, you're so bad. Who would have thought that You Know Who drinks tea from a mix? And I've just got to see that recliner before I leave."

"Maybe she doesn't drink tea, Mama. Maybe—" I had to cut myself short. You Know Who had just entered the room, and she was bearing a silver tray piled high with sizzling rumaki. Those certainly did not come from a can.

"The ones on the left are scallops," she said. "The ones on the right prawns."

Mama, bless her heart, is as fond of shellfish as I am of liver, but she gamely helped herself to one of each. I, on the other hand, virtually cleaned out the prawn side of the tray.

"So," Queen Priscilla said, finally alighting on a veilleuse, a sort of glorified daybed, "what have you ladies been up to?"

Mama smiled. Her fifteen minutes of fame had finally arrived.

"Well, I've been thinking about being a missionary to Africa, you see—"

"How wonderful!" Priscilla said, even as she turned to me. "And what are you up to—Allie, isn't it?"

"It's Abby," I said through clenched teeth. "And I've just been working."

Priscilla took a sip of Mama's Bolivian merlot. "I

bet you have. That wonderful little shop of yours must keep you awfully busy. Dusting those little knick-knacks all the time. I can't imagine how you find time to volunteer in a nursing home on the side."

"But I don't—"

"Abby," Mama said sternly, "you never told me this." She turned to the Queen. "I've been a member of the Episcopal Church Women for forty years. I don't personally volunteer in nursing homes, but our group does many worthwhile things. One year, we made cute little baskets of toiletries for the homeless. I supplied the aftershave cologne."

Priscilla arched an imperial brow and sipped again. She was, of course, an Episcopalian, but the ECW was far beneath her playing field. Much better to write a fat check when, and if, the spirit moved her than to associate with professors' wives.

Mama shrank under the inquiring gaze. "The homeless need to smell nice, too," she said weakly.

"How very interesting." Priscilla smiled and turned to me. "Now, dear, let's talk about you."

"But Mama does lots of other worthwhile things," I said quickly. "She—well, last year she went off to be a nun."

Mama paled. "Abby, not here."

Imperial brows raised. "Oh?"

"They wouldn't take me," Mama wailed. "They accused me of singing too much. Too much! Can you imagine that? And I did not wear curlers under my wimple! That was a bald-faced lie. Sister Margarita was jealous, that's all."

The royal noggin nodded. "Jealousy can be a crippling disease. Believe me, I know all about that. Of course, with me, it's not my hair that people envy."

"Oh, it wasn't Mama's hair that Sister Margarita envied. It was her tattoo."

Priscilla's eyes widened while Mama's closed. I struggled in vain to remove the foot from my mouth.

"It's a very small tattoo, and it's discreetly placed where folks can't see it."

Our hostess fanned herself delicately with a cocktail napkin. The woman has self-control, I'll grant her that.

"My, what an interesting woman you are, Mozella. What about you, Abby? Any secret tattoos?"

"Oh, no, I'm too big of a chicken for that. I hate needles."

"Really? You seem like such a . . . well, spunky woman."

"I'm a wimp, a total coward. It's Mama who's the brave one."

"That's true," Mama said. "I cut my thumb on a broken glass once and drove myself down to Piedmont Medical Center. There was blood all over the place—ruined my best crinoline. Abby would have fainted dead away."

"Yes, I'm sure," Priscilla said. She hadn't even looked at Mama. "But I saw you bidding the other night at the church auction. You were anything but a coward, Libby."

"That's Abby. And auctions don't require bravery, just money. Besides, the painting didn't go for all that much."

"About the painting—"

"Please, we've already covered that subject. I will not reveal my client's name."

"Fair enough. I can respect that. Perhaps, though, you could ask your client if he or she would consider selling the painting to me."

Mama was gasping like a fish out of water. "Abby, I didn't know you sold that painting. You never said a word."

"Well, it was no big deal."

"It is to me. I thought you were going to give it to me for my birthday."

Uh-oh. I'd completely forgotten. Mama's birthday was coming up in less than two weeks. Normally she barrages me with hints two months in advance.

"You wanted that painting, Mama?"

"Of course not. It was disgusting, just like you said. But you seemed to want it so bad. That's why I thought you were getting it for me."

"Well, I—don't worry, Mama. I'll buy you something really nice for your birthday. I promise."

"Like what?"

"You name it. The sky's the limit."

"A diamond bracelet."

"Done."

Mama giggled and glanced at Priscilla. "Abby, we're being silly."

"No, we're not. My ship has finally come in." If loose lips can sink ships, then mine can sink an entire navy. But I felt a need to impress Priscilla in front of Mama, and besides, in a day or two everyone would know I was rolling in dough. Matt Lauer would invite me on the *Today* show to talk about *Field of Thistles*, and Jay Leno would start cracking short jokes.

Mama blushed. "Please, Abby, don't embarrass yourself."

"I am not embarrassing myself, Mama. I'm going to be—I mean, I am—a very rich woman." Believe me, You Know Who's ears perked up when I said the R word.

"Ah, yes," she said, "the stock market. Still, one needs investment capital. Those knickknacks you sell must be quite profitable."

"It has nothing to do with the market or my antiques. But it has everything to do with that hideous painting I bought Wednesday night."

Priscilla swallowed a sip of merlot. "I'm afraid I don't follow."

"I do," Mama said excitedly. "You found a bundle of bills tucked into the frame. I found ten dollars tucked in a library book once."

"No, Mama. I found a painting. Vincent van Gogh's *Field of Thistles.*"

"You what?" Priscilla Hunt's hand trembled, and deep red merlot stains instantly found the wrinkles that were hiding in her linen suit.

Mama sprang to life. "Quick, paper towels! Abby, find some paper towels and club soda!"

I jumped to my feet.

"Wait a minute! Salt! Get salt as well. It will suck the color right out of linen."

"Sit!" Her Majesty ordered.

I sat.

"Tell me about this painting."

"Well, like I said, it's a van Gogh and—"

"Nonsense! You wouldn't find a real van Gogh at a church auction."

"But I did. And it's worth between ten and fifteen million dollars. More if the Japanese get involved."

Mama's eyeballs were in danger of landing in her lap. "Abby, is this really true?"

"Yes, Mama. Maybe now you can finally be proud of me."

"Don't be ridiculous, dear. I've always been proud of you."

"As proud of me as you are of Toy? Because it's always Toy this, Toy that. You'd think he hung the moon and stars. Well, let me tell you something, Mama, last time I spoke to Toy out in Hollywood, he bragged about mooning the stars."

"Oh, Abby, don't be jealous," Mama wailed. "I only carry on about Toy because—well, because he's such a loser, and I don't want you thinking ill of your brother. But you've always been my favorite child."

"Honest?"

"Honest. I love you very much. You know that, don't you?"

"Yeah. And I love you, too, Mama."

"This is all very touching," Priscilla said and drained what remained in her wineglass. "But would you mind terribly if we get back to the painting?"

"Ah, yes! My ten-million-dollar baby."

"So you've found a buyer already?" The quaver in Her Majesty's voice made her sound like the real queen.

"Not yet, but I've found a broker who just happens to be the world's expert on van Gogh. He flew out from New York this morning and pronounced it the real thing. Of course, he needs to do some routine lab tests, but—"

The sudden infusion of wine must not have agreed with our hostess. Her face had gone cotton-white, and the blue-blooded lips had actually turned blue. The same thing happened to my daughter, Susan, once when I let her stay too long in the swimming pool.

"Are you all right, Priscilla?"

There was no response.

"Mrs. Hunt?" I called louder.

"Huh?" was the best Her Majesty could do.

Mama was back on her feet. "Maybe she's in shock on account of the spilled wine."

"What should we do?" I wailed.

"I think I read we're supposed to put her feet up. And loosen her garments. Or was it the other way around? No, that wouldn't make any sense because—"

"Mama, you loosen her feet. I'll get some water."

"Water?"

"That's what they do in the movies," I wailed. "They make them drink water."

I ran into the kitchen, located a crystal goblet in the first cupboard I opened, and filled it with tap water. I was gone only a matter of seconds, but when I returned, Priscilla lay on the floor, her feet propped against the back of the veilleuse. Mama was standing over her, looking particularly grim.

"Did you loosen her blouse?" I demanded.

"I did," Mama moaned. "But it didn't do any good. She's dead."

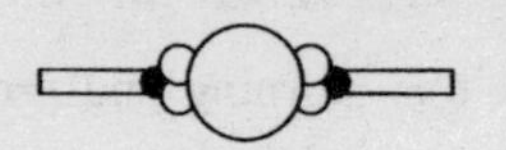

25

"Dead?"

"It was my Bolivian wine, wasn't it?" Mama wailed. "I killed her."

I knelt over Priscilla Hunt's prostrate body. Mama was right. She didn't seem to be breathing.

"Maybe she had a heart attack. Mama, don't you know CPR?"

"Me? Don't you?"

I glanced around for a telephone, but there was none. I ran back into the kitchen and, after wasting even more precious seconds, spotted a white cordless phone attached to a white cupboard panel. I made the call.

"Any change?" I asked when I returned.

Mama shook her head. "Oh, Abby, do you think they'll send me to jail?"

"Of course not, Mama. But even if they do . . . well, you always did look good in stripes."

"Really? Horizontal or vertical?"

"Definitely vertical. And go for pastel if you get a choice."

"Yes, pink is my color."

"Mama, I'm only kidding! No one's going to send you to jail for giving someone a five dollar bottle of wine. Even if they tried, I wouldn't let them. Buford and I might not get along, but he was always very fond of you. Still asks about you, in fact. Anyway, I'm sure Buford is buddies with all the best lawyers in both Carolinas, and if anyone has a pocketful of judges, it's him."

Mama nodded absently. No doubt she was already planning the seersucker curtains for her barred window, and a bed set in complementing colors.

Unfortunately, there was nothing either of us could do but wait until the paramedics showed up. Although it wasn't dark yet, I flipped on the porch light and left the door ajar to make the house easier to find—not that it was necessary, mind you. In my panic, I had blurted out, "The queen is dead! Long live the king!" The dispatcher, bless her soul, had known exactly whom I meant and where she lived.

I wrung my hands while Mama, bless her heart, decorated her cell. The loud knock on the door made us both jump.

"The paramedics," Mama gasped. "They're finally here."

I gasped as well. A burly man with a wide nose and deep-set eyes was standing in the doorway. I may not have recognized the man's face, but I sure as shooting recognized the grommet-studded vest.

"He's not a paramedic, Mama. He's a motorcyclist."

Mama was too distraught to hear. "The police? Tell them the bottle had a cork in it when I bought it. I made sure of that. It wasn't one of those twist-off kinds you wanted me to buy. It was real wine. From Bolivia!"

I positioned myself between Mama and the intruder. "What do you want?"

"I thought something might be wrong," he said in a surprisingly gentle voice.

"Wrong? Why ever would you think that?" I felt behind me for a fire poker or heavy vase with which to conk him on the head. But life is not like the movies, and all I got was a fistful of crinoline.

"The door was open and—" The deep-set eyes widened a fraction. He had seen Priscilla Hunt. "What happened here?"

"It's none of your business," I shrieked. "The paramedics will be here any second!"

"My name's Freddy. I've had some paramedic training." He knelt beside the still form of Priscilla Hunt and felt for a pulse. "How long has she been this way?"

"I don't know," I wailed. "But it couldn't be more than a few minutes."

"You try CPR?"

"I don't know how!"

"Step back, please."

Mama and I stepped back and watched wordlessly as Freddy worked to resuscitate Priscilla. He placed his hands on her sternum, one on top of the other, and pumped rhythmically. Then he pinched her nose and breathed directly into her mouth. He repeated the process a number of times, and every now and then he stopped and listened for a heartbeat. Finally, he looked up at us and grinned.

"Got a good beat going," he said. "And I can hear the sirens. The paramedics will be here any minute. I think she'll make it."

"Thank heavens!" Mama's eyes rolled back in her head, and she collapsed in my arms.

I staggered under her weight, and it was only with Freddy's help that I managed to lay her gently on the floor beside Priscilla Hunt. One might incorrectly assume that Mama was suffering from the same condition as Priscilla, but only if one does not know Mama. As Freddy and I lowered Mama to the antique Persian carpet, her tiny hands smoothed her skirt beneath her, and when she was all settled, she rearranged her pearls.

"Will she be all right?" Freddy asked. His concern was touching.

"She'll be as fine as frog's hair. She just wants you to resuscitate her."

"I do not!"

"Then sit up, Mama."

Mama sat and fluffed the hair at the back of her head. "Honestly, Abby, I don't know where you get some of your ideas."

I was about to tell her where I got them when the loud wail of sirens announced the paramedics' arrival. I ran to the door to wave them inside. When I looked back, Freddy was gone.

The Rock Hill paramedics were a marvel to watch. They had Priscilla Hunt hooked up to oxygen and loaded into the ambulance before you could flip a flapjack. No doubt it was a heart attack, they said.

Just as many women die from heart attacks as men. But not to worry—Her Majesty would be well taken care of in Piedmont Medical Center's fine new cardiac care wing. She was lucky, though, to have two knowledgeable friends like us to give her what she needed.

The Rock Hill police were as nice as they could be. They assured Mama that her Bolivian merlot was not an issue. The bottle was on the kitchen counter, still unopened. They offered to give us a ride back to Mama's house, but of course there really was no need. Mama and I had a light supper of leftovers while we polished off the crossword puzzle in the *Observer.* I was just saying good night, about to head for the door, when the police called, asking us to come down to the station. A few details had come to light, they said, and they wanted our take on them.

Mama, ever the worrier, called Greg. This was despite my protestations and after I made it perfectly clear to her that Greg, as a member of the Charlotte-Mecklenburg police department, had no jurisdiction in South Carolina. It was a moot point, however, because Greg wasn't even home. Nonetheless, Mama left a tearful message informing him of our imagined plight and entreating him to come to our rescue.

Now it was beginning to look like she had done the right thing. We were seated in a small, but not unpleasant, room in the Rock Hill Police Department, just across the street from York County Public Library, and we were being asked a million questions. Officer Yoder, a man who looked young enough to be my son, did most of the asking.

"What is your relationship to Mrs. Hunt?" he asked, in a voice that still changed registers.

"We're dear friends."

"Mama!"

"All right, maybe we're not dear friends, but I've known the woman her entire life. She goes to my church."

"Mama and Mrs. Hunt operate on different social levels," I said by way of clarification.

"That's not true, Abby. She just has more money. We belong to the same clubs."

"Mama!"

"Well, one, at any rate."

"The Allergy Club," I said.

"That's Apathia Club, and it's the most exclusive club in Rock Hill."

Officer Yoder bit his Bic. He had teeth like a rabbit, and the pen was deeply marked.

"I see, and what was the nature of your visit to her house tonight?"

"We were invited there for dinner." The pride in Mama's voice was almost touching.

"Was anyone else invited?"

"No."

"Was Mr. Hunt there?"

"No. Priscilla said he had to take a last minute business trip."

Priscilla? What ever happened to Her Majesty? Soon Mama would reveal that she and the Queen had slit their fingers as girls and commingled their blood.

"And what were you served?" The Bic paused above a writing pad for a second and then returned to Officer Yoder's mouth. No doubt it felt much more at home there.

"Well, we didn't have a chance to eat dinner," I offered, "but we had some delicious rumaki for appetizers."

By the look on Officer Yoder's face, it was clear that he had no idea what I meant. I hastened to explain.

"Traditionally, rumaki is marinated chicken livers and water chestnuts, wrapped in bacon. Cooked, of course. Some people prefer scallops to chicken livers, however. Mrs. Hunt served scallops and shrimp. I just love shrimp."

"Abby took half the plate," Mama whined.

Officer Yoder laid down his pen just long enough to blow his nose on a wad of well-used tissue. "What did you have to drink?"

Mama grimaced. "The worst sweet tea this side of China. It was one of those canned mixes."

"I had a crisp sauvignon blanc with herbal undertones," I said. "It was mostly undertones."

"What did Mrs. Hunt have to drink?"

"It wasn't my merlot," Mama wailed. "The officer there said the bottle wasn't even opened."

I nodded vigorously to underscore Mama's point. "But it was a red wine—well, a red beverage, at any rate."

"Was any other food or beverage served?"

"No," Mama said. "We didn't even get to find out what she was planning for an entrée."

"Chicken, ma'am. Our detectives found a roast chicken in the oven."

"Chicken? Her Majesty was going to serve us roast chicken?"

"Maybe she was going to doctor it up with a sauce," I said gently. It had been a long day for Mama, a woman who wouldn't dream of serving something as mundane as roast chicken to her guests. If it didn't have four legs, it wasn't fit for company.

"How long do you estimate you were at Mrs. Hunt's house?" Officer Yoder asked.

"Twenty minutes," I said. "Maybe half an hour, if you include the incident."

"Was Mrs. Hunt ever out of your sight?"

"Yes, when she went to get the drinks."

"And how long did that take?"

Mama snorted. "As long as it takes to make tea from a mix."

Officer Yoder put his pen down. He seemed to age ten years before our eyes.

"Now, tell me about the incident."

"It was like this," I said, before Mama had a chance to muddy the waters. "Priscilla and I were chatting, and suddenly her eyes glazed over and she sort of slumped into her chair."

"Then what?"

"Then I ran into the kitchen—there wasn't any phone in the drawing room—and dialed 911."

Officer Yoder turned to Mama. "Mrs. Wiggins, what did you do while your daughter called for help?"

"I lifted her legs and loosened her clothes."

"It was all on the up-and-up," I said quickly.

He nodded. "Miss Timberlake, what were you and

the victim talking about when the incident happened?"

"A painting."

"You mean like art?"

"Absolutely not. This painting was a piece of garbage I picked up at a church auction sale."

"If it was garbage, why did you buy it?"

"To help raise money for the youth group. They need a new van."

"I donated wooden salad bowls," Mama said. "Real teak salad bowls from Thailand."

Officer Yoder treated us to a sliver of a smile. "I believe my wife bought them."

"You're an Episcopalian?"

"Not by a long shot. My wife loves sales, though. She saw the ad in the paper."

"Tell her I have a matching serving fork and spoon. I'll be glad to part with them for a song."

"I'll do that. Now, Mrs. Wiggins, are you much of a gardener?"

"Am I ever! You should see my perennial beds. They won first prize in the Rock Hill Garden Club competition the year before last. And behind the house I have a little vegetable plot with the biggest, juiciest tomatoes in York County. Of course, Abby here makes fun of me because you can buy such a wide variety of produce at the supermarket these days, but it isn't the same."

"You're right about that, ma'am." He turned to me. "Do you garden?"

"I rotate my crops. One week I shop at Harris Teeter; the next, Winn Dixie; then Hannaford's. It saves on calluses."

He turned back to Mama. "Are you familiar with malathion?"

"Of course. It's an insecticide."

"Do you ever use it?"

"Look, officer," I said, "this garden chat is all very interesting, but it's almost ten o'clock."

"It's more than interesting, ma'am. Mrs. Wiggins, please answer my question."

"Well—I . . . uh . . . I think I used some last year when the Japanese beetles were so bad. I know they say to use one of those less toxic powders, but it was my turn to supply flowers for the church, and those powders don't wash off very easily. I couldn't very well have white-blotched roses up there behind the altar, now, could I?"

"I see. Was there any malathion left over?"

"Of course. I didn't use that much."

"What did you do with the leftover?"

I didn't like where this was leading. "Now wait just one minute—sir. My mama knows better than to dump toxic substances down the drain. I know for a fact that she turns her unused poisons in to the city during their annual collection program."

Mama squirmed. "Actually, Abby, last year I didn't. That stuff is very expensive, you know. I think it's still sitting in the garage."

"Yes—but, Mama, this has nothing to do with Priscilla Hunt's heart attack. There is no reason he can't talk to you about this tomorrow."

Officer Yoder picked up the pen, made a new dent

in the cap, and laid it down. "Mrs. Hunt didn't have a heart attack. Not tonight, at any rate. She was poisoned."

"Poisoned?" Mama and I echoed.

"Malathion."

"But that's impossible," I cried. "Did she tell you this?"

"Oh, no, ma'am. Priscilla Hunt died minutes after reaching the hospital."

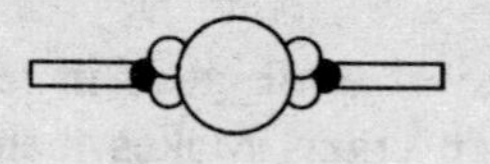

26

Mama and I exchanged shocked glances.

Officer Yoder spun the pen, which lay on the table between us. "But then, of course, you anticipated that, didn't you?"

"We most certainly did not," I said. Mama, bless her heart, could barely catch her breath.

For the first time, Officer Yoder consulted his pad. "Let's see . . . your exact words to the dispatcher were 'the queen is dead, long live the king.' "

"Yes, I thought she was dead. But only in the beginning. Then the biker showed up and performed CPR and got her breathing again. She was very much alive when they put her in the ambulance. Check with the paramedics—they'll tell you that!"

The pen spun out of control and shot off the corner of the desk. Officer Yoder looked torn between retrieving it and asking what I knew would be his next question. Picking up the pen delayed the inevitable by only a second or two. Much to my surprise, he actually began to use it.

"A biker, you say?" He scribbled on the pad. "You mean one of those guys in speedos who drive motorists crazy?"

"I believe, sir, that would be a cyclist. This is the

other kind—one of those guys in leather who drive middle-aged men crazy. Makes them all want to be Jack Nicholson and Peter Fonda in *Easy Rider*."

"Are you saying that a motorcyclist just happened to stop by Mrs. Hunt's house shortly after she consumed the malathion?"

"Yes, sir, I am."

"Describe this man to me. It was a man, wasn't it?"

"Definitely," Mama said, her eyes glazing over.

"Would you describe him please, Mrs. Wiggins?"

Mama sighed. "He was dreamy."

Officer Yoder wisely turned to me. "Ma'am?"

"Well, sir, he's tall and kind of burly, with little pig eyes and a nose that looks like it's been kissed by a Mack truck."

"Those are lies," Mama wailed.

The pen was finally being put to good use. "How tall is tall, ma'am?"

I hoped he wasn't being facetious. Just because I'm vertically challenged doesn't mean I don't recognize society's conventions.

"He was six foot two and a half," I said emphatically.

Officer Yoder smiled. "Weight?"

"Well over two hundred pounds. Maybe two hundred and fifty. But, like I said, burly—not fat."

"It was all muscle," Mama moaned.

"Had either of you ever seen this man before?"

Mama shook her head.

I braced myself for the fallout. "I have."

"What? Abby, that's not true! Tell the officer you were only kidding."

"Yes, Mama, it *is* true. I have seen the biker before, but only from a distance."

"When was that?" Officer Yoder asked calmly.

"That night at the church auction, for one thing, and then out near Pine Manor—"

Mama was beside herself. "You really did go out to Pine Manor?"

"I wanted to give Adele Sweeny my condolences," I said. That was partly true. I would have done just that if the poor woman had been aware of her son's death.

"Abby, I thought you were just trying to yank my chain."

"Moi?" I turned and addressed Officer Yoder. "I think the man's been following me."

He scribbled some more. "Do you have any idea why he would do that?"

Mama, of course, felt free to jump in. "Maybe he was looking for a chance to meet me."

We both ignored her.

"I can't prove anything," I said, "but I have my suspicions."

"Care to enlighten me?"

"I think it has to do with a very valuable painting I acquired this week."

"It's worth ten million dollars," Mama gushed. "Abby's going to buy me a diamond bracelet."

That seemed to jump-start Officer Yoder's engine. Call it vanity on my part, but I'd swear under oath that the first thing he did was look at my ring finger.

"You think this man—this motorcyclist—is after your painting?"

"That's just a guess, since he was there when I bought it. Only he had no way of knowing that unless he works for Marina Weiss. Of course, that's it! She hired him to help keep tabs on me."

If Officer Yoder ever wanted to switch careers, he would do well to consider medicine. The marks he scribbled on his pad could be read only by a pharmacist.

"Miss Timberlake, to your knowledge, did this man—the one who appeared to have resuscitated Mrs. Hunt—have any relationship to her? Gardener, chauffeur, something like that?"

"How should I know?" I snapped. "I am not my sovereign's keeper."

Our interrogator turned to Mama. "Had you ever seen this man before?"

"Unfortunately, no."

"I beg your pardon?"

"He's to die for," Mama said, practically drooling. "He makes Mel Gibson look like chopped liver. Say, he's not a suspect, is he?"

"Ma'am, I'm not at liberty to say."

Of course, Mama jumped to conclusions. Then again, it is one of the few exercises there is in which one can engage while wearing spike heels.

"You've arrested that dreamy man, haven't you?"

"I didn't say that."

"But you know something you're not saying. At least tell me this: does South Carolina allow conjugal visits?"

"Mama!"

Officer Yoder stood. "Well, that's it for now. If you

can think of any other details that might help me get a fuller story, give me a call." He handed us each a card.

"That's it?" Mama wailed. "You dragged us out of bed, asked us a few questions, told us the woman we were about to dine with was dead, asked us a million more questions, and then excused us like we're the morning kindergarten class?"

"Mama," I said gently, "you weren't in bed. We had just finished the crossword puzzle, and I was leaving to go home, remember? Anyway, it's time for us to go. Officer Yoder is through with us."

"But maybe I'm not through with him. Is he the only one who gets to ask the questions?"

"Yes. I'm afraid that's the way the system works."

Mama crossed her arms in front of her cinched waist. Her crinolines billowed below them.

"It isn't fair."

"That may be, but there is nothing you can do about it."

"I could hold a sit-down strike. Isn't that what you did in the seventies?"

"Mama, you really could end up in the jail," I whispered.

I grabbed her elbow and tried to steer her toward the door of the room, but she wouldn't budge. It was like her spike heels had drilled through the linoleum and were embedded in the concrete subfloor.

"Please, Mama, don't make a scene."

"What color are your uniforms?" she demanded.

"Excuse me?"

"I look best in pastels. Preferably pink. And I really

don't mind the stripes. Abby here says I look good in stripes. But they need to be vertical."

I positioned myself behind Mama, lifted my right foot, and pushed firmly but gently on the soft spot behind her right knee. Mama lurched forward, and, before she could regain her balance, I had her halfway out the door. Momentum was on my side from then on.

After making sure Mama was really in bed, I drove home the back way. Even at that late hour, I-77 was clogged with Buckeyes and Quebecers who'd had their fill of Myrtle Beach, and I didn't feel like playing Carolina tag. It was still very warm out, but not suffocating, and I had the window down. There is something exhilarating about being on a country road, at night, with the wind blowing through one's hair. So what if my hair got greasy and I perspired a little? There's a first time for everything, isn't there? And besides, when I got home I planned to do two things: feed Dmitri a can of gourmet cat food (it was way past his feeding time) and take a nice, long soak in the tub.

Unfortunately, my path took me right past the new Burger King in Pineville, and the smell of charbroiled beef through the open window was irresistible. I would have taken advantage of the drive-through, except that I suddenly realized I had to use the bathroom. A few more minutes weren't going to hurt a cat that could go for days sticking up his nose at the most tempting morsels money could buy. I made a silent pledge that if my ten-pound bundle of joy forgave me my tardiness, I would give him a thorough combing and a pinch of catnip.

I used the ladies room, got my order—burger, fries, and a medium strawberry shake—and it wasn't until I started scouting for a place to sit that I saw them. I wisely put my tray down on the nearest empty table and then willed my rubbery legs to transport me across the room.

"Well, look who's here," I said. I couldn't bring myself to look directly at Greg. Or Hooter, for that matter. I let my eyes wander back and forth between C. J. and Sergeant Bowater.

"Hey, Abby, sit down," Greg had the nerve to say.

Of course, there wasn't any place to sit, and I wouldn't have sat even if that booth was on the last train out of hell. From the corner of my vision, I saw Hooter scoot over against the wall, her enormous breasts jiggling like a pair of Santa Claus bellies.

"C. J., how could you?" I moaned.

She blushed. "I didn't know you could see under the table, and we're only holding hands."

"I'm not talking about you, dear, I'm talking about them! How could you betray me like this with them?"

"Abby!" Greg said sharply. "This wasn't C. J.'s idea. We just happened to run into them."

"And I suppose you just happened to run into her," I said, still not looking at Greg or his bovine companion.

"Would you believe it if I said yes? Because, as a matter of fact, I did just run into her."

Hooter jiggled indignantly. "Hey, I have a name."

"Is it Moo?"

"Abby! You're above that."

"I am?" I finally was too mad to cry and could afford to look at him. Those deep blue eyes had the affrontery to stare calmly back.

"Hooter was getting out of her car when I pulled up. It would have been rude not to ask her to join me."

"Indeed."

"And then we arrived." C. J. looked at Sergeant Bowater and cooed just like a pigeon. "This man's a keeper, Abby. I don't know how I can ever thank you."

"By never making that disgusting noise again, dear."

"Okey-doke. Anyway, Abby, they didn't even want to sit together after we joined them. Hooter kept trying to slide into the booth beside me. But I said, 'No way.' I've been down that road, done that. I wanted to sit with my Bo-Bo."

"Your Bo-Bo?" Greg, Hooter, and I said in unison.

"So, Abby, you don't have anything to be mad about. Greg is crazy about you. That's all he's been talking about. It's about made us sick to our stomachs."

Hooter and Sergeant Bowater nodded vigorously.

"I don't know what to say," I said, "besides 'I'm sorry.' "

"Oh, it ain't nothing," Hooter said and jiggled closer to the window. "Come on, Gregory. Scoot over and let Abby sit."

I took a step back. "No, I don't deserve to."

"Sit!" everyone ordered.

I thought it over for a nanosecond and then sat. It was a decision I still regret.

27

It is not my place to judge others, but I only sleep with married men. Perhaps that did not come out the way I intended. What I mean is, I do not sleep with men to whom I am not married. Greg and I parted amicably, and somewhat tenderly, in the parking lot of Burger King. We had plans to see each other the following evening. There was no need for him to come home with me—and besides, I had another, younger male already waiting.

"Dmitri," I called before I even had the key out of the lock. "Mama's home."

No answering meow, no fat yellow tummy rubbing against my leg.

"Dmitri!"

Except for the ticking of the ship's clock on the mantel, my house was silent.

"Dmitri! If you forgive me and come out now, I'll scratch under your chin for—what the hell?"

There was a yellow stick-up note on the mantel straight ahead. Dmitri may be uncommonly bright, even for a cat, but he doesn't leave me notes. Mama does, and sometimes my children, Charlie and Susan, do. In any of these cases, unfortunately, the notes tend to be whining reminders of how I have failed somebody by not reading their mind and being home upon demand.

I strode to the mantel and ripped loose the bright scrap of paper.

Go to Pine Manor nursing home. Bring painting with you. Be there, midnight sharp—or you won't see your cat again.

Mouse

P.S. Tell anyone, and it dies.

I gasped, read the note again, and dropped it on the floor. It was 11:35. Pine Minor nursing home was a good forty-five-minute drive, more like an hour if I obeyed all traffic laws. I couldn't very well call there and ask if someone named Mouse had catnapped my pussy, now, could I? And there certainly wasn't any time to waste calling friends and family to see if this was just a sick joke. I knew in my bones that it wasn't. No one but Mama was even aware I had been out there to see Adele Sweeny, and Mama loves—well, tolerates—my yellow bundle of joy. Besides, I had yet to tell her about Mouse. No, there was no time to do anything except comply with the demands of the note.

I ran into the guest bedroom, threw back the covers, and, for one agonizing minute, stared at *Field of Thistles.* Then I did what any normal, red-blooded American mother would do in my size-four shoes; I snatched up the canvas and made a beeline for Pine Manor.

* * *

I burned up the highway getting to Rock Hill, and from there I was a menace on the byways. It was a wonder I didn't have an accident, much less get a string of tickets. It was 12:08 when, amidst a spray of gravel, I jolted to a stop in front of the tiny nursing home. There were two other vehicles in the parking lot: a black Cadillac and Mouse Trap's van.

Please don't tell me what I should, or should not, have done. That's all water over the Rock Hill dam now. What I did was barge straight into the nursing home with a ten-million-dollar painting under my arm. I expected to confront the evil Mouse, but what I didn't expect was to see him sitting on the couch, along with his brother Johnny and Hortense Simms.

"Did they hurt you?" were the first words out of my mouth, thereby proving that I am not entirely self-absorbed, and that I do value human life over feline life—although sometimes just barely.

Much to my surprise, Hortense smiled. "My cousins would never hurt me."

"What?"

"Johnny and Mouse. My cousins from Shelby."

"Actually, we're first cousins once removed," Johnny said. "Pull up a chair, Abigail. It's good to see you."

"Oh, for Pete's sake," Hortense said, "close your mouth, or flies will get in."

"At night, it's likely to be mosquitoes," Mouse said. The three of them laughed.

I sat, but only because my legs would no longer support me. "Where's Dmitri?" I croaked.

Hortense and Mouse both rolled their eyes.

"I think she means her cat," Johnny said.

"You're damn square, I do. Where is he?"

"He's safe," Johnny said.

Mouse reached behind Hortense and cuffed Johnny's right year. "He ain't safe for long."

"Harm one hair on his yellow head, and you'll pay for it," I growled.

"You see what I mean?" Johnny said. "She's a tough little thing."

Mouse cuffed his brother again. "Ah, she ain't so tough."

"Maybe I'm not, but I'm not afraid of you."

"You ought to be."

Johnny sighed. "You see, she reminds me of Mama."

"Your mama is dead," I snapped. "You boys killed her, remember?"

Johnny paled. "We did no such thing."

"Oh, yes, you did. Y'all killed both your parents and used to brag about it at school. In fact, you—," I said to Johnny,—"wrote a prize-winning short story about it."

Johnny grinned. "Yeah, it was a good one. I later made it the basis for one of my mystery novels. Say, how did you know about that?"

"I know all about you, buster. I know, for instance, that y'all's last name isn't Trap, but Westerman."

Three pairs of eyes widened. "Okay, so it was Westerman," Johnny said, "but I wanted a pen name."

I turned to his brother. "And what was your excuse, Albert?"

Albert Westerman, alias Mouse Trap, could sound tough if he wanted, but he was powerless to stop his ears from turning bright red. "How the hell do you know that?"

"I don't reveal my sources. Now give me Dmitri."

"We get the painting first."

I pried *Field of Thistles* loose from under my arm and, using every last ounce of strength, handed it to Johnny.

He smiled. "Thanks, Abigail. I tried to warn you to stay away from my brother, but you wouldn't listen."

"Thanks, nothing," I hissed. "Y'all owe me ten million dollars. Now where's my cat?"

Mouse Trap laughed. "Maybe she ain't even here."

"Dmitri's a he, you nincompoop! Dmitri! Dmitri!"

Hortense put a finger to her lips. "Shhh. You'll wake Mama."

"Too late," I said.

Three heads swiveled. Adele Sweeny was standing in the semi-lit corridor that led to the sleeping rooms. She was dressed in the same blue chenille robe and blue, fussy slippers she'd worn at my last visit, but she didn't look at all the same. This woman had fire in her eyes, and there was still a spring in her step. Somehow, I was not surprised.

"It's about time you joined us," I said.

"What day is it?"

"Drop the act, Adele. I know your game. You're not the confused old woman you pretend to be."

"Don't you be calling me by my given name!"

"Sorry," I said instinctively. As a custom, I defer

to octogenarians. "Now, where's my cat?"

"That sweet little thing is curled up fast asleep on my bed."

"Mrs. Sweeny—"

"Don't you be calling me that, either. The name is Trap. Mrs. Trap, to you."

"Mrs. Trap?"

"You don't think I'd keep the name Sweeny, do you? Gilbert Senior was a real wienie."

They all laughed, including Johnny.

"Gilbert Junior was a wienie, too."

I gasped again. "You killed your own son?"

Adele stepped out of the shadows. "Stepson, and the man was a menace. You can't keep a business going with a weak link like that in the chain of command."

"Face it, Auntie Adele," Mouse said. "Gil was plain stupid."

"He had scruples," Hortense said in disgust.

"Just look at the walls!" Adele Trap waved her arms like a chenille-clad conductor. "He actually thought I would never miss it. He really wanted to raise money for a church van. Can you imagine that?"

Hortense snorted. "It was just dumb luck that he picked the best painting. He had no idea what was really behind that frame."

I stared at the awful collection of what passes for art in far too many homes. "There are real paintings behind those?"

"The da Vinci is a sketch. The rest are paintings."

"You have a da Vinci hidden somewhere behind a paint-by-number?"

Hortense chortled. "And a Renoir and a Rembrandt. Mama, do we still have a Monet?"

The shock was almost too much for me to bear. My heart was racing like it did during the early days of my marriage to Buford. I tried to speak, but nothing came out. I tried again.

"You're supposed to be a helpless little old lady," I finally wailed. "How can you be the ringleader of an art-smuggling gang?"

Adele perched on the arm of the couch next to Johnny. "I *am* an old lady—I was eighty last birthday. But don't get me wrong; I still have my wits about me."

"My aunt's as sharp as a tack," Mouse said proudly.

Adele smiled. "Thank you. Now, boys, y'all know what to do with her."

"Do with me?" I echoed.

"Auntie Adele," Johnny said quietly, "do we have to?"

Hortense stood. "Well, I'm out of here. Y'all know how I feel about violence."

Mouse snickered. "Good one, cuz. I suppose poisoning Her Majesty doesn't count."

"You poisoned Priscilla Hunt?"

"Nosiest woman who ever lived," Hortense said. "I did Rock Hill a favor."

I caught my breath. "Of course, the malathion! You are Hortense Scissorhands, after all."

"I'm a Master Gardener," Hortense huffed. "I make things grow. Johnny was happy to do the honors for me."

Johnny Trap beamed. "She owed me one, for making me write that awful book."

Hortense rearranged herself on the couch between her big-eared cousins. "Hey, it was a best-seller."

"Thanks to Oprah." Johnny turned to his aunt. "Let me have Abigail. Please. She's a feisty little thing, but I could tame her. And she likes to read, Auntie Adele. We were made for each other."

Adele cocked her head, apparently giving it some thought.

I needed to distract her. "What are y'all? Nazis?"

Everyone laughed.

"It isn't funny! Those paintings were stolen from their rightful owners by Nazis. Is that what you were, Mrs. Trap? A Nazi? You're the right age."

"My daddy was no Nazi!" Hortense was red in the face.

"Yeah? Well, I know for a fact that there is a private detective hot on the trail of paintings the Nazis stole, and *Field of Thistles* is one of them."

"Auntie Adele, let me off her now," Mouse begged.

Adele frowned at her eldest nephew. "Be patient." She turned to me. "My first husband, Leonard Trap, was a lieutenant in the U.S. Army. He found these paintings in a German *schloss*."

"Bull," I said.

Adele stared at me.

"You see why I want her," Johnny whined. "Abigail lights my fire."

I glared, first at him and then at his gaping aunt. "Even if your husband did find them in a *schloss* somewhere, he had to have known they were taken from Jews and others who were sent to concentration camps."

"He knew no such thing."

"Then he was just as stupid as you."

I heard a metallic click and glanced at Mouse. For the first time, I noticed that he was holding a small handgun. Perhaps he had just pulled it from a holster. At any rate, I know next to nothing about weapons, but I knew all I needed to know about this one. It was pointed directly at my head.

Adele smiled. "That's my nephew. Take her outside first, Mouse. Pinky has enough work around here. And you might wake the ladies."

"I'm not going without my baby," I wailed. "Dmitri!"

Meow. My precious pussy appeared out of nowhere and began rubbing his cheeks against one of Mouse's shoes. Mouse looked down in surprise.

I still don't know why I did it, but in that split second when Mouse was distracted, I leaped from my chair, straight at his aunt. And I can only guess that Johnny intended to cooperate because he leaned to one side, allowing me to tackle the old biddy.

Yes, I realize that tackling an elderly woman—knocking her off the couch arm and onto the floor—is not something one should normally brag about, but surely there are exceptions. Adele went down cleanly, and I landed neatly on top of her.

"Mama!" Hortense shrieked.

The next thing I heard was the crack of gunfire.

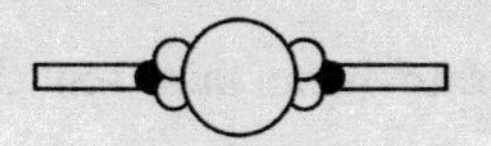

28

"That shot," Mama said proudly, "was fired by Freddy."

There were ten of us sitting around Mama's dining room table, polishing off what had been a magnificent late breakfast. Besides Mama and myself, the ten included Greg, C. J., Sergeant Bowater, Wynnell, both Rob-Bobs, the lovely Marina, and, of course, Freddy.

"And it was a good shot," I said. "It knocked the gun right out of Mouse Trap's hand, but the bullet never touched him. Too bad it tore a hole clean through a Cezanne."

Rob moaned.

"So, Abby," Bob boomed, "what were they going to do with you if Freddy hadn't showed up?"

"Plug me with the pistol and then plant me in a cotton field."

"Some farmer would have had a bumper crop," Greg said. Everyone laughed.

"I planted a feather once," C. J. said, "and it grew into a chicken. Or did I dream that?"

"You dreamed that!" we all chorused.

I helped myself to another slice of Mama's bacon, crisp on the ends but with a little play in the middle.

"I guess it pays to have the U.S. Customs Service tailing you."

Freddy grinned. He was still wearing a studded leather vest. Seated next to Mama, he looked positively boyish, too young even for my daughter, Susan.

"You're a hard one to keep up with, Ms. Timberlake. But the department is grateful that you discovered the van Gogh. And I bet Ms. Weiss is grateful as well."

"You bet," she said, her lovely mouth full of Mama's cinnamon toast.

"We couldn't have done it without you," Freddy said.

Marina swallowed. "Freddy and I both knew the missing paintings were in the Charlotte area. We also suspected that Adele Trap was involved, but that was getting very difficult to prove. We'd both been grabbing at straws, and then we—well, Freddy—observed the suspect's stepson removing a painting from the nursing home. So we followed it to the auction."

Mama put a biscuit on Freddy's plate and smothered it with red-eye gravy. "What made you suspect Adele? Isn't she senile?"

"Far from it," I cried. "The woman is craftier than a sailboat regatta. She was the brains behind the whole thing. Did you know that she owns Pine Manor nursing home, lock, stock, and barrel?"

Greg cleared his throat. "From what I can share of the police report, she handpicked the elderly women who reside there. None of them knew what was going on, of course—none of them was capable of knowing.

None of them had any living relatives, either. It made an excellent cover for her operation."

"She nearly froze the poor dears," I cried. "Kept them sluggish that way. Meanwhile, the old biddy was wearing long johns under her chenille robe."

Mama shook her head. "And to think that was going to be my final earthly home."

"Mama!"

Wynnell poured herself a second glass of fresh-squeezed orange juice. "How's Dmitri?"

"Don't ask!" I wailed.

Wynnell's eyebrows met in a hedgerow. "He's not . . . I mean . . . he didn't—"

"He's fine! He's asleep on Mama's bed. For all I know, he had been sleeping on her chest. I hope he put his foot in her mouth. I hope she gets some horrible litter box disease. Maybe they'll all catch it."

"Abby!" Mama said, genuinely shocked.

"Well, they're wicked people—except for Johnny."

Greg reached for his coffee. "How's that?"

"Well, he didn't really fit in. He really was a writer, and he lived modestly. Besides, he could have stopped me from tackling Adele."

"But he killed Mrs. Hunt. Surely you don't condone that."

"No. I forgot about that. I guess Johnny just seemed nicer than the rest."

"Appearances can be deceiving," Mama said, shamelessly making goo-goo eyes at Freddy.

I turned to C. J. "You know, I really didn't believe you at first, but you were right. The Trap brothers were from Shelby. Only I don't think they killed their parents."

"They didn't," Greg said. "I already checked that out. Their parents died in a plane crash."

C. J. didn't hear us. She was too busy nibbling on a sausage that Sergeant Bowater was hand-feeding her.

Bob leaned to one side as Rob poured him a second cup of coffee.

"Let me get this straight. Lieutenant Trap found a cache of the world's finest paintings and kept them for his personal enjoyment?"

Rob sighed. "Can you blame him?"

Freddy frowned. "They weren't his to keep. At any rate, after Trap died Adele began selling them off—a little bit at a time in order to avoid suspicion. That was clever on her part. However, when her second husband, Gilbert Sweeney, Sr., died five years ago, she got greedy and sold three paintings in a short period. *That* was her first mistake."

"What was the second?" I asked.

"The second was that these last three were all major works."

"As important as *Field of Thistles*?"

Marina shook her braids. "No. Very few paintings can compare with that. My clients—the rightful owners—expect it to bring fifteen million at Sotheby's. And that's without the Japanese."

Rob moaned again.

"Well, I think my Abby should get a reward," Mama said loyally.

"She will," Marina said softly.

"How much?" Mama demanded.

Marina looked at me.

"Go ahead; you can tell them," I said. Marina, who'd been on the phone much of the night, had in fact just told me minutes before we sat down.

"One hundred thousand dollars."

"Is that all?" Mama wailed.

C. J. stopped sucking sausages and came up for air. "Ooh, Abby, what are you going to do with all that money?"

I smiled. "Well, for one thing, the youth group is going to get a van."

"And?"

"And Mama is getting a trip to Africa."

Mama gasped. "I am?"

"Yes, Mama, but a photo safari. You don't have to be a missionary to get to Africa, you know."

"And?" C. J. was relentless.

"Y'all get to go with her if you want."

"Ooh!" C. J. wasn't the only one to squeal with delight.

"Look," I said, when everyone had quieted down, "I'm really sorry for being such a jerk."

"That's okay," C. J. said. "We love you anyway."

"Thanks." I reached for Greg's hand. "But there is one more thing—*if* there is any money left."

"What?" the group demanded in unison.

"I've decided to take a vacation." I squeezed Greg's hand. "How does Maui sound?"

Greg squeezed back.

We hope you have enjoyed this Avon mystery. Mysteries fascinate and intrigue with the worlds they create. And what better way to capture your interest than this glimpse into the world of a select group of Avon authors.

Tamar Myers reveals the deadly side of the antique business. The bed-and-breakfast industry becomes lethal in the hands of Mary Daheim. A walk along San Antonio's famed River Walk with Carolyn Hart reveals a fascinating and mysterious place. Nevada Barr encounters danger on Ellis Island. Deborah Woodworth's Sister Rose Callahan discovers something sinister is afoot in her Kentucky Shaker village. Jill Churchill steps back in time to the 1930's along the Hudson River and creates a weekend of intrigue. And Anne George's Southern Sisters find that making money is a motive for murder.

So turn the page for a sneak peek into worlds filled with mystery and murder. And if you like what you read, head to your nearest bookstore. It's the only way to figure out whodunnit . . .

December

Abigail Timberlake, the heroine of Tamar Myers' delightful Den of Antiquity series, is smart, quirky, and strong-minded. She has to be—running your own antique business is a struggle, even on the cultured streets of Charlotte, North Carolina, and her mean-spirited divorce lawyer of an ex-husband's caused her a lot of trouble over the years. She also has a "delicate" relationship with her proper Southern mama.

The difficulties in Abby's personal life are nothing, though, to the trouble that erupts when she buys a "faux" van Gogh at auction . . .

ESTATE OF MIND

by Tamar Myers

You already know that my name is Abigail Timberlake, but you might not know that I was married to a beast of a man for just over twenty years. Buford Timberlake—or Timbersnake, as I call him—is one of Charlotte, North Carolina's most prominent divorce lawyers. Therefore, he knew exactly what he was doing when he traded me in for his secretary. Of course, Tweetie Bird is half my age—although parts of her are even much younger than that. The woman is 20 percent silicone, for crying out loud, although admittedly it balances rather nicely with the 20 percent that was sucked away from her hips.

In retrospect, however, there are worse things than having your husband dump you for a man-made woman. It hurt like the dickens at the time, but it would have hurt even more had he traded me in for a brainier model. I can buy most of what Tweetie has (her height excepted), but she will forever be afraid to flush the toilet lest she drown the Ty-D-Bol man.

And as for Buford, he got what he deserved. Our daughter, Susan, was nineteen at the time and in college, but our son, Charlie, was seventeen, and a high school junior. In the penultimate miscarriage of justice, Buford got custody of Charlie, our house, and even the dog Scruffles. I must point out that Buford got custody of our friends as well. Sure, they didn't legally belong to him, but where would you rather stake your loyalty? To a good old boy with more connections than the White House switchboard, or to a housewife whose biggest accomplishment, besides giving birth, was a pie crust that didn't shatter when you touched it with your fork? But like I said, Buford got what he deserved and today—it actually pains me to say this—neither of our children will speak to their father.

Now I own a four bedroom, three bath home not far from my shop. My antique shop that is, the Den of Antiquity. I paid for this house, mind you—not one farthing came from Buford. At any rate, I share this peaceful, if somewhat lonely, abode with a very hairy male who is young enough to be my son.

When I got home from the auction, I was in need of a little comfort, so I fixed myself a cup of tea with milk and sugar—never mind that it was summer—and curled up on the white cotton couch in the den. My other hand held a copy of Anne Grant's *Smoke Screen*, a mystery novel set in Charlotte and surrounding environs. I hadn't finished more than a page of this exciting read when my roommate rudely pushed it aside and climbed into my lap.

"Dmitri," I said, stroking his large orange head, "that 'Starry Night' painting is so ugly, if van Gogh saw it, he'd cut off his other ear."

Some folks think that just because I'm in business for myself, I can set my own hours. That's true as long as I keep my shop open forty hours a week during prime business hours and spend another eight or ten hours attending sales. Not to mention the hours spent cleaning and organizing any subsequent purchases. I know what they mean, though. If I'm late to the shop, I may lose a valued customer, but I won't lose my job—at least not in one fell swoop.

I didn't think I'd ever get to sleep Wednesday night, and I didn't. It was well into the wee hours of Thursday morning when I stopped counting green thistles and drifted off. When my alarm beeped, I managed to turn it off in my sleep. Either that or in my excitement, I had forgotten to set it. At any rate, the telephone woke me up at 9:30, a half hour later than the time I usually open my shop.

"*Muoyo webe*," Mama said cheerily.

"What?" I pushed Dmitri off my chest and sat up.

"Life to you, Abby. That's how they say 'good morning' in Tshiluba."

I glanced at the clock. "Oh, shoot! Mama, I've got to run."

"I know, dear. I tried the shop first and got the machine. Abby, you really should consider getting a professional to record your message. Someone who sounds . . . well, more cultured."

"Like Rob?" I remembered the painting. "Mama, sorry, but I really can't talk now."

"Fine," Mama said, her cheeriness deserting her. "I guess, like they say, bad news can wait."

I sighed. Mama baits her hooks with an expertise to be envied by the best fly fishermen.

"Sock it to me, Mama. But make it quick."

"Are you sitting down, Abby?"

"Mama, I'm still in bed!"

"Abby, I'm afraid I have some horrible news to tell you about one of your former boyfriends."

"Greg?" I managed to gasp after a few seconds. "Did something happen to Greg?"

"No, dear, it's Gilbert Sweeny. He's dead."

I wanted to reach through the phone line and shake Mama until her pearls rattled. "Gilbert Sweeny was never my boyfriend!"

January

From nationally-bestselling author Mary Daheim, who creates a world inside a Seattle bed-and-breakfast that is impossible to resist, comes Creeps Suzette, *the newest addition to this delightful series . . .*

Judith McMonigle Flynn, the consummate hostess of Hillside Manor, fairly flies out the door in the dead of winter when her cousin Renie requests her company. As long as Judith's ornery mother, her ferocious feline, and her newly retired husband aren't joining them, Judith couldn't care less where they're going. That is until they arrive at the spooky vine-covered mansion, Creepers, in which an elderly woman lives in fear that someone is trying to kill her. And it's up to the cousins to determine which dark, drafty corner houses a cold-blooded killer before a permanent hush falls over them all . . .

CREEPS SUZETTE

by Mary Daheim

"As you wish, ma'am," said Kenyon, and creaked out of the parlor.

"Food," Renie sighed. "I'm glad I'm back."

"With a vengeance," Judith murmured. "You know," she went on, "when I saw those stuffed animal heads in the game room, I had to wonder if Kenneth wasn't reacting to them. His grandfather or great-grandfather must have hunted. Maybe he grew up feeling sorry for the lions and tigers and bears, oh, my!"

"I could eat a bear," Renie said.

Climbing the tower staircase, the cousins could feel the wind. "Not well-insulated in this part of the house," Judith noted as they entered Kenneth's room.

"It's a tower," Renie said. "What would you expect?"

Judith really hadn't expected to see Roscoe the raccoon, but there he was, standing on his hind legs in a commodious cage. The bandit eyes gazed soulfully at the cousins.

"Hey," Renie said, kneeling down, "from the looks of that food dish, you've eaten more than we have this evening. You'll have to wait for dessert."

Judith, meanwhile, was studying the small fireplace, peeking into drawers, looking under the bed. "Nothing," she said, opening the door to the nursery. "Just the kind of things you'd expect Kenneth to keep on hand for his frequent visits to Creepers."

Renie said goodbye to Roscoe and followed Judith into the nursery. "How long," Renie mused, "do you suppose it's been since any kids played in here?"

Judith calculated. "Fifteen years, maybe more?"

"Do you think they're keeping it for grandchildren?" Renie asked in a wistful tone.

Judith gave her cousin a sympathetic glance. So far, none of the three grown Jones offspring had acquired mates or produced children. "That's possible," Judith said. "You shouldn't give up hope, especially these days when kids marry so late."

Renie didn't respond. Instead, she contemplated the train set. "This is the same vintage as the one I had. It's a Marx, like mine. I don't think they make them anymore."

"Some of these dolls are much older," Judith said. "They're porcelain and bisque. These toys run the gamut," Judith remarked. "From hand-carved wooden soldiers to plastic Barbies. And look at this doll house. The furniture is all the same style as many of the pieces in this house."

"Hey," Renie said, joining Judith at the shelf where the doll house was displayed, "this looks like a cutaway replica of Creepers itself. There's even a tower room on this one side and it's . . ." Renie blanched and let out a little gasp.

"What's wrong, coz? Are you okay?" Judith asked in alarm.

A gust of wind blew the door to the nursery shut, making both cousins jump. "Yeah, right, I'm just fine," Renie said in a startled voice. "But look at this. How creepy can Creepers get?"

Judith followed Renie's finger. In the top floor of the half-version of the tower was a bed, a chair, a table, and a tiny doll in a long dark dress. The doll was lying face-down on the floor in what looked like a pool of blood.

The lights in the nursery went out.

February

Carolyn Hart is the multiple Agatha, Anthony, and Macavity Award-winning author of the "Death on Demand" series as well as the highly praised Henrie O series. In Death on the River Walk, *sixtysomething retired journalist Henrietta O'Dwyer Collins must turn her carefully-honed sleuthing skills to a truly perplexing crime that's taken place at the luxurious gift shop Tesoros on the fabled River Walk of San Antonio, Texas. See why the* Los Angeles Times *said, "If I were teaching a course on how to write a mystery, I would make Carolyn Hart required reading . . . Superb."*

DEATH ON THE RIVER WALK

by Carolyn Hart

Sirens squalled. When the police arrived, this area would be closed to all of us. Us. Funny. Was I aligning myself with the Garza clan? Not exactly, though I was charmed by Maria Elena, and I liked—or wanted to like—her grandson Rick.

But I wasn't kidding myself that the death of the blond man wouldn't cause trouble for Iris. Whatever she'd found in the wardrobe, it had to be connected to this murder. And I wanted a look inside Tesoros before Rick had a chance to grab Iris's backpack should it be there. That was why I'd told Rick to make the call to the police from La Mariposa.

The central light was on. That was the golden pool that spread through the open door. The small recessed spots above the limestone display islands were dark, so the rest of the store was dim and shadowy.

I followed alongside the path revealed by Manuel's mop. It was beginning to dry at the farther reach, but there was still enough moisture to tell the story I was sure the police would understand. The body had been moved along this path, leaving a trail of bloodstains. That's what Manuel had mopped up.

The sirens were louder, nearer.

The trail ended in the middle of the store near an island with a charming display of pottery banks—a lion, a bull, a big-cheeked balding man, a donkey, a rounded head with bright red cheeks. Arranged in a semicircle, each was equidistant from its neighbor. One was missing.

I used my pocket flashlight, snaked the beam high and low. I didn't find the missing bank. Or Iris's backpack.

The sirens choked in mid-wail.

I hurried, moving back and forth across the store, swinging the beam of my flashlight. No pottery bank, no backpack. Nothing else appeared out of order or disturbed in any way. The only oddity was the rapidly drying area of freshly mopped floor, a three-foot swath leading from the paperweight-display island to the front door.

I reached the front entrance and stepped outside. In trying to stay clear of the mopped area, I almost stumbled into the pail and mop. I leaned down, wrinkled my nose against the sour smell of ammonia, and pointed the flashlight beam into the faintly discolored water, no longer foamy with suds. The water's brownish tinge didn't obscure the round pink snout of a pottery pig bank.

Swift, heavy footsteps sounded on the steps leading down from La Mariposa. I moved quickly to stand by the bench. Iris looked with wide and frightened eyes at the policemen following Rick and his Uncle Frank into the brightness spilling out from Tesoros. I supposed Rick had wakened his uncle to tell him of the murder.

Iris reached out, grabbed my hand. Rick stopped a few feet from the body, pointed at it, then at the open door. Frank Garza peered around the shoulder of a short policeman with sandy hair and thick glasses. Rick was pale and strained. He spoke in short, jerky sentences to a burly policeman with ink-black hair, an expressionless face, and one capable hand resting on the butt of his pistol. Frank patted his hair, disarranged from sleep, stuffed his misbuttoned shirt into his trousers.

When Rick stopped, the policeman turned and looked toward the bench. Iris's fingers tightened on mine, but I knew the policeman wasn't looking at us. He was looking at Manuel, sitting quietly with his usual excellent posture, back straight, feet apart, hands loose in his lap.

Manuel slowly realized that everyone was looking at him. He blinked, looked at us eagerly, slowly lifted his hands, and began to clap.

March

Nevada Barr's brilliant series featuring Park Ranger Anna Pigeon takes this remarkable heroine to the scene of heinous crimes at the feet of a national shrine—the Statue of Liberty. While bunking with friends on Liberty Island, Anna finds solitude in the majestically decayed remains of hospitals, medical wards, and staff quarters of Ellis Island. When a tumble through a crumbling staircase temporarily halts her ramblings, Anna is willing to write off the episode as an accident. But then a young girl falls—or is pushed—to her death while exploring the Statue of Liberty, and it's up to Anna to uncover the deadly secrets of Lady Liberty's treasured island.

LIBERTY FALLING

by Nevada Barr

Held aloft by the fingers of her right hand, Anna dangled over the ruined stairwell. Between dust and night there was no way of knowing what lay beneath. Soon either her fingers would uncurl from the rail or the rail would pull out from the wall. Faint protests of aging screws in softening plaster foretold the collapse. No superhuman feats of strength struck Anna as doable. What fragment of energy remained in her arm was fast burning away on the pain. With a kick and a twist, she managed to grab hold of the rail with her other hand as well. Much of the pressure was taken off her shoulder, but she was left face to the wall. There was the vague possibility that she could scoot one hand width at a time up the railing, then swing her legs onto what might or might not be stable footing at the top of the stairs. Two shuffles nixed that plan. Old stairwells didn't fall away all in a heap like guillotined heads. Between her and the upper floor were the ragged remains, shards of wood and rusted metal. In the black dark she envisioned the route upward with the same jaundice a hay bale might view a pitchfork.

What the hell, she thought. *How far can it be?* And she let go.

With no visual reference, the fall, though in reality not more than five or six feet, jarred every bone in her body. Unaided by eyes and brain, her legs had no way of compensating. Knees buckled on impact and her chin smacked into them as her forehead met some immovable object. The good news was, the whole thing was over in the blink of a blind eye and she didn't think she'd sustained any lasting damage.

Wisdom dictated she lie still, take stock of her body and surroundings, but this decaying dark was so filthy she couldn't bear the thought of it. Stink rose from the litter: pigeon shit, damp and rot. Though she'd seen none, it was easy to imagine spiders of evil temperament and immoderate size. Easing up on feet and hands, she picked her way over rubble she could not see, heading for the faint smudge of gray that would lead her to the out-of-doors.

Free of the damage she'd wreaked, Anna quickly found her way out of the tangle of inner passages and escaped Island III through the back door of the ward. The sun had set. The world was bathed in gentle peach-colored light. A breeze, damp but cooling with the coming night, blew off the water. Sucking it in, she coughed another colony of spores from her lungs. With safety, the delayed reaction hit. Wobbly, she sat down on the steps and put her head between her knees.

Because she'd been messing around where she probably shouldn't have been in the first place, she'd been instrumental in the destruction of an irreplaceable historic structure. Sitting on the stoop, smeared with dirt and reeking of bygone pigeons, she contemplated whether to report the disaster or just slink away and let the monument's curators write it off to natural causes. She was within a heartbeat of deciding to do the honorable thing when the decision was taken from her.

The sound of boots on hard-packed earth followed by a voice saying: "Patsy thought it might be you," brought her head up. A lovely young man, resplendent in the uniform of the Park Police, was walking down the row of buildings toward her.

"Why?" Anna asked stupidly.

"One of the boat captains radioed that somebody

was over here." The policeman sat down next to her. He was no more than twenty-two or -three, fit and handsome and oozing boyish charm. "Have you been crawling around or what?"

Anna took a look at herself. Her khaki shorts were streaked with black, her red tank top untucked and smeared with vile-smelling mixtures. A gash ran along her thigh from the hem of her shorts to her kneecap. It was bleeding, but not profusely. Given the amount of rust and offal in this adventure, she would have to clean it thoroughly and it wouldn't hurt to check when she'd had last had a tetanus shot.

"Sort of," she said, and told him about the stairs. "Should we check it out? Surely we'll have to make a report. You'll have to write a report," she amended. "I'm just a hapless tourist."

The policeman looked over his shoulder. The doorway behind them was cloaked in early night. "Maybe in the morning," he said, and Anna could have sworn he was afraid. There was something in this strong man's voice that told her, were it a hundred years earlier, he would have made a sign against the evil eye.

April

Sister Rose Callahan, eldress of the Depression-era community of Believers at the Kentucky Shaker village of North Homage, knows that evil does not merely exist in the Bible. Sometimes it comes very close to home indeed.

"A complete and very charming portrait of a world, its ways, and the beliefs of its people, and an excellent mystery to draw you along."
Anne Perry

In the next pages, Sister Rose confronts danger in the form of an old religious cult seeking new members among the peaceful Shakers.

A SIMPLE SHAKER MURDER

by Deborah Woodworth

At first, Rose saw nothing alarming, only rows of strictly pruned apple trees, now barren of fruit and most of their leaves. The group ran through the apple trees and into the more neglected east side of the orchard, where the remains of touchier fruit trees lived out their years with little human attention. The pounding feet ahead of her stopped, and panting bodies piled behind one another, still trying to keep some semblance of separation between the brethren and the sisters.

The now-silent onlookers stared at an aged plum tree. From a sturdy branch hung the limp figure of a man, his feet dangling above the ground. His eyes were closed and his head slumped forward, almost hiding the rope that gouged into his neck. The man wore loose clothes that were neither Shaker nor of the world, and Rose sensed he was gone even before Josie reached for his wrist and shook her head.

Two brethren moved forward to cut the man down.

"Nay, don't, not yet," Rose said, hurrying forward.

Josie's eyebrows shot up. "Surely you don't think this is anything but the tragedy of a man choosing to end his own life?" She nodded past the man's torso to a delicate chair laying on its side in the grass. It was a Shaker design, not meant for such rough treatment. Dirt scuffed the woven red-and-white tape of the seat. Scratches marred the smooth slats that formed its ladder back.

"What's going on here? Has Mother Ann appeared and declared today a holiday from labor?" The powerful voice snapped startled heads backwards, to where Elder Wilhelm emerged from the trees, stern jaw set for disapproval.

No one answered. Everyone watched Wilhelm's

ruddy face blanch as he came in view of the dead man.

"Dear God," he whispered. "Is he . . . ?"

"Yea," said Josie.

"Then cut him down instantly," Wilhelm said. His voice had regained its authority, but he ran a shaking hand through his thick white hair.

Eyes turned to Rose. "I believe we should leave him for now, Wilhelm," she said. A flush spread across Wilhelm's cheeks, and Rose knew she was in for a public tongue thrashing, so she explained quickly. "Though all the signs point to suicide, still it is a sudden and brutal death, and I believe we should alert the Sheriff. He'll want things left just as we found them."

"Sheriff Brock . . ." Wilhelm said with a snort of derision. "He will relish the opportunity to find us culpable."

"Please, for the sake of pity, cut him down." A man stepped forward, hat in hand in the presence of death. His peculiar loose work clothes seemed too generous for his slight body. His thinning blond hair lifted in the wind. "I'm Gilbert Owen Griffiths," he said, nodding to Rose. "And this is my compatriot, Earl Weston," he added, indicating a broad-shouldered, dark-haired young man. "I am privileged to be guiding a little group of folks who are hoping to rekindle the flame of the great social reformer, Robert Owen. That poor unfortunate man," he said, with a glance at the dead man, "was Hugh—Hugh Griffiths—and he was one of us. We don't mind having the Sheriff come take a look, but we are all like a family, and it is far too painful for us to leave poor Hugh hanging."

"It's an outrage, leaving him there like that," Earl said. "What if Celia should come along?"

"Celia is poor Hugh's wife," Gilbert explained. "I'll have to break the news to her soon. I beg of you, cut him down and cover him before she shows up."

Wilhelm assented with a curt nod. "I will inform the Sheriff," he said as several brethren cut the man down and lay him on the ground. The morbid fascination had worn off, and most of the crowd was backing away.

There was nothing to do but wait. Rose gathered up the sisters and New-Owenite women who had not already made their escape. Leaving Andrew to watch over the ghastly scene until the Sheriff arrived, she sent the women on ahead to breakfast, for which she herself had no appetite. The men followed behind.

On impulse Rose glanced back to see Andrew's tall figure hunched against a tree near the body. He watched the crowd's departure with a forlorn expression. As she raised her arm to send him an encouraging wave, a move distracted her. She squinted through the tangle of unpruned branches behind Andrew to locate the source. *Probably just a squirrel,* she thought, but her eyes kept searching nonetheless. There it was again—a flash of brown almost indistinguishable from tree bark. Several rows of trees back from where Andrew stood, something was moving among the branches of an old pear tree—something much bigger than a squirrel.

May

Once upon a time Lily and Robert were the pampered offspring of a rich New York family. But the crash of '29 left them virtually penniless until a distant relative offered them a Grace and Favor house on the Hudson.

The catch is they must live at this house for ten years and not return to their beloved Manhattan. In In the Still of the Night *Lily and Robert invite paying guests from the city to stay with them for a cultural weekend. But then something goes wildly askew.*

IN THE STILL OF THE NIGHT

by Jill Churchill

"I realized that Mrs. Ethridge wasn't at breakfast and she hasn't come to lunch either. I kept an eye out for her so I could nip in and tidy her room while she was out and about and she hasn't been."

"She's not in the dining room?" Lily said. "No, I guess not. There were two empty chairs."

"She might be sick, miss."

"Have you knocked on her door?"

"A couple times, miss."

"I'll go see what's become of her," Lily said.

Robert, who had been ringing up the operator, hung up the phone. "I think it would be better for me to check on her."

"But Robert . . ." Lily saw his serious expression and paused. "Very well. But I'll come with you."

They went up to the second floor and Robert tapped lightly on the door. "Mrs. Ethridge? Are you all right?" When there was no response, he tapped more firmly and repeated himself loudly.

They stood there, brother and sister, remembering another incident last fall, and staring at each other. "I'll look. You stay out here," Robert said.

He opened the door and almost immediately closed it in Lily's face. She heard the snick of the inside lock. There was complete silence for a long moment, then Robert unlocked and re-opened the door. "Lily, she's dead."

Lily gasped. "Are you sure?"

"Quite sure."

"Oh, why did she have to die *here*?" Lily said, then caught herself. "What a selfish thing to say. I'm sorry."

"No need to be. I thought the same thing. It's not as if she's a good friend, or even someone we willingly invited."

"What do we do now?"

"You go back to the dining room and act like nothing's wrong while I call the police and the coroner."

"The police? Why the police?"

"I think you have to call them for an unexplained death. Besides, if we don't, what do we *do* with her? Somebody has to take her away to be buried."

Patricia Anne is a sedate suburban housewife living in Birmingham, Alabama, but thanks to her outrageous sister, Mary Alice, she's always in the thick of some controversy, often with murderous overtones. In Murder Shoots the Bull, *Anne George's seventh novel in the Southern Sisters series, the sisters are involved in an investment club with next door neighbor Mitzi. But no sooner have they started the club than strange things start happening to the members . . .*

MURDER SHOOTS THE BULL

by Anne George

I fixed coffee, microwaved some oatmeal, and handed Fred a can of Healthy Request chicken noodle soup for his lunch as he went out the door. Wifely duties done, I settled down with my second cup of coffee and the *Birmingham News*.

I usually glance over the front page, read "People are Talking" on the second, and then turn to the Metro section. Which is what I did this morning. I was reading about a local judge who claimed he couldn't help it if he kept dozing off in court because of narcolepsy when Mitzi, my next door neighbor, knocked on the back door.

"Have you seen it?" She pointed to the paper in my hand when I opened the door.

"Seen what?" I was so startled at her appearance, it took me a moment to answer. Mitzi looked rough. She had on a pink chenille bathrobe which had seen better days and she was barefooted. No comb had touched her hair. It was totally un-Mitzi-like. I might run across the yards looking like this, but not Mitzi. She's the neatest person in the world.

"About the death."

"What death?" I don't know why I asked. I knew, of course. I moved aside and she came into the kitchen.

"Sophie Sawyer's poisoning."

Mitzi walked to the kitchen table and sat down as if her legs wouldn't hold her up anymore.

"Sophie Sawyer was poisoned?"

"Arthur said you were there yesterday."

"I was." I sat down across from Mitzi, my heart thumping faster. "She was poisoned?"

"Second page. Crime reports." Mitzi propped her elbows on the table, leaned forward and put a hand over each ear as if she didn't want to hear my reaction.

I turned to the second page. The first crime report, one short paragraph, had the words—SUSPECTED POISONING DEATH—as its heading. Sophie Vaughn Sawyer, 64, had been pronounced dead the day before after being rushed to University Hospital from a nearby restaurant. Preliminary autopsy reports indicated that she was the victim of poisoning. Police were investigating.

Goosebumps skittered up my arms and across my shoulders. Sophie Sawyer murdered? Someone had killed the lovely woman I had seen at lunch the day before? I read the paragraph again. Since it was so brief, the news of the death must have barely made the paper's deadline.

"God, Mitzi, I can't believe this. It's awful. Who was she? One of Arthur's clients?"

Mitzi's head bent to the table. Her hands slid around and clasped behind her neck.

"His first wife."

"His what?" Surely I hadn't heard right. Her voice was muffled against the table.

But she looked up and repeated, "His first wife."

by

TAMAR MYERS

LARCENY AND OLD LACE
0-380-78239-1/$5.99 US/$7.99 Can

GILT BY ASSOCIATION
0-380-78237-5/$6.50 US/$8.50 Can

THE MING AND I
0-380-79255-9/$6.50 US/$8.99 Can

SO FAUX, SO GOOD
0-380-79254-0/$6.50 US/$8.99 Can

BAROQUE AND DESPERATE
0-380-80225-2/$6.50 US/$8.99 Can

ESTATE OF MIND
0-380-80227-9/$6.50 US/$8.99 Can

A PENNY URNED
0-380-81189-8/$6.50 US/$8.99 Can

NIGHTMARE IN SHINING ARMOR
0-380-81191-X/$6.50 US/$8.99 Can

SPLENDOR IN THE GLASS
0-380-81964-3/$6.99 US/$9.99 Can

Available wherever books are sold or please call 1-800-331-3761 to order.

TM 0502